ALWAYS HER COWBOY

"How does this happen?" Her voice was soft when she spoke. "Why are we here?"

"Why are we where?"

"We're two healthy, consenting adults with a real, tangible attraction to each other. Why is it like an unscalable mountain between us instead of a bright, vivid sign that screams *Go*?"

It was the question that got him.

No, Chance amended to himself, it was actually that shift in tone.

Any hints of provocation or attempts at goading him were gone.

A man was only so strong, after all.

Charlotte's hand went to his chest as he bent his head to brush his lips to hers. As their mouths met, Chance knew the truth. No matter how badly he needed to resist her, there was no amount of self-control that could walk away from this woman pressed up against his chest.

Because in that moment the blaze had already consumed him.

By Addison Fox

ALWAYS HER COWBOY
FORGET ME NOT COWBOY
THE COWBOY SAYS YES

ALWAYS HER COWBOY

Rustlers Creek

ADDISON FOX

AVONBOOKS

An Imprint of HarperCollins*Publishers*

ALWAYS HER COWBOY. Copyright © 2023 by Frances Karkosak. All rights reserved. Printed in the United States of America. No part of this book may be used or reproduced in any manner whatsoever without written permission except in the case of brief quotations embodied in critical articles and reviews. For information, address HarperCollins Publishers, 195 Broadway, New York, NY 10007.

First Avon Books mass market printing: May 2023

Print Edition ISBN: 978-0-06-313530-7
Digital Edition ISBN: 978-0-06-313526-0

Cover design by Amy Halperin
Cover illustration by Larry Rostant
Cover images © Shutterstock (background, sky)

Avon, Avon & logo, and Avon Books & logo are registered trademarks of HarperCollins Publishers in the United States of America and other countries.

HarperCollins is a registered trademark of HarperCollins Publishers in the United States of America and other countries.

FIRST EDITION

23 24 25 26 27 BVGM 10 9 8 7 6 5 4 3 2 1

For my grandparents.
Rudolph & Eleanor and Frank & Frances.

Forever in my heart.

ALWAYS HER
COWBOY

Chapter 1

Charlotte Wayne put on her best and brightest smile in an effort to avoid clamping her jaw so tight she might as well have welded it. She'd grown up around cowboys, was the daughter of one and a sister, too. She understood the pride and promise that lived in a man's breast when he worked the land and built a profitable business from his labors.

But she had no time for the ones who thought they were smarter than her, needed to protect her or saw her goals and ambitions in life as some amusing object of humor.

Her father was one of the most well-known cowboys in all of Montana, and he didn't treat her that way. Her brother Zack, equally as well-known as their father, didn't do it, either. Neither did the ranch hands at Wayne and Sons.

And she sure as shit wasn't taking it from these jerks. Jerks she'd invited to one of the finest steakhouses in Bozeman after having spent nearly thirty hours proactively building out a kick-ass marketing plan to pitch them.

"Tom. Merrill. I'm getting the sense you didn't read the proposal I shared in advance of this meeting."

The soft, dim lighting in the dark-paneled steakhouse couldn't hide their quickly dropped gazes, nor did it hide their twin reaches for drinks to wet their throats.

Merrill Harvey and his son Tom ran a ranch outside of Bozeman. She'd focused on them because, while not the most progressive males on the evolutionary chain, they had done some incredible work with herd rotation and sustainability practices. They'd also recently started a vitamin line to add to feed. Her sister-in-law's sister was engaged to a large-animal vet, and Dr. Gray McClain felt there was real promise in what the Harveys offered.

And Charlotte was unequivocally positive she could help them market the heck out of the product.

"Look, Ms. Wayne," Merrill started in. "I'm sure you've got some good ideas, but I don't see why we need a PR firm. We've done just fine without one to date."

"You're part of the Montana Ranchers' Association. You take part in their activities."

"Well, yeah. I've been a part of the MRA for years."

"Then you're well aware marketing is one of the key items on their agenda in their ten-year plan."

"Plans, Charlotte, are all they are." Tom scoffed as he took another sip of his whiskey before re-settling his glass. "No one I know wants to put a ton of money into ads to support someone else's business."

Charlotte avoided pasting on another smile in favor of appealing to Tom's business sense. And the fact that he still had a lot more years of ranching ahead of him. "It's good business for all of you, Tom."

"It's a waste of money."

"I'm sorry to have taken up so much of your time, then."

Merrill gave her an indulgent smile. "It's never a poor use of time to share a meal with a beautiful woman. And your daddy's one of my favorite people in Montana." The older man shook his head. "Even if the sonofabitch beats me every time we play poker."

When she had made the decision to go out on her own, leaving the PR firm where she'd worked since graduating college, she'd known it would be hard. Montana wasn't the center of the marketing world, and she'd made the choice a long time ago to stay in the northern reaches of the Western wilderness instead of going to New York or LA. She loved her home and her family and—for her—believed in staying where she'd been put.

But she had little care for people who were

overly comfortable or lacked ambition. A person could stay in the place they called home and still make something of it.

She also had never wanted to trade on her family notoriety, even as she knew people paid attention to the name Wayne in this part of the country.

Admittedly, it was hard to ignore or hide since her brother Zack had more than doubled the size of Wayne and Sons's output since taking over the management of the ranch from their father. And their family-name recognition had only gone global as Zack's wife, Hadley, became a major Cooking Network celebrity.

But it didn't mean Charlotte didn't want to make something of herself all on her own.

Merrill excused himself, leaving her and Tom alone at the table. The younger man had been respectful, but Charlotte hadn't missed the appreciative gaze in his eyes or his overly touchy demeanor. He'd already laid a hand on her lower back as they'd walked to their seats—a move she'd deliberately shaken off by beelining toward another table to say hello to her parents' friends— and then he'd brushed his fingers over hers as he'd taken her menu to hand it to their waitress.

"How long are you staying in Bozeman?"

"I head home first thing tomorrow. I have an early meeting I need to get back for."

"But you're here this evening. Maybe we can go get a nightcap after we finish dinner."

"Thank you for the offer, but I'm not going to be able to."

His smile dimmed, but he pressed on. "It's one drink, Charlotte."

She kept her voice steady but pumped the slightest bit of steel under her even tone. "I believe I said I wasn't able to join you."

"And if Dad and I were signing on the dotted line of your damn proposal? How would you feel then?"

It wasn't the first time she'd been propositioned and, tiring though it may be, she recognized the eternal dance behind modern dating. Tom was single and unattached, and the dating pool in this part of the country wasn't huge. She didn't blame him for taking a shot.

But she sure as hell blamed him for thinking she'd prostitute herself on the altar of her business.

"You've made it perfectly clear you don't care one goddamn for my work or my efforts to improve your business. And that's entirely within your right." She lifted a hand and made the universal gesture for the check to their waitress. "I won't, however, sit here and be called a whore."

"That's not what I meant—"

Tom looked about to argue further when his father wove his way back to the table. Merrill arrived just as the waitress did, and Charlotte already had her credit card out, handing it over without looking at the check, adding one final instruction. "Please add one more round of drinks for these lovely gentlemen. I'm the one who has to end our evening early."

When Tom remained sullen and his father looked about to protest, Charlotte added, "Merrill,

I apologize for my abrupt departure, but I'm afraid I need to head out. You've both been so kind to give me so much of your time, but I need to prepare for a meeting tomorrow as well as the early drive back to Rustlers Creek."

As excuses went it was one of the types she hated—pandering to her elders to get what she wanted. At the same time, the world was small, and she couldn't afford to go around pissing off the very people her business depended upon.

Especially because she couldn't afford to alienate any of them.

"I do appreciate your time, and if you have a chance to think about what I said, I'd love to review my proposal with you should your perspective change." She signed the check with a flourish, pleased when the waitress had sensed the mood shift and already arrived with the next round of drinks. "You enjoy the rest of the evening."

The men stood in unison as she got up, Tom offering a sullen thank-you for the dinner and Merrill sending his best to her parents. And in moments, Charlotte was breathing the fresh fall air as she trekked across the parking lot toward the hotel she favored when she stayed in Bozeman.

And refused to let a single frustrated tear slip over her cheeks.

CHANCE BEAUMONT HADN'T meant to eavesdrop from his perch at the end of the bar. Or *sightdrop*, as it were, since he couldn't hear what was being said. But as he'd watched the tableau play out across the restaurant, off and on as he ate his meal, he had a pretty damn good idea of what had happened.

The fact that he had a difficult time tearing his gaze off of Charlotte Wayne under the best of circumstances had little to do with his observations. He normally couldn't keep his gaze from wandering to her, but it had been a marvel to have an opportunity to do it with little fear of getting caught.

The two of them had managed a low-level sort of animosity since grade school. It was a state that, while initially his fault, had morphed into a sort of Olympic sport of sheer stubborn will. They'd go months at a time without seeing each other, but no matter how long it had been, their mutual aversion managed to flare high and bright within a matter of minutes of being in one another's company.

Even if he'd struggled to ever find a single thing about Charlotte he actually, legitimately found distasteful.

Still, it was their love language, as he'd heard Hadley Wayne jokingly refer to it once. A state that had changed only modestly about six months ago when Hadley's sister, Harper, had come back to town. Harper had reconnected with several of them when she'd come back to Rustlers Creek from Seattle, and it had put Chance and Charlotte in each other's way a bit more often than usual.

Often enough that they'd shared an incendiary kiss still haunting his dreams.

He'd seen Charlotte a handful of times since that night, but she'd avoided him to just shy of basic politeness, and he'd kept his distance, oddly disappointed they couldn't even find their way back to the arguing and bickering that had characterized most of a lifetime of experiences with each other.

Not that it mattered, he kept telling himself. He was focused on reviving his business back from being nearly dead, the damage his late father had done to Beaumont Farms shockingly deep. He needed to focus on the life and business he wanted, not pine away for the cool beauty who'd never be his.

This trip to Bozeman was a perfect example of why he needed to focus. He'd come in for a meeting with a potential supplier and had sprung for a night in a hotel. A gamble that had been worth it when his long day of meetings turned into a follow-up appointment the next morning.

The small chain of all-natural grocery stores in Bozeman was expanding, and they wanted a local beef producer they could feature in their stores. Beaumont Farms was in the final running for the deal.

The celebratory glass of bourbon—the only one he'd allowed himself—was his determined attempt not to be superstitious and to appreciate a good, productive day.

And then he'd seen Charlotte.

He didn't know she was working with the Harveys, but based on the frustration that covered her gorgeous face as she'd marched from the restaurant, Chance was guessing they weren't working together any longer.

If they ever had been.

He'd already signed off his own check and took the last sip of what was left in his bourbon glass and slipped out of his high bar chair. He might have a wild, raging crush on Charlotte, but he also knew when a friend needed an ear. And he was pretty sure she needed one now.

The Harveys were the only people he knew in the steakhouse, and he was far enough away from them to make an exit unnoticed. In moments he was outside, Charlotte's retreating form still visible at the other end of the parking lot, heading for the hotel on the opposite end. He picked up his pace and managed to intercept her just as she hit the edge of the lobby.

"Charlotte!"

She whirled at her name, her face set in firm lines. "Chance? What are you doing here?"

"I was in Bozeman for some business today and saw you leave the restaurant."

"Oh. Yes, well, my meeting was over."

"Not a great meeting, I take it?"

Although his and Charlotte's history was fraught at best, he'd only lied to her once, when they were both in the fourth grade. It had made him feel awful and had set the trajectory for their relationship for the next twenty-plus years, but he'd vowed at ten that he'd never do it again.

Along with never lying to her, he'd also made it

his personal policy never to bullshit her. Between her family's reputation and her stunning looks, nearly everyone he'd ever observed spent their time weaving heaps of bullshit around Charlotte Wayne. And since he'd never been a big joiner—*and* all that BS felt too close to lying—he'd adopted a sort of Honest Abe vibe around her.

Plus, he liked her too damn much to insult her like that.

And God, why did he always somehow manage to forget just how much of a stunner she was? No amount of thoughts or memories ever quite replicated what it was like to be in her company and look at her. The severe cut of her black business suit did nothing to diminish the long, lithe frame and the lean curves he knew were underneath.

And his memories never quite reproduced the soft look of her skin or the way her high cheekbones set off intelligent, observant, *intense* brown eyes.

"The meeting was"—she stopped, and he got the briefest sense she was debating a lie of her own before she sighed—"not the outcome I was hoping for after working really hard to prepare for it."

"Why don't you join me for a drink and tell me about it?"

"I have an early meeting."

He tilted his head toward the bar. "And it's not even nine. You deserve a vent session, and I'm all you've got at the moment. Plus, you barely touched your lone drink at dinner."

"You watched me?"

"You're hard to look away from, but I was also eating at the bar by myself. You and the Harveys caught my attention, and let's say I didn't like Tom's intense intention."

"Caught your attention? That's your excuse for watching me all through dinner?"

Despite her accusations, she'd already started toward the bar and Chance followed, taking his first easy breath since he'd seen Tom Harvey lay a hand on Charlotte's back as the hostess led them to their table.

He liked Tom. He'd even say Tom Harvey was a good guy. But Chance had seen a hell of a lot of shades of red as the man touched Charlotte.

They took two oversize leather seats that cornered each other near a small cocktail table. A waiter took their orders—a glass of red wine for each of them—and discreetly disappeared.

It was only as their waiter walked away that Chance saw the real misery stamped on Charlotte's face. "Want to talk about it?"

"Not really."

"Why not?"

She turned that vivid gaze on him, but her voice softened to a tone she didn't normally direct his way. "Because I'm not in the mood to get embarrassed all over again."

Chance had already admitted to watching her business dinner from a distance. Wasn't he the one who should feel embarrassed?

"I'm here to listen. And for the record, nothing you do is embarrassing."

"Yeah, well, this is. And I'm guessing you're here on business, and I want you to get a chance at succeeding. Making an enemy of the Harveys isn't in your best interests."

An enemy?

"I'm not doing business with the Harveys. So what the hell is this about, Charlotte?"

"Nothing I couldn't handle. Or haven't been handling for a long damn time."

Their waiter arrived with their drinks, and Chance gave Charlotte an opportunity to collect herself. He wasn't giving up on this, but he figured he might need to change his strategy a bit.

Because his head wasn't fully in the game, nor was the air between them as clear as it once was.

Ever since the kiss they'd shared six months ago, Charlotte had taken on a sort of mythic quality. She'd always intrigued him—likely more than she should—but that kiss had messed with his head.

So he needed to tread lightly here.

But what the hell *had* happened at dinner?

While he'd admitted to watching the proceedings, he hadn't sat and stared at her the whole time. He'd eaten his own meal and shot the shit with a few of the men seated nearby as well as the bartender who'd covered their end of the bar. Had something happened while he'd looked away?

Chance took a sip of his wine and considered how to play things. It was only when he caught a single tear slip down her cheek that he realized something was really wrong.

"Please tell me. Whatever ridiculous comments or nonsense the two of us manage to cook up between us, I do hope you count me as a friend."

"I do. Which is why this is so humiliating."

"I won't repeat it."

Charlotte shifted her gaze then, all that intensity laser-focused on him. He felt her size him up, take his measure. No matter what he'd always believed about himself, it never failed to lift him up that whatever she seemed to see when she looked into his eyes met with some inner approval. He'd felt like that at ten and every time he'd been in her company since.

It was all sorts of intoxicating, even though it was at direct odds with all he'd ever believed about himself.

"No, I believe you won't."

She hesitated for another second before seeming to come to a decision. "Tom asked me out for a drink after dinner."

"I'd suspected as much."

"You did?"

"Charlotte, you're a beautiful woman. He's not seeing anyone, if the fact that he came alone to the last Cattle Baron's ball is any indication. The guy's only human."

"Which is what I thought. I was kind, but I rebuffed the invitation."

"And?"

"He suggested I'd have been more amenable to

a nightcap if he and his father had signed on the dotted line of my proposal."

"The bastard."

"Yes, he is. Was." Charlotte shook her head. "*Is.* But the worst part is that I don't think he even realized how insulting he was."

"Like that's some fucking excuse?"

Chance had gone very still at her reveal—one she still wasn't entirely sure why she'd shared—but he was already up and out of his seat.

"Chance!"

He hadn't slowed down at her calling him back, so she got up, quickly walking through the bar until she could grab his arm. "Please come back."

"Tom Harvey doesn't get to talk to you like that."

"Chance, please keep your voice down." A wholly odd feeling settled itself in her chest. A sort of soft glow that not only defused how bad she'd been feeling but also made her inwardly preen at his quick defense.

While she appreciated it more than she could say, Charlotte suddenly wanted to find a way to deescalate the situation.

Because for one strikingly clear moment, it suddenly dawned on her that she and Chance could have far more interesting conversations about a lot of other things that didn't involve her shitty evening or the frustrating outcome of her business dinner.

She pitched the Harveys' business. They'd said no.

Tom Harvey tried for a date. She'd said no.

The fact that he was a raging asshat and too dumb to realize just how insulting he'd been was on him.

"Come on. Seriously, I handled it and put him in his place to boot. I'd rather sit and talk to you." Charlotte glanced down and realized her hand was still on his arm. "Please. Come on back."

Something must have registered, because that hard glint never left his gray eyes but his arm did relax beneath hers. "I don't have to like it."

"Neither do I. But let's not let it spoil our drink."

They took their seats back in the bar, everything just where they'd left it. There was a steady hum around them, but it faded away as Charlotte leaned into her innate skill for conversation.

"What brings you to Bozeman?"

"I had a meeting with the Complete Grocer. They started as a small health-food store but are expanding into more of an all-natural grocery store to compete with some of the higher-end specialty retailers. They like my work with grass-fed beef, and they also want a local provider."

"Chance, that's amazing."

He took a sip of his wine, eyeing her over the glass. "You're trying to divert me with compliments."

"Is it working?"

He finally smiled at that. "A bit."

The good humor was short-lived, though, as

he settled his glass on the small table in front of their chairs. "I thought Tom was a decent sort. You don't deserve that treatment."

"No, I don't. But beating him up isn't going to help the situation, either."

"How do you know I was going to beat him up?"

"I have two older brothers. I recognize that glint in the eye."

"For the record, I don't feel particularly brotherly toward you."

"And I don't feel sisterly toward you. It still doesn't change the fact that I recognize that glint."

She kept her motions casual, reaching for her glass and trying to ignore the mortifying realization of what she'd just confessed.

Aside from the mind-bending kiss she'd initiated six months ago, she diligently avoided anything that suggested even a whiff of attraction to Chance. Even if she had an intense infatuation with the man that had only gotten more pronounced since then.

Which was why she'd ended it and pulled away. And in the months since, because it had become increasingly clear that the verbal poking and jabbing they'd handed each other over a lifetime had been a front for something else.

Attraction that, if she'd read the situation right when they kissed—and she had no doubt she had—was mutual.

"Why don't you at least cheer me up and tell me what amazing PR strategy Tom and his old man were too dumb to take you up on."

"What do you know about specially mixed vitamins to optimize herd grazing, digestion and muscle growth?"

Chance propped his chin on his fist as he gazed over at her. "Oooh. Tell me more."

Chapter 2

Charlotte couldn't remember when she'd had such an enjoyable evening. When she factored in how terrible the night had started, the contrast of this time with Chance only served to further prove her point.

She enjoyed his company.

Maybe it was being a few hours outside of Rustlers Creek, with minimal chance of people recognizing them. Or maybe it was just a friendly face after a bad meeting. But one glass of wine had turned into two, and she was seriously contemplating a third, early-morning commitments be damned.

All the baggage they carried seemed to have vanished as the conversation had flowed from one topic to another. And the people they'd become—full-fledged grown-ups who had shed their childhood thoughts and actions years ago—could just *be*.

No one watching them like specimens under a microscope.

No one waiting for the latest tidbit of gossip when the two of them clashed on something.

And no one taunting or teasing about just how many sparks actually flew between the two of them.

And, wow, were there some sparks.

Each time their gazes met, she felt another wave crash over her. She'd always thought him attractive. Hell, she could still remember how her fourth-grade heart used to beat wildly when he walked into class in the morning. That damnable sensation had never really left her, and each and every time she was in his presence she felt both ten again and most definitely like a woman.

One with needs, who now understood attraction on an entirely different level.

It wasn't just his looks, either. He was intensely attractive, broad-shouldered and well-muscled, but there was an intelligence in his gaze as well as a deep level of emotional acuity that never failed to captivate her. She hadn't understood that either, as a child, but she'd instinctively sensed it. The way he knew all the math problems but also stayed after class to help Jason Trowbridge learn his multiplication tables. Or the way he could dominate the playground at recess yet still make sure the less popular kids were selected for a team.

Chance Beaumont was special.

Which made his seeming inability to see it that much more of a frustration.

With that in mind, Charlotte asked the question that had been hovering on the tip of her tongue all night. "Do you ever get tired of all the attention, coming from a small hometown?"

"You get more attention than most. Your family's well-known, and that only grows by the day with your sister-in-law's fame."

"Yeah, sure, there are some extenuating circumstances for my family. But we all grew up there. You. Me. Gray. Harper and Hadley. You don't think it would be different to live in a bigger place?" Charlotte glanced out the nearby window to the well-lit parking lot beyond. "Even Bozeman feels like a place where you could get lost a bit, freed from everyone's scrutiny and attention."

"Do you want to go somewhere else?"

Charlotte had considered it. She'd even discussed it with Harper when her friend had first come back to Rustlers Creek from Seattle. No matter how appealing the idea of disappearing into the crowd was, Rustlers Creek was her home. It always had been. Even if she had more ambition than often seemed wise in a town so small, she didn't want to live anywhere else.

"I love my home, and I always have. It's just a lot, sometimes. The everyone-knows-everyone vibe and the fact that we put each other in a box. People don't live that way, you know?"

Something serious filled his eyes, and Charlotte realized she was holding her breath, waiting for what he'd say. Although she usually saw the serious beneath the easygoing demeanor he always projected, it was fascinating that he didn't try to hide himself from her.

"No, they don't. But we like our mental shorthand of one another because then we don't have to go deeper or get into uncomfortable spaces."

"What's your mental shorthand of me?"

That grin flashed, broad and wide. It was a devilish grin, one that caught her low in the chest and made her think of sin. The delightfully naked kind. "And why should I tell you that?"

"Curiosity?"

The smile faded, replaced with something more thoughtful. "I'll only tell you if you go first."

"Not fair."

"I'd say it's exceedingly fair." He settled his nearly empty glass on the small table, the forearms he'd exposed when he rolled up his dress sleeves lightly flexing with the movement.

She should stop this now. They'd had a nice, diverting close to the evening, and she should stop.

End it before it went to a place she couldn't come back from.

But damn it, just like the devil, he'd tossed out a challenge she couldn't resist.

If she were honest with him, he'd tell her what he thought of her. And somehow, that was just too enticing an offer to pass up.

She *wanted* to know what he thought of her.

Hell, she'd wanted to know since she was in

the fourth grade. Proof that some questions could linger for decades, remaining elusive and just out of reach.

Should she reach for it?

How could she not?

CHANCE WASN'T SURE how their conversation had covered herd rotation, cow digestion and small-town emotional politics, but he and Charlotte had discussed it all.

And now he actually wanted her to tell him what she thought of him?

Hadn't he ruined his chances there years ago? Or even if his ten-year-old behavior could be excused—because, you know, *childhood*—his teasing, taunting and all-around asshole act since adulthood likely negated that one.

"I think you're a deep thinker. One who sees a lot more than he lets on. And I think you're not nearly as much of a bad boy as you pretend to be."

Chance laid a hand over his heart. "You wound me. No man wants to be told he's a milquetoast."

"There!" Charlotte pointed a finger. "Right there! *Milquetoast*. That's a serious word. Not one some fly-by-night pretty boy uses."

Since she'd hit a bit closer to home than he'd ever expected, Chance felt himself leaning even harder on the humor he'd relied on since childhood to get through the conversation. "You mean I'm not pretty, either?"

"Oh, you're plenty pretty. That's not what I meant."

Well, wasn't this interesting?

He wasn't blind, nor was he ignorant to what others saw when he and Charlotte got within twenty feet of one another. He *knew* the two of them had an attraction. It hummed between them and if he could feel it so intensely, he had no doubt others saw it, too. That fiery, all-consuming kiss back in the spring only proved it.

But her perceptions were a bit more spot-on than he was comfortable admitting.

"No one expects a Montana cowboy to have deep thoughts."

"That doesn't mean you don't have them."

"Then let me rephrase my point. No one expects Trevor Beaumont's offspring to have deep thoughts."

"Was he that bad?"

He rarely mentioned his father and certainly not in relation to how he saw himself, so it was startling to see Charlotte hit the mark once again.

Even more disconcerting to *feel* it.

"I shouldn't have brought him up."

"It's okay if you don't want to talk about him. I just—" She stopped, seeming to search for her words. It was a very *un*-Charlotte-like thing to do, and combined with the steady gaze that held questions and curiosity but not an ounce of pity, he surprised even himself when he began to speak.

"You just what?"

"I get the sense that he's in the way, somehow. For you. I know grief doesn't vanish overnight, nor should it, but your father is this ghost that hovers over your shoulder."

Chance wanted to be mad. He half wondered why the ire any mention of his father usually sparked was nowhere in evidence, especially since *grief* wasn't the term he'd normally apply to his feelings. Yet that gut-churning anger never manifested.

Instead, like some freaking beautiful magician, she seemingly pulled the words out of him.

"My father is a ghost. And it's all his own making. He threw a long-enough shadow in life that death hasn't managed to erase it yet."

Hadn't that been the most surprising thing about the old man's passing? He'd made life a living hell while he was alive, and other than the absence of that steady beatdown of verbal abuse, not much had changed since Trevor Beaumont had died two and a half years before.

Life was still a grind, every damn day.

Had the old man planned it? Or was he just such a ruthless sonofabitch that it was bound to happen anyway?

His father had run Beaumont Farms into the ground, leaving a mound of debt and a barely functioning ranch in his wake. Chance still cursed himself for not realizing how poorly things had been run, but they were moving cattle and selling product and he'd had no idea just how bad the books had been.

More to lay at his own feet.

He'd spent the first year barely keeping his head above water as he'd unearthed problem after problem. From bad books to crippling debt, his father had mortgaged the hell out of the ranch and had left little behind. Other than the value of the land itself, Chance had been shocked to realize how little they had.

It was such a contrast to Charlotte's life and the business her father and now her brother had constructed. A strong enterprise that was well-run, productive and the home of a staff who loved what they did and who they did it for.

Beaumont Farms couldn't quite say the same.

Chance had managed to claw back some team members who'd left, disillusioned with Trevor's management of the ranch, and he'd had enough conversations with them to know their loyalties had shifted and several were looking to settle in and stay for a while.

But there was so much to do.

"You want to talk about it?"

"Someday." Chance nodded. "Someday I think I will. But I had a really good day today, and I'm not willing to spoil it, if you don't mind."

"No." She shook her head, her smile firmly intact. "I don't mind at all."

Something about that smile snuck beneath his defenses. He always wanted more of her—more of her time and attention—but something had shifted between them. As if his willingness to open up had taken the normal edge off their interactions.

He'd felt it the night they'd kissed, too. They'd both been at Gray's house, helping him wrap up construction on his barn for the horse rescue he'd started. The day's work had flowed straight into dinner and then on into an evening of conversation between friends. He and Charlotte had experienced their first détente that night.

He wanted that again. And an evening like tonight made him feel like there might be room for something between them.

"Chance!"

The conversational din of the bar couldn't block out the loud, slightly slurred voice that matched the weaving form of a man walking toward them.

Chance recognized Johnny Cox immediately. The man had been one of his father's friends—to the extent Trevor actually had any—and had always fancied himself something of a ranching expert. Johnny had gotten Trevor into several bad schemes that had contributed to the mismanagement of Beaumont Farms and some of the debt Chance was still digging out of now. Schemes that Cox's own ranching operation was more than large enough to sustain.

With a murmured apology to Charlotte, he stood and greeted the older man as Johnny approached their seats. "Good to see you, sir."

"You, too, my boy." Johnny's red-rimmed eyes

drifted over to Charlotte, and Chance saw the moment recognition dawned. "Charlotte Wayne?"

"Yes, it is. Hello, Mr. Cox."

Chance had spent enough time around her through the years to gauge her moods. Most often her emotional freeze ray was directed at him, but that typically cool demeanor had nothing on the frosty politeness she aimed at Johnny.

"I didn't know you two were seeing each other."

"We're both in town for business and saw each other coming back from our respective dinners. We're just catching up."

Although Chance would have said the words first, something about Charlotte's matter-of-fact recounting of their relationship stuck in his throat.

He had no interest in their evening becoming a point of gossip, but that quick brush-off still stung. Ridiculous, he inwardly acknowledged, yet true.

"It's good to see the next generation making their place in the world." Johnny shook his head, his gaze on something he only saw in his memories. "Never had a son of my own. That fact pains me to today."

"I see Jane and Loretta from time to time. Neither were interested in ranch life?"

Although her smile remained firmly in place, Charlotte's questions about Johnny's two daughters—bookends to Chance and Charlotte in age—struck Chance as determinedly forced.

"I needed a son for that. I love my girls, but they're doing what they were meant to. Both found good men and are off making babies."

Charlotte lifted her glass, the very last sip of wine sloshing in the bottom. "Well, then. Happy breeding to them both."

Johnny's mouth tilted down slightly, the thinly veiled insult not exactly landing, but it was obvious the man sensed it on some level. Even with the cues that suggested he wasn't welcome, the older man grabbed a seat and pulled it over, all without being asked.

Their unexpected guest gestured for a fresh round of drinks, and their server had clearly sensed a rising tip with the arrival of the elder statesman. The waiter practically leaped into action, arriving in a matter of moments with fresh glasses of wine for Chance and Charlotte and a double whiskey for Johnny.

"I meant what I said. It sure is great to see the next generation making their mark." Johnny lifted his whiskey, and Chance and Charlotte politely clinked their glasses with his.

"How's your daddy doing, Charlotte? Your mamma, too?"

"They're well, Mr. Cox. Thank you."

"Heard the two of 'em went a few rounds last year." Johnny cackled. "Heard she kicked his old ass out."

"Then you heard wrong." Charlotte took a small sip of her wine, eyeing Johnny over the top of the rim. "I'd kindly ask that you not repeat those sorts of lies about them, too."

Johnny nearly choked on his sip of whiskey, coughing hard. "I don't tell lies."

"Then I guess we're agreed, and you won't repeat that."

"Just telling you what I heard."

"And I'm just setting the record straight."

Chance had heard the rumors, too, at the time, but they had a distinctly different tone and tenor. The root cause of Charlie and Carlene Wayne's marital struggles had been tied to Charlie's unwillingness to reduce his workload on the ranch. A state that bruised his pride and put his marriage at risk.

Charlie had eventually seen reason—and his wife's patience while he found it was a testament to Charlotte's mother in every way.

And Johnny's thoughts on it—just like his expectations for his daughters—were one more example of how little progress his father's generation had made.

Charlotte's smile had remained firmly in place, but ice seemed to encase her body from head to toe. Although he wasn't interested in amping up unfounded gossip about the two of them, their feet were close enough that he could tap the tip of her high heels with his toe. It wasn't much, but it kept their communication out of Johnny's line of sight, and the answering smile from Charlotte confirmed it was the right move.

"How's your business doing, Chance?" Johnny scratched the tip of his nose. "Heard you sold off some acreage to Gray McClain. I wish I'd've known you were selling. I'd have been happy to buy some of your land. Would be even happier in future should you choose to sell. I told your daddy that for years, but he hung on."

"The transaction with Gray was a private matter."

"Nothing private about real estate." Johnny gestured to the waiter for a refill on his whiskey. "So you be sure to keep me in mind."

"Like I said, the transaction with Gray was a private matter. The rest of my land isn't for sale."

Although he'd had no issue with selling off a parcel of land to his friend so Gray could start his blind-horse rescue, Chance knew what people thought of the transaction. It was seen as the first hole in the dam, a way for Chance to claw back some income for the ranch.

While technically true, it hadn't been the reason he'd sold. Gray's childhood had been as shitty as his own, and it was when Chance saw an opportunity to help—a real one that ensured the large-animal vet could combine his professional passion with a personal one—that he had wanted to take part.

To hell with what everyone else thought.

Gray was his friend, and what he chose to do for a friend had nothing to do with how he ran the business.

His business.

He might have spent far too many years in the dark about his father's ranching practices, but Trevor Beaumont's contemporaries had clearly had a handle on those poor business decisions for a while. Rumors had flown on swift feet throughout Rustlers Creek that Beaumont Farms might go on the market, and Johnny Cox wasn't the first to note his interest in buying.

Suddenly aware he didn't have much else to contribute, their small circle got very quiet as their waiter set down Johnny's refill. So it was a surprise when Charlotte picked up the conversational gambit.

"I understand Loretta is chairing the Cattle Baron's ball this winter."

"She is. That girl's not happy if she's not juggling six different projects. Like her mother, that one. But she's going to do a damn fine job of it."

Whatever male bravado and clueless reaction to female accomplishment this was, Charlotte did warm to Johnny's fatherly pride. "I'll have to reach out to her and offer my help."

"I think she'd like that. You're doing marketing work now, right?"

"Public relations, yes. I have my own firm."

"I guess ranch life wasn't for you, either."

Charlotte's deflection was smooth, but Chance saw the slight curl of her lower lip before it smoothed out.

"It's my brother's love. And while Wayne and Sons means the world to me, it's always meant a bit more to him. I thought it best that he have the opportunity to build his dream. My dreams took a different path."

"The world's changing." Johnny drained his glass and stared at the remaining ice with a philosophical air Chance wouldn't have expected from the man. "People want different things."

"Some do, some don't." Charlotte shrugged before winking at Chance. "The important thing is giving people an opportunity to figure it out."

Chance had gotten the distinct sense the man was about to order a third round when he seemed to think better of it.

"I'll let you two get back to your visit, then." He nodded his head to Charlotte. "Miss. Good to see you."

"Enjoy your evening, Mr. Cox."

Chance waited until the older man was out of earshot before he turned to Charlotte. "That was some impressive shade."

"Which part?"

"Most of it. The man's insides were roasting, and he had no idea."

"I suspect all his work pickling that liver of his put up a considerable barrier." She sighed before tapping the edge of her nearly full glass. "He tried to screw my father out of a deal when they were both young ranchers ages ago. He then made the serious mistake of trying the same on my brother a few years back. There's not a Wayne in Montana who wouldn't love to rip the man's eyes out."

"Bloodthirsty *and* unfailingly polite. It's a potent mix, Miss Wayne."

"And one more reminder of this evening's failure of a dinner." She settled her glass down on the table. "And since I'm bringing that back up again, it's proof I don't need any more wine. I can feel the maudlin stirrings settling in."

"Let me just get our check, and I'll walk you up."

"I'm good."

He hadn't missed the appreciative glances that came her way all evening. And while he had no qualms that she was safe and secure in a crowded, well-staffed hotel, he would see her to her room. "Humor me."

The waiter headed over, and Chance dug his credit card out of his wallet. He handed it over without looking at the bill, amused when Charlotte let out a low sound.

"What's that about?"

"The bastard stiffed you on the check."

Chance didn't want to laugh—his bank account might be in a sorry state but he *could* afford to buy an old cowboy a few drinks—but the look of sheer irritation had him smiling all the same.

"I've got it."

He signed off on the check—and made sure the waiter received a more-than-fair tip—and set the leather folio down on the cocktail table. The quiet bubble that had seemed to envelop them before Johnny's arrival had vanished, and the noise—a lot louder than when they'd first walked in—throbbed around them as they wove their way back out of the bar.

Chance didn't recognize the new crowd Johnny had sidled up to, but he was pleased to see the man's back was to them. He was only walking

Charlotte up to her room, but it wouldn't do to have any unsavory rumors spreading around.

Especially when all he wanted to do was drag her into his arms and give the likely gossip some credence.

"You're made of some seriously stern stuff, Beaumont." Charlotte patted his shoulder as they waited for the elevator. His suit jacket should have blunted the heat, but he could have sworn he felt the shot of electricity from her fingers clear through to his muscle fibers, layers of fabric be damned.

"How's that?"

She glanced over her shoulder at him as she stepped into the elevator. "Stiffed on the check *and* cock-blocked by an aging cowboy. Yet here you are, cool as a cucumber."

Chance wasn't sure about cool.

Or composed.

Especially since every ounce of blood in his body had just landed squarely in that cock she'd so casually mentioned.

CHARLOTTE RECOGNIZED THE difference between a buzz and drunk. She knew how to manage her alcohol consumption, and the basic equivalent of three drinks over a five-hour evening wasn't anywhere near to drunk.

Which only left one alternative.

She was horny as hell and unsteady on her feet. Damn Chance Beaumont and his sexy gray gaze and sharp jaw and his willingness to actually *listen* to her. Even his unfailing politeness to an elder rancher who didn't deserve the respect stuck a landing somewhere deep inside the gooiest parts of her.

Why did it all add even more pluses and hearts and freaking cupids to the *Yes, please* column when it came to the man?

She didn't need this.

They'd proven over and over that the two of them were a bad idea.

It had become an easy go-to in her mind to use that first incident—the mother of all embarrassments—as the reason they couldn't be together. But it was more.

So much more, steeped in a lifetime of small-town living, vastly different upbringings and a subtle yearning that neither of them had the guts to do anything about.

So they teased and swiped and circled each other.

And through it all, they'd found a way to successfully lead very separate lives all while maintaining an odd, but real, friendship.

Losing sight of that wasn't only dumb but it set her up for a heartache that was far worse than a rejected Valentine's card when she was ten.

More to the point, love was all about risk. She might have only been ten when she'd done it, but she'd risked her heart for him, and he'd stomped on it with all the finesse that came in a pair of size-six worn-thin Nikes.

If that had been all, she'd have found her way past that initial heartache. But Chance Beaumont had never—not once—made a move since that suggested he felt otherwise. Even their kiss six months ago had ended, nothing coming from it other than heated dreams and the feel of him that she still caught on her lips from time to time.

It had left her with a notion—one that might have been more fantasy than truth—that somewhere along the way, they'd gotten stuck in the assumptions of who they were. Her from one of the most successful ranching families in Montana, and him from a life that he had to claw out each and every day to pay for the bad business dealings of his father.

Whether she was right or not, she wasn't mistaken on the attraction. But there wasn't much either of them could do unless they moved past those half-formed impressions. Especially since that conversation with Johnny Cox had reinforced the lingering idea, making it seem less like fantasy and far more like the truth.

She was the daughter of Charlie and Carlene Wayne, a successful couple, with a successful ranch and a successful family. Her oldest brother had taken that already-productive ranch and more than doubled its output. Her next-oldest brother was a top-tier player in the NFL. Her sister-in-law was known throughout America for her cooking empire.

The Wayne name meant something.

And all Chance's name meant was an opportunity to buy land on the cheap.

It wasn't fair and it wasn't right that it all stood between them. She didn't see him that way. But she would be playing ignorant if she didn't acknowledge that others did.

The real question was why Chance believed them.

Chapter 3

Ghosts.

After that escape from the hotel bar, Chance was half convinced they were real.

One ghost in particular.

He'd never been a big believer in the idea of souls stuck on earth, lingering through their after-life, but the persistent impact of his father's life on his own had made Chance start to wonder. And Charlotte's assessment of his father's ongoing in-fluence was insightfully spot-on.

He wasn't a stranger to death. His mother had died when he was a kid, and while he had wisps of memories that floated through his mind—good ones from a happier time—he'd been so young that they had minimal form or substance.

But Trevor Beaumont?

The man haunted his life in every way, every day.

Tonight was one more example of that fact.

Today had been a good day. He'd nearly wrapped up a new business deal—a solid, productive one that supported his business goals—and he'd had drinks with a woman who challenged him and interested him in every way.

And smack in the middle of it was a fat-ass reminder that he'd never really escape the old man.

Heard you sold off some acreage to Gray McClain. I wish I'd've known you were selling. I'd have been happy to buy some of your land. Would be even happier in future should you choose to sell. I told your daddy that for years, but he hung on.

He'd bet every last dime—and every acre of that property he was so fiercely determined to keep—that no one went around asking Zack Wayne to sell off some land. No one would even think to ask.

Yet Chance was fair game.

Charlotte stopped in front of a hotel door and dug her key out of a small purse. "I'm sorry tonight ended on such a sour note. I did have a nice time. Thanks for the drinks and a chance to get out of my own head."

"You're welcome."

"And, look—" She broke off, her heavy exhale sending small wisps of hair floating around her face. "It takes a big man to still be nice to an aging cowboy like Johnny Cox. You did a good thing tonight, and you were a hell of a lot nicer than I was."

"You were unfailingly polite."

"It's not polite when there are insults laced beneath the words."

"The *happy breeding* comment was inspired."

She smiled then, the tension riding her features fading as the laughter took over. "The shame of it all is that I really do like his daughters. And their kids are adorable. It's the insinuation they've failed their father somehow that's so maddening." Her good humor faded. "And it's a cop-out to say he's only that way because he's older."

"It is a cop-out. Your parents aren't that way. And my father was a raging bastard but he wasn't so . . . *old* in his thinking."

"So what's to be done?"

"Correct them where you can. I noticed you didn't take any shit about your parents' marriage. Land a direct hit or two whenever possible. And keep the polite smile in place and hope like hell you don't turn out that way."

"Some might say it's inevitable."

"A lot of things feel inevitable. That doesn't mean they are."

Even as he said the words, Chance felt the ground tilt beneath him. Were they talking about old cowboys or the realities of aging any longer?

Because Charlotte Wayne had felt inevitable for a long time, too.

Not her cock-block insinuation earlier—that somehow the two of them were on a path for the evening, circumvented only by Johnny Cox's arrival. No, he admitted to himself, it was something more.

It was the way he was so aware of her and had been for most of his life.

It was the increasing connections between them, their friends and family coupling up and building lives that had put them firmly in each other's orbit.

And it was the additional reality that neither of them had successfully made a go of another relationship that had resulted in marriage and family.

Those things carried weight. And when you added their shared history, it all felt more real, somehow.

More tangible.

And a whole lot less like a mistake if he reached out and pursued what he'd always wanted.

Charlotte moved up into his space, her already-tall form and added height from her heels putting them eye to eye. "Chance? Please don't walk away."

The shift toward what *could be* between them—so like his own thoughts—had his head spinning, but Chance was determined to keep them on level ground.

"I'm not sure this is a good idea."

"Why does it have to be any sort of idea? Why can't it just be a choice? Tonight."

His desire for her—whether he gave in to it or not—had nothing to do with some ridiculous aging cowboy without social graces. Yet because of the interruption during drinks, he couldn't help but feel there was a significance there.

A large, blinking sign that warned him to slow down.

Fate offering him one last lifeline before he

made an irrevocably stupid decision with irreversible consequences.

His hormones didn't agree, but that deep-seated sense of self-preservation—the one he could never fully ignore—had sparked to life.

"I know you had a difficult evening. I invited you to a few drinks as a friend, Charlotte. Not to get inside your hotel room."

"I know that."

Did she?

Because for all their attraction, he hadn't carried an ulterior motive when he'd left the steakhouse. Hadn't even dreamed that they'd be standing here a few hours later.

He saw something flicker in the depths of her rich gaze. "But now that we're here, I'm suggesting we make the most of our time. Why are you backing away?"

Even as he cursed himself for it, Chance moved a fraction of a step closer, unable to ignore the brewing argument. "I'm not backing away from anything."

"Could have fooled me."

"You were the one who backed away six months ago."

He hadn't allowed himself to voice that reality—even in his most reflective moments—for fear he'd read too much or too little into that kiss. Which was the real proof that her ending things *had* affected him.

Especially since he realized it was the same choice that stood in front of him now.

Her gaze fell before returning fully to his. "Because I knew better than to put myself on the line. In fact, I'm questioning why I'm even doing it now."

He'd dodged an emotional bullet that night, and he could hardly blame her for doing the same. So once again, he tried for cool logic, even if he didn't feel a single bit of it. Especially with that light scent of hers tangling up his senses and wrapping his whole damn body in a tight fist. "Which brings us right back to where we always end up. We're friends. We've known each other forever. It's enough."

"What if it isn't?" Charlotte asked.

The rising wave of frustration crashed against the shore at her quietly uttered words. "It has to be."

He knew it. Understood it, even if she didn't. It was a decision that lived in the crossroads of that elevated place where the Wayne name sat in the Montana ranching community. The hallowed air of reverence that name took on in Rustlers Creek. And the very real, very tangible fact that a man who barely knew how to keep his business afloat didn't take up with ranching royalty.

The idea might be as old and antiquated as Johnny Cox's views on the world, but it didn't make it wrong.

And since it was his heart and his pride that were liable to get obliterated in the crossfire, he had a right to stand by his decision to keep away from her.

He was a grown man. He knew how to control

his urges, and he knew damn well not to touch the things that would burn him into oblivion.

But God, why did she have that soul-destroying face? From fierce and earnest to sharp and alert—and about every other expression he'd practically memorized since the age of ten—Charlotte Wayne was a fucking heartbreaker.

"Why does it have to be anything at all? Why can't it just be fun?"

And there it was.

The swirling, eminently *practical* temptation he himself had thought of far too many times. That sly inner voice, as destructive as the snake in the garden who offered Eve the apple. The one that suggested they could just give in to what was between them. What would be the harm?

That they could take advantage of the mutual heat and need, and it wouldn't have to cause problems or change their dynamic. Because, after all, it was two consenting adults simply scratching an itch.

Nothing more.

Nothing of substance.

Even though Chance knew it was utter and total bullshit.

"How does this happen?" Her voice was soft when she spoke, the subtle taunts that had hovered underneath her words since they got to her hotel door nowhere in evidence. "Why are we here?"

"Why are we where?"

"We are two healthy, consenting adults. We do have a real, tangible attraction to each other. Why is it like an unscalable mountain between us instead of a bright, vivid sign that screams *Go*?"

It was the question that got him.

No, Chance amended to himself, it was actually that shift in tone.

If she'd continued to press him, that subtle taunt lacing her words, he'd chalk the moment up to all the times they'd verbally tussled with each other in the past and step away.

Only now, any hints of provocation or attempts at goading him were gone.

A man was only so strong, after all.

He could only resist and come up with excuses for so long. Excuses that were a hell of a lot easier to muster up when he couldn't breathe in that tantalizing scent of honeysuckle that lightly emanated from her skin. Or when he couldn't see her pulse tripping at the base of her throat.

Because when the woman was Charlotte Wayne, how in the ever-loving hell was a man supposed to walk away?

Charlotte's hand went to his chest as he bent his head to brush his lips to hers. As their mouths met, Chance knew the truth. No matter how badly he needed to resist her, there was no amount of self-control that could walk away from this woman pressed up against his chest.

Because in that moment the blaze had already consumed him.

PURE FEMININE TRIUMPH flooded her veins, but
Charlotte had no time to consider the victory.

Chance's large body was pressed to hers, his
hands splayed across her back as he pulled her
against his chest. Just like their first kiss six
months ago, something elemental and ferocious
arced between them.

Fierce.

Savage.

Feral.

Desire wasn't supposed to be like this. Something that rattled a person from the inside out.
A feeling that literally removed all of the calm
veneer she lived with and, maybe even more important, *believed* in.

But with Chance she had no other way to be.
The man literally pulled her outside of herself. Her
freaking personality *changed* around him. From
the way they teased and taunted each other to this
desperate need that had claws so sharp she wasn't
sure how she was still standing.

Hell, even this moment was a testament to that
fact. She'd damn near begged him to come into her
hotel room, to give in to this attraction that never
seemed to fade, even when their common sense
or years of history or all-around mutual surliness
clanged like a bell for the next round.

She was *different* around Chance, and yet, in
some ways, she was most herself.

Absently, she reached behind her with the
hotel-room key card, trying to get the door open.
With a smile against her lips he murmured, "Give

it," and managed to keep their mouths in perfect contact all while unlocking the door.

The wall of the door at her back swung open, and she stepped through it backward, unable to see where she was going yet bone-deep sure in the knowledge Chance had her safe in his arms.

Whatever was between them might be fierce and raw, but it was honest.

She wouldn't fall with him. He wouldn't let her.

Yet, she was deeply afraid of falling anyway. A state she only ever felt around Chance. He was temptation personified, but he was more than that, too. She *liked* him. With a genuine sort of affection that went beyond the complex chemistry that always sizzled between them.

Or maybe the chemistry was simple and it was the genuine affection that made it all so complex?

Whatever the reason, it all added up to a constant seesaw of thoughts.

From their walk to the elevator, when she'd convinced herself that nothing could or would happen, to now, when it most assuredly *was* happening, she didn't quite know how to take it all in.

Nor was she entirely comfortable with the whip-quick changes in her own emotions and behavior. But . . .

But *God*, the man could kiss.

Had she ever felt anything like it? Sure, she dated. And she'd enjoyed being part of several mutually satisfying relationships over the years. Just because they hadn't turned into anything lasting hadn't diminished the time spent in them.

But they hadn't ever fired her blood like *this*.

Even memories of really good sex came nowhere close to the feeling of Chance's large hands splayed against her hip and lower back.

Not by a long shot.

The hotel room wasn't large, and in a matter of steps he'd backed her past the bathroom to the king-size bed that dominated the space. She'd left one of the bedside lamps on, and it cast a warm glow over the room.

"Chance." She murmured his name on a sigh as those clever hands drifted from her waist to trace a soft, teasing line along her stomach. Her muscles quivered under that light, tantalizing touch, shockwaves echoing off her nerve endings at the simple play of his finger.

Charlotte gave in to her own exploration, burying her hands beneath his sport coat before thinking better of it and pushing the heavy material off his body in one deft move. Thick muscle met her seeking palms as she stroked sculpted shoulders.

She was a woman who'd grown up around fit men. Living on a ranch ensured that physical labor—and the resulting body that came from it—was a given in her life. Add on her brother Jackson's lifetime in sports and she recognized what the human body was capable of. But to feel all that heat up close, against her palms, was heady.

Because she sure as hell didn't look at her brother or his friends the way she looked at Chance.

And didn't that just make all the difference?

"That's an amused smile if I've ever seen one." His gaze had become an even darker shade of gray, a reflection of the softer lighting and the clear stamp of his desire.

"I was just admiring these very broad shoulders, Mr. Beaumont. They're impressive."

"The mark of the laborer."

His smile never dimmed but she heard it all the same. That subtle disdain even in the midst of a compliment. "I was thinking it was the mark of a man who works hard. One who's determined to make something out of what's his."

"Whatever works, sweetheart."

She nearly argued right there at his quick self-deprecation but stopped. Not because she believed he was right, but because giving in and arguing only brought them right back around to where they usually ended up. Two people on opposite sides of a circular disagreement that was easy to get into and difficult to get out of.

Maybe it was time to stop.

Or, even better, perhaps it was time to listen and figure out a new way into the problem. One that was less provocation from her own tender, close-to-the-surface feelings.

Besides, an eminently rational voice whispered through her mind, she'd gotten what she wanted.

Chance Beaumont all to herself, with the promise of sharing considerably more heat in delightfully intimate places. Why was she looking for reasons to pick a fight?

And then her thoughts shattered into a million fragments as his hand closed over her breast, the brush of his thumb drawing her already-tight nipple into an even harder peak. She wrapped her arms around his neck—talking rarely got the two of them anywhere productive anyway—and pressed herself into his palm as his thumb continued that erotic play through the layered materials of her blouse and bra.

He kept up the steady kisses against her lips, her jawline, breathing lightly over the shell of her ear before moving on down her neck. Charlotte felt the sweet answering tug of desire between her thighs, even with both of them still fully clothed.

God, where did the man learn to kiss like that?

He had kissing down to a suave art. Just the right amount of tongue. Firm lips used with perfect pressure against her skin. And those hands . . .

Charlotte's head fell back as his fingers shifted to the row of buttons on her blouse, his mouth covering the throbbing of her pulse just above her cleavage. His tongue flicked along her skin, heated breath warming her even as the erotic sensations had delicious tension lighting up her nerve endings, shooting shivers down her spine.

Those light shivers took another trip up and down the length of her spine when her blouse came fully open, his wide palm lying flat against her ribs. And then he upended the moment by neatly spinning her around so that her back was pressed to his chest. The hand that covered her stomach shifted so that he once again palmed her breast, his clever fingers plying the hard peak of her nipple.

Charlotte was helpless to do anything but revel in the moment, her head pillowed against the solid curve of his shoulder as pleasure erupted over her skin, matched only by an increasing restlessness between her thighs.

And when his free hand slipped lower, beneath the waistband of her skirt, Charlotte was half convinced Chance was a mind reader.

A soft whimper—was that her?—fell from her lips as one finger, then two, snuck under the elastic of her panties. The whimper shifted into a hard moan as those fingers swept over her clit, a shocking intrusion of pleasure. With slow, erotic circles he centered his ministrations—just *there*—and Charlotte's knees buckled. He tightened his hold on her, the move seeming instinctive, without ever breaking that steady, *insistent* demand of her body.

His lips pressed against her ear, his breath sending more erotic shockwaves over yet another erogenous zone, and Charlotte nearly forgot to breathe as sensation after sensation flashed over her. The warmth of his body was a welcoming cradle, but it was the heat of his words—a mix of reverence and erotically dirty suggestions—that had her release coming on her with an overwhelming rush.

"Come for me, Charlotte. Come for—" He broke off, something raw and vibrantly real shimmering to life around them. "*Fuck*, there you are."

Her body tightened around his fingers, a savage moan falling from her lips as her release simply overwhelmed her.

And as her body shattered, she never doubted the man who held her in his arms would hold her through it.

Fuck.

That lone word played over and over in his mind, but Chance couldn't figure out if he was cursing himself to hell or simply expressing exquisite shock and awe at the glorious woman in his arms.

Whatever he'd expected—and he'd had a lot of years of imagining this—touching her like this had been better than every fantasy he'd ever had.

She was . . . exquisite.

It was the only word that fit, in every single way. And in her climax—one he still rode her through—he was humbled, dazzled and damn near hypnotized all at once.

He glanced down, his gaze unerringly caught on the way his hand still slipped beneath the waistband of her skirt. The silky material of her blouse was featherlight against his skin, and the wet heat of her was proof of what they'd just shared. Erotic images of that same heat covering his dick shot his already-tight body nearly into orbit, tremors echoing through his legs and nearly buckling his knees.

A small voice whispered through the clanging in his head. Chance had the irrational urge to shake it all off and return to that glorious place where it was just him and Charlotte.

But no matter how he tried, something reasonable and fucking *rational* kept notching that inner voice louder and louder, a steady drumbeat that rose several decibels at a time.

Run.

Run as fast as you can, Beaumont.

Run, goddammit!

"Chance?"

That soft, breathy tone floated up to his ear. There was welcome there, and so much promise. And, maybe, he realized with abject misery as he gently removed his hand from her skirt, there was belief there, too.

Belief in him.

Belief in *them*.

Even as he questioned—just as he always had— why she had any at all.

Caught between the demands of his body and the choking need to leave before they did have sex and altered the landscape between them forever, he stilled at the peal of his phone. Glancing in the direction of his discarded sport coat, he felt her subtle nod. "Get that."

"It's Gray's ring, otherwise—" He heard his hollow words, well aware of the shocking relief doing battle with his aching body.

"Answer it."

The call might have provided a handy excuse, but it was also his livelihood, and his friend and ranch vet didn't call from his work phone—which Chance kept on a special ringtone—if there wasn't good reason.

The call was quick—clinical, even—but it did give Chance the excuse he needed to leave.

"I'm sorry, Charlotte, but I need to go. There's a problem with one of the heifers. Gray thinks he's going to lose her."

It was a financial blow he could hardly afford, but it was Charlotte's empty gaze—even as she nodded her head in acceptance—that had him inwardly cringing.

She'd already whirled away, the silk of her blouse whipping against him in her rapid movements.

"I am sorry. For all of it."

"You're sorry? For all of what, exactly?" Arousal had stained her skin a gorgeous pink, but it had nothing on the growing ire that arced between them.

He knew he'd overstepped, yet the words kept tumbling out, insistent truth bombs that lit the room on fire. "I shouldn't have started this. I should have left you at the door. I never should have allowed this to go so far."

"That's a lot of *should*s, Chance. And what a marvel to realize how you *allowed* it all to happen. Like some fucking benevolent sex dictator."

He'd seen a myriad of emotions on Charlotte's face over the past two decades, but the sheer mix of incredulous fury and hurt was unlike anything he could ever remember. It tore at him, that dark, bleak pain that had a sharp set of claws.

Her blouse hung open, the disheveled evidence of what they'd shared, but as Charlotte stood to her full height, Chance saw none of it.

Instead, he saw a regal queen, well able to rise above the likes of him. It was the place she belonged and the place she needed to stay. Now and always.

He wanted her.

He wanted her like he needed breath and sustenance, but he couldn't have her. A few moments of losing his head wouldn't—worse, it *couldn't*—change that.

Which was why he bent down to pick up his sport coat and draped it over his arm, covering the hand that had so recently pleasured her.

"I'm sorry I let this go so far, Charlotte. You don't deserve this."

"No, I don't."

He stood there a few beats more, forcing himself to hold her gaze. He'd stand there and take it—all her ire and hurt and layers of frustration at what was between them—because it was what she deserved, yes.

But more, because he couldn't look away.

There was nothing he wanted more than to stay right there and finish what they'd begun. Nothing he wanted more than to look into the darkest depths of her eyes and believe he was worthy.

He finally turned away, the impasse between them insurmountable, even as need and desire still lingered in the air, curling around them like smoke.

It was only when he got to the door that she finally spoke. It was a small, broken sound, so unlike the furious fire that had threaded her words only moments before.

"You know, Chance. You don't deserve this, either."

He might not deserve it, but he knew no other way to be. It was why he said nothing. Instead, he stepped through the door and refused to look back.

Chapter 4

Charlotte wasn't a big believer in regrets. A person made decisions with the information in front of them. Regretting those choices later when the bright light of hindsight shimmered clear as a bell was an insult to your former smart, educated, decision-making self.

She was proud of being an independent, *smart*, freethinking woman.

But hell and damn, she wasn't sure what she'd possibly been thinking the night before.

"Oh yeah, right," she muttered at herself as the sign for the Rustlers Creek exit came up on the interstate, "you were thinking with your hormones."

Every last glorious hormone that could still send orgasmic aftershocks through her system as she thought about Chance on the entire drive home.

And his hands.

And those clever fingers that had managed to . . .

The man had stripped her bare and still walked away.

Bastard.

Worst of all, she wasn't sure what had her more upset. That he walked away or that he'd walked away before they'd had sex and not the equivalent of what she might have expected after a high-school football game.

If she hated the idea of regrets, Charlotte hated emotions that vacillated between *petty* and *childish* even more.

Yet here she was.

Right back to the same place she and Chance always ended up. Except this time she'd finally rounded a few sex bases before getting the time-out warning.

And since her thoughts had veered back dangerously close to high school again—because really, *sex bases*?—Charlotte focused on navigating off the highway and attempting to channel her inner adult instead of the fifteen-year-old who seemed to have set up shop this morning in her head.

She nearly succeeded when she came down Main Street and saw Harper Allen just coming out of Hadley's latest Rustlers Creek project-slash-flash-of-marketing-genius, the Trading Post. Harper might be Charlotte's sister-in-law's sister, but as far as she was concerned, the woman was family. They'd been friends since they were kids, and she was beyond happy Harper was back in Rustlers Creek to stay.

Or as much as living a life in two places could be considered staying, yet Harper did it with effortless cool and an ability to balance her personal life in Rustlers Creek and her business life in Seattle with enviable grace.

Charlotte pulled up along the sidewalk and rolled down the window, letting out a hard whistle first. "Well, that's a successful career woman if I've ever seen one!"

Harper turned at the noise, confusion giving way to a broad smile. "Takes one to know one! What are you doing here?"

"I had business in Bozeman yesterday and an early call I wanted to take from my office. I ended up taking the call from the car anyway when the client asked if I could move things up by an hour."

"That's an early and productive morning." Harper waved a hand toward the opposite end of the street. "Since I know you like nothing better *and* I know you well enough to know you haven't eaten, let's go get pancakes."

"You're on."

Charlotte found a parallel spot beside the sidewalk a few car lengths down and parked. As soon as Harper caught up to her, Charlotte swooped her up in a hug. It was only when Harper pulled back, confusion in her gaze, that Charlotte had to admit she might have held on a bit too hard.

"You okay?"

"Better than okay." Charlotte put on her breeziest smile. "You're looking at a woman who just extended a PR contract through all of next year."

While the new contract wasn't a lie, Charlotte knew damn well what Harper had felt in that too-tight hug.

Which meant she had to navigate pancakes with a bit more finesse than she normally did.

Should she tell Harper about what had happened with Chance?

Would it feel too much like a gossip session?

Or should she keep all these feelings—including the delicious ones she couldn't quite shake—to herself for a bit?

And damn it all, why was she still channeling high school? Was that all she and Chance were? Some childhood mistake she couldn't get over?

Even as she thought it, Charlotte disregarded the notion. Whatever else might exist between her and Chance, what happened last night was most decidedly adult. More, prior to that, their ability to talk about their lives outside of the scrutiny of Rustlers Creek had ensured they actually had a conversation like two adults out for the evening.

Was that why what happened after had left such a sour taste?

She knew their attraction was mutual. Whatever else last night was—and his abrupt departure was hard on the ego—it hadn't been about lack of want or need or attraction.

Which had been little consolation when she'd spent the night all alone in bed.

Shaking it off, Charlotte stepped into the diner with Harper. Things were busy, but there were still seats, and in a matter of minutes they were ensconced in a booth with coffee in hand and pancake orders on the way.

"This is a pleasant surprise." Harper added a small drop of cream into her coffee, and Charlotte couldn't help but smile.

"Very pleasant. But why do I get the sense you're going to suck down that coffee with your teeth gritted tight the whole time?"

"I can handle it."

"Oh come on. This is an abomination to you and your yuppie coffee and you know it."

Harper had worked in the tech industry for more than a decade when she'd given it all up to buy a small coffee chain in Seattle. She'd had the business about a year, and in that time had seen wild success with her chain, Coffee 2.0. Her focus on custom blends created by algorithms was a bona fide hit, and she could barely keep up with demand.

Magic in a cup was how Charlotte saw it, and she had already gotten hooked on her own custom blend.

"I wouldn't quite go to *abomination*, but it wouldn't hurt them to change out the brew basket more than once every three years."

Charlotte took a sip, so desperate for the brew she was willing to put her own special blend out of her mind. "And I think you're being generous. I'd give that cleaning at least five years."

Harper took a sip, then reached for more cream. "They could do better."

"And I have no doubt you'll sell them your own version of a Rustlers Creek special blend before the year's out."

"I've tried, but Mo's been stubborn."

Charlotte waved a hand. "Tell him you'll toss in some new coffee machines and put him on your website. He'll listen then."

Harper's eyes widened. "That's a great idea."

"PR, baby. It's what I do."

"Is that why you were in Bozeman?"

"I was there for a dinner, pitching some business."

"How'd it go?"

"About as well as you and Mo." Charlotte hated the dry tone and couldn't help but frown at the remembered dinner with the Harveys. "And I'm mad about it because I really thought it would go in my favor."

"They went with someone else?"

"They don't believe they need PR and didn't even read the proposal."

Harper's mouth dropped open. "That's shitty."

"Extremely."

"Did you tell them off?"

"Sort of."

Their waitress arrived with their pancakes so Harper waited until they were alone again before pressing that one. "You're not a *sort of* kind of girl. What happened?"

"It's just irritating. And it makes me irritated

that I'm irritated so I'm just more irritated about the whole thing."

Harper took another sip of her coffee, minus the grimace this time. "Sounds like you're actually mad."

"Yeah, that, too. I met with a ranch owner from up in that area and his son. They've got a good business, and they're launching some new vitamin products I think can really go somewhere with some marketing support."

"Sounds ripe for some press."

"Exactly!"

Harper's attention to Charlotte's pitch was far more sincere than Tom and Merrill Harvey's had been the night before, and Charlotte found herself oddly grateful she'd found her friend as she was driving back into town.

"They think it's a waste of time."

"Amateurs." Harper shook her head as she smothered her pancakes in syrup. "I worked on some of the most complex pieces of software known to man, and we still marketed the shit out of them. It's bad, narrow-minded business to think people are just going to magically find your work."

"It got worse."

Harper stilled with a forkful of pancakes in hand. "How?"

"The son suggested I could stay and have a drink with him after the old man left. When I declined, both because I didn't want to and because I had an early drive home this morning, he insinuated I'd have been happy to stay if they were buying my proposal."

"Asshole."

"I agree. The jerk was out of line and I'm still mad I didn't kick his ass."

The deep voice filtered over them in response to Harper's astute assessment, and Charlotte nearly jumped out of her skin as she turned around to see Chance standing behind her.

"Chance." Every moment of the night before and how they'd left each other—as well as all the sexy moments *before* they'd left each other—hit her in one gigantic wave. "What are you doing here?"

"Came in to take out some breakfast. I—" For all her lingering ire and embarrassment, she saw the pain in his eyes. "We lost one of the heifers to hardware disease."

As a rancher's daughter, Charlotte immediately knew the problem, but Harper looked genuinely confused. "What is that?"

"We try to manage it, but there are a lot of foreign objects on a ranch. Wires, bolts, nails. They can all come off the fencing or fall out of the ranch equipment. One of the cows ingested some nails while grazing."

"Chance, I'm so sorry." Despite the lingering frustration from the night before, Charlotte slid over in her booth, gesturing for him to sit down before pointing to her still-untouched plate. "These just arrived. Why don't you eat, and I'll get something else."

The man was asleep on his feet, whisker stubble covering his jaw and clad in a gray sweatshirt that molded to his shoulders with soft, well-worn cotton, fraying along the collar.

"I didn't mean to interrupt, but I saw you both over here and came to say hi while I was waiting for some takeout. And when I overheard your story I felt the urgent need to editorialize."

"You were there?" Harper's question was a simple ask between friends, but Charlotte knew damn well it was anything but innocent.

She thought about saying something, but one look at Chance's bloodshot eyes and she realized arguing was a petty, jerk move. He'd had a shitty go of things, and since he'd made the two-hour drive back to Rustlers Creek in the middle of the night, it was obvious they hadn't spent the evening together.

Highlighting it would only put Harper's antennae up. Or would set them to quivering, Charlotte amended to herself, since they were clearly up and on high alert.

"I was in Bozeman for work, too. Charlotte and I were at the same restaurant." Chance stilled as he cut into the pancakes. "So were half the cowboys in Montana, come to think of it."

"Is there anything we can do to help?" Charlotte asked, anxious to change the subject of where they both were the night before.

"Gray's been over since early this morning. He did what he could."

Chance stiffened beside her, and Charlotte

didn't need to know the rest of the story to know that Gray had euthanized the animal. She laid a hand on his shoulder. "I am sorry."

"It's fine. It's the business."

"Yes, it is."

Harper was already digging out her phone before she excused herself. "I'm going to go call Gray. When he left in the middle of the night, I was half-asleep and obviously not paying attention. I didn't realize he was headed out to help you."

"Let him know I've got breakfast and will bring it back in about fifteen minutes."

Charlotte shook her head. "Harper, why don't you take the food back to the ranch, and I'll drive Chance over once he's done eating."

"I'm good."

"Humor me," she said, channeling the no-nonsense voice she'd learned at a young age from her mother. "You're dead on your feet. I'll drive you, and we can get your truck later."

"Thanks."

"Eat."

"You sure you don't mind if I head out?" Harper asked, taking the stack of food containers from their waitress.

"Of course not." Charlotte's mind was already whirling with the realities of sitting in a car with Chance on the ride out to Beaumont Farms.

Realistically she knew the disastrous evening the night before hadn't eradicated Chance from her life. Despite what had happened, it wasn't like they'd never talk again.

But somehow she'd expected she'd have more than eight hours to get used to having had an orgasm at his highly capable hands.

In his hands? By his hands?

Shaking off the grammatical flight of fancy, she caught Harper's pointed stare. "I still want the rest of this story from last night's dinner." Her friend repositioned the stack of take-out boxes in her hand. "Including whatever it is you're leaving out."

"I'm not leaving anything out."

"It's an asshole story. Of course you're leaving something out."

Before Charlotte could argue the point, Harper was already moving back through the diner at a clip, and Charlotte was once again alone with Chance.

The already-tense air grew electric as they sat there, neither saying anything. Which had Charlotte searching for something to mitigate the awkwardness. "Fancy seeing you here."

"Fancy that." He barked out a short, tired laugh. "Things sure can change in a few hours."

"You think?"

She heard the terse edge to her own voice and wasn't quite sure what to do about it. She wasn't interested in playing the hurt woman, nor did she want to enter shrew territory. She took full, personal responsibility for her choices last night and didn't owe anyone anything for it.

Chance didn't, either.

Which made his forlorn expression something of a surprise.

Whatever else she and Chance did well, it was their mutually assured cocky veneers that refused to show their vulnerabilities to the other.

Yet all she saw in that moment was an ocean of vulnerable in his tired gaze. Chance took a deep breath before turning to face her in the booth. "Charlotte, I'm not going to give you an empty apology."

"So give me a sincere one."

"I can't make a different choice."

"No, you can't. The horse is out of the barn, as they say. And in more ways than one."

"I'm sorry I let things go so far."

"I'm not."

His eyes, bloodshot and tired, widened at her words. "You can honestly sit there and say that to me? After—"

"After you left me still wanting? Yes, I damn well can."

"Charlotte—" His gaze moved around the diner meaningfully. "Come on, not here."

"Then where, Chance? Everyone already thinks we regularly screw around. Why not feed the fire?"

"This is no one's business."

"That hasn't stopped anyone from making it their business."

His gaze never wavered, but there was a bleakness there that spoke of the coldest days in February. "Why can't you leave this alone?"

Why couldn't she?

Why was this one man an endless temptation she couldn't seem to shake?

"Why'd you come over here to talk to Harper and me?"

"It would have looked pretty bad if I stood six feet away and ignored you."

"My back was to you, and Harper and I were talking. We weren't exactly watching the door."

"Yes, but people were watching me."

"So it was a pity hello."

"Damn it, Charlotte." He balled up his napkin and tossed it on the table. "Quit fucking around with my words."

"Then quit acting like you owe anyone in here anything."

"I didn't—" He broke off, nodding his head. "You're right. And I am sorry for that."

"Since you're here, you might as well finish those pancakes. Then I'll drive you home."

"I can make the drive."

"Humor me. And I've got twenty that says we won't pass the end of Main Street before you're fast asleep."

As if sensing it was better to give in than argue, Chance reached for a few napkins in the small dispenser on the table. The edge of his forearm just brushed her breast as he reached, and they both stilled at the accidental contact.

Words she hadn't realized she was holding inside suddenly filled her throat, spilling out in a rush. "If you don't want me, that's the breaks. What I can't tolerate is walking away or being treated like I don't matter."

Although he shifted just slightly, so that his

body didn't touch hers on the return trip to his lap, Charlotte felt Chance's full focus on her with all the impact of a winter squall, eradicating everything until you lost all sense of the world around you.

But it was his words that hit with the full force of a rampaging avalanche.

"Last night was about a lot of things, but not a single one of them was me not wanting you."

CHANCE KNEW THAT exhausted and sad made for a miserable state to attempt a serious conversation. Hell, to attempt any conversation at all.

But here they were.

And whatever last night was, he'd be damned if Charlotte was walking away from it thinking he didn't want her.

He wanted her so damn bad his fingers burned from the memory of touching her. Walking away from that intimate act that had nearly cost him his sanity. And then, to have those lingering memories on the long ride home, with nothing but regrets and a lot of time to think.

To curse himself.

And to curse the strange, swirling circle of their lives that seemed to pull them together and spin them back apart, over and over.

What were the odds she'd be in Bozeman at the same time he was? And then layer on the same restaurant and the same hotel. Sure, they ran in similar circles, but there was something uncanny about how directly they'd fallen into each other's orbit.

"Then what was last night about?"

"Attraction. Need. Whatever this thing is between us."

"So you do agree there's something between us?"

The temptation to leave it as a rhetorical question beckoned, but he'd started this. And not just this moment, but last night, too.

He'd asked her to drinks.

He'd walked her to her room.

He'd leaped in with both feet when the sands shifted between them as he'd known they inevitably would.

They were magnets, and they never quite pulled far enough away to break their unerring attraction.

"Come on, Charlotte, you know there is. To the bigger point, the whole damn town knows there is."

"Then why do we keep running away from it?"

"Because I'm a Beaumont and you're a Wayne."

He felt her bristle at that, and on some level, he recognized that his argument was about as rational as believing in the tooth fairy or hanging a horseshoe over his barn door for luck.

At the same time, he knew he wasn't wrong.

They might run in the same circles, but they occupied a very different place in the strata that made up those circles.

"That's nothing but an excuse."

"Is it? Is it really? Because I can guarantee

Johnny Cox walked away from last night's visit with us thinking you're slumming."

"Chance! I—"

"He did, and you know it. If he didn't think that, he'd never have brought up buying my ranch. Not in front of you."

"Come on, I know that was a dick move and it upset you, but it's other people and whatever misguided bullshit they want to believe."

"You've built a professional reputation understanding people's bullshit perceptions drive their choices. Don't try and forget that now."

Her lips had opened, and she looked ready to argue when her mouth closed abruptly. When she finally did say something, her words were vintage Charlotte.

Still challenging.

Still pushing him.

"So that makes it okay?"

"Hell no. But it doesn't make it any less true."

"Yet, it is a block to you and me acting on some healthy, adult attraction."

Once again, temptation struck swift and hard. A not-so-subtle lure that suggested sex with this woman would be easy.

Simple.

Even as he full well knew that nothing about Charlotte Wayne was simple. Least of all the feelings he never seemed to get a firm grip on. "Unless you've rewritten last evening, we did act on some healthy, adult attraction."

"We half acted."

Unbidden, something in the prim set of her mouth and suddenly stiff shoulders had him grinning. "I'd say we fully acted."

"But you didn't—" A blush crept up her neck.

"I didn't what?"

"You know."

For as miserable as he'd felt walking into the diner, he couldn't quite deny how good it felt to see that blush stain her cheeks or how much more comfortable he was in this place, when banter and irritation formed both a cocoon around them as much as a protective wall between them.

"Maybe you need to say it. I haven't had much sleep, and I'm not sure I'm understanding your point."

"Chance Beaumont." She smacked him against the shoulder, obviously unconcerned if anyone around them noticed. "Quit being an ass."

"About?"

She shot him a side-eye then before she reached for the last piece of bacon still on the plate. "Everything."

Although it was comfortable to sink back into the familiar, something had changed last night.

"We don't have to be those people, you know," Charlotte finally said. "The ones trapped in everyone else's expectations."

"Some days I can believe that more than others."

"And on the days you can't?" she pressed, obviously unwilling to let it go.

"On those days I am firmly grounded in the world we live in. The one we grew up in and that made us.

The one that's embedded so deep in our blood you can't separate it from the rest of our DNA."

"It doesn't make it any less of an excuse."

"Maybe so, but it's a powerful one."

And it was.

For all his belief in his work ethic and in the fact that he could still make something of Beaumont Farms, Chance knew the truth.

He was hanging on by a shoestring.

His father's debts were nearly overwhelming, and no matter how hard he worked, he was one disaster away from losing it all.

Hadn't last night proven that?

It was a reality of ranch life that not every animal under their care would make it. They ran that risk each year with the calves and the complexities of nature that never fully went away. He had no doubt Zack Wayne hated to lose an animal just as much as Chance did.

But Zack's ranch didn't live or die by one animal's survival.

And Beaumont Farms damn near did.

That's what he couldn't make Charlotte understand. Couldn't seem to get her to see that they might have been raised by ranchers half a town apart from each other, but it didn't mean they had a single thing in common.

She didn't understand it in the fourth grade when she'd blindsided him with the biggest Valentine's card in class. And she still didn't understand it, with all the additional wisdom they'd both acquired in the ensuing twenty-plus years.

A jaded part of him wondered if it was purposeful, but however much he knew about Charlotte, one thing stood out above all.

She didn't lie.

Which meant somewhere deep inside she not only believed he was worthy of her attention but that he was a man of value.

And *that* was the real temptation.

Chapter 5

It was the fastest twenty bucks she'd ever made.

Charlotte glanced over at Chance just as she hit the stoplight at the far end of Main Street. His head tilted back against the passenger seat, and sleep was evident in the steady cadence of his deep, even breathing.

The strange, restless thoughts that had accompanied her on the entire drive back to Rustlers Creek from Bozeman suddenly seemed insignificant now that she had Chance sitting in the seat beside her.

How did this one man tie her up in knots? And with the world's dumbest arguments to boot.

Did he honestly think there was some power imbalance between them because her father was Charlie Wayne and his was Trevor Beaumont?

It was like something out of an eighties-era soap opera, yet it took up a massive amount of space in Chance's psyche.

For all she thought she understood about him, this one roadblock suggested she actually knew very little. And she hated not knowing something.

Which was the only reason she allowed her mind to wander as she made the last turnoff for Beaumont Farms and took in the view outside her front car window.

For all her attraction to Chance and nearly a lifetime of knowing each other, she'd only been out here a handful of times. And it was with that knowledge that Charlotte tried to really see what he believed was the difference in their lives.

Weather-roughened fence bordered the long driveway that led from the road to the main house. Although the fence posts were straight and the wood fitted, she could see clear wear and tear in the structure. Not rotten, per se, but weathered to the point of needing repair.

It was the sort of ranch enhancement her father and now her brother replaced on their own farm every couple of years but which Chance had obviously had to leave alone.

Due to finances? Lack of ranch help? On some level, Charlotte knew, weren't they the same?

She'd grown up with a world of support all around her. Even now, she never went over to Wayne and Sons without seeing someone in the fields, riding a horse or working in pairs on some task that needed doing around the ranch. From

branding day to burning day and every possible
job in between, there was always activity humming at Wayne and Sons.

Yet as far as she could tell, the fields around
Chance's property were quiet.

It was pretty, she thought, the flat land slightly
rolling as far as the eye could see. But parts of
it were clearly unworked. Those burning days
she knew her father had practiced religiously—a
practice her brother now followed—ensured
unproductive brush was burned off to provide
newer ground and fresh grass for grazing. Some
of the land had obviously been managed, but as
she looked farther she could see a lot of brown
in the far reaches of the field. It was a missed opportunity and, even more, a sign his land wasn't
being used to maximum potential.

And it was in that moment that Charlotte had
the briefest inkling of what Chance had meant at
the diner and why Johnny Cox's casual offer to
buy his land had struck so deep.

They'd spent a lot of time the past twenty-four
hours talking about ambition and work, and he
was clearly in her corner when it came to her own
achievements. But no matter how much support
he showed her, stubborn pride had its place, too.

Especially when all that pride was inwardly
directed.

What was to be done about it?

"We're here already?" Chance's hushed rumble
of a voice shot straight to her belly. It hovered in
a similar range as his voice last night, low and

gravelly in her ear, and her body lit up with the mere memory of it.

"Yep." Ignoring the slight squeak in her voice, she swallowed around her suddenly dry throat. "And you owe me twenty bucks."

"For what?"

"You were asleep before we hit the stoplight on Main. Just like I bet you'd be."

He grinned at that. "That's a sucker bet if I've ever heard one."

"I'll take the self-righteous satisfaction that I called it right, then."

The grin faded as she pulled into a spot near his stables. "Thanks for driving me out here. I was dead on my feet. And it might have only been fifteen minutes, but I feel a hell of a lot better."

"You're welcome. I can hang around and drive Harper back in to get your truck if you want."

"Nah, one of the hands'll drive me in later."

"Okay, then."

He'd already reached for the handle when her hand shot out, almost of its own accord, landing on his forearm and stilling his movements.

"Losing that cow isn't your fault."

"I didn't say it was."

"You didn't have to. It telegraphed off you in waves."

He leaned back in the seat, his gaze focused on the ceiling of her sedan. She didn't miss the tight bands of muscle that corded his neck or the sheer disgust that turned down that sculpted mouth.

"It's a careless mistake. We keep up with the

tools on the ranch, but there's always something to watch out for. Some loose metal you weren't expecting or didn't even know you'd lost off a piece of equipment."

It was a sad fact of ranching. The increasing humanity and sustainability they'd brought to husbandry still couldn't erase every implication of using man-made tools. And the loss of metal parts, be it bolts or nails or other small nondigestible objects, was a reality of the business. Especially when the cattle they raised weren't able to address the problem on their own when they fed.

"I'd say Zack loses a few animals a year to hardware disease. And that's with all the proper precautions anyone can possibly take."

"Zack can afford to lose a few animals."

She might be willing to accept the fact that her brother's ranch and Chance's had different levels of productivity, but the comment still stung. "It's never good to lose an animal. I realize not everyone understands the business, and they don't have to. But to suggest a rancher doesn't care for his herd—*all* of his herd—is unfair."

"No, you're right." He removed his hand from the door and laid it over hers where it still lay on his forearm. "That wasn't fair of me."

"Okay."

They sat there like that without moving, the intimacy of the night before arcing between them. It would be so easy to force his hand. To make him admit that there was something there between them.

But he does know.

Which was the truth Charlotte came back to over and over.

It was the thought that had accompanied her observations as she wended her way through the ranch property. It was also the instinct and awareness she'd carried since she was young in the way the two of them just *were* with each other.

The problem wasn't that Chance didn't want her.

The problem was that he did.

CHANCE KNEW HE needed to get out of the car. He needed to take his hand off Charlotte's, effectively disengaging them both from the contact, and he needed to get away.

He'd cursed himself in any number of ways for the night before, but no harder than this moment when he could still remember the way her body hummed against him. The soft skin of her breasts and stomach. The way his lips seemed to fit perfectly against that dip between her neck and shoulder.

And the hot, sexy heat of her against his fingers as he pleasured her to orgasm.

It was that last bit that finally had him moving.

He needed to get away from her and that damned subtle understanding of hers that truly *got* all the things he wasn't actually saying when he talked about a dead cow or the differences in their families.

He'd made it a lifetime habit to bait her—and

he'd be a liar if he didn't admit to enjoying it—but none of it ever seemed to get quite the outcome he was going for. Like a bullet ricocheting off a target and hitting the shooter, something about his engagements with Charlotte always ended up in him taking the hit.

It was the damnedest thing, but somehow when she looked at him, the veneer of the smooth, easygoing, devil-may-care rancher faded away. It was the facade he showed everyone else, and they seemed to buy it.

Why not Charlotte?

"Chance!"

His name was muffled, but he heard it through the quiet in the car. Gray was waving his hand and running toward them from the direction of the barn.

He glanced over at Charlotte, and she was as intrigued as he was, both of them jumping out at Gray's enthusiastic welcome.

"What is it?"

Something strong and happy telegraphed through Gray's exhausted features and bloodshot blue eyes as he came up beside the car. "Call me Miracle Max."

"What?" Chance recognized he should know the reference but the events of the past twenty-four hours had dulled his ability to put coherent thoughts together.

"*The Princess Bride*," Charlotte and Gray both said together.

When confusion obviously remained on his face,

Charlotte pressed on. "Billy Crystal. He played the medicine man, Miracle Max. The one who brought Westley back from the dead?" She shook her head. "Sheesh, Chance. Westley was only *mostly* dead."

"Okay, fine, I get the reference. What does any of that have to do with us?"

"The heifer, Chance," Gray said. "Sorry, man. I know we're both walking zombies, but try to keep up with me. The heifer. The hardware disease. We saved her. Which"—he slapped Chance on the shoulder—"you're so writing the recommendation for my intern. Sameena is going to make one hell of a large-animal vet."

"The cow didn't die?"

"Not on my watch." Gray glanced back over his shoulder in the direction of the barn and corrected himself. "On our watch."

Chance pictured the young woman who'd helped Gray over the past few hours. Her petite features and long black hair made her look like she was both about twelve and barely able to lift a bird, let alone operate on a cow. Yet she'd kept up with Gray's every request and had done an admirable job handling an animal that had more than four hundred pounds on her.

"That's incredible."

"It's a testament to the preventative care you invested in. The cow magnet did its job, and we were able to manipulate it enough to catch most of the problem and then operate on the rest."

"But when I left an hour ago, the heifer was on the barn floor. You did all that in under an hour?"

Chance had struggled a bit with leaving, but when it looked like the cow wasn't getting any better he'd suddenly needed to get away from the ranch and the large barn they used when animals needed treatment or euthanization. He wasn't normally willing to walk away from a problem on the ranch—captain of the ship and all that crap—but something about the night before and the ridiculous conversation with Johnny Cox over buying his land, plus his chickenshit excuses to walk away from Charlotte, had all coalesced in his mind.

Add on the lack of sleep, a race of a drive home at two in the morning and the thought of losing one of his livestock, and all of it had just struck a deeply sour chord.

"Sameena read a case recently in one of her textbooks. The procedure hasn't been tested extensively, but there was minimal risk in trying and maximum benefit if we succeeded."

That willingness was one of the things he treasured most about his friendship with Gray. "I'm grateful that you acted so quickly."

"And made medical history in the process."

Chance suddenly realized that Charlotte had been uncharacteristically quiet, and he turned to her. If Gray was at all surprised Charlotte had driven him to the farm, he didn't let on. Instead, he tilted his head in the direction of the barn, obviously still excited about his medical success. "I'm going to get back in there. We do have to clean up a bit, and I want to be prepared for when the heifer comes out of anesthesia, but I heard you pull up, and I wanted to let you know."

"Where's Harper?" Charlotte looked around. "I thought she'd beat us over here."

"She's feeding half the hands right now." Gray smiled, pride shining through his exhaustion. "She has more of her sister in her than she realizes. And, Chance, I think your food budget just jumped. She's spoiled your hands over the coffee in the bunkhouse and seems a bit too proud of herself that she got them to revolt over the economy-size generic stuff they've been buying at Walmart."

"God help us." Chance gave a mock shudder even as he knew he was hardly one to complain. He'd already gotten a bit too used to the blend Harper made up for him. And while he'd never personally participated in the drug trade, he had a suspicion Harper had taken a page out of the standard pusher's playbook. She was more than willing to give everyone a free taste of her coffee blends.

And once hooked, they all came back to her for more.

Gray headed back toward the barn, and Chance turned to face Charlotte. Their casual, if fraught, conversation at the diner had faded, replaced by the stilted self-consciousness now that they were around friends. It killed him that things had gotten so awkward between them, but no matter how much he cursed himself, he couldn't go back and change last night.

It wasn't like you should apologize to a woman for sex. Even if he did feel an overwhelming urge to somehow atone for walking away last night, something on a cellular level told him that going down that path over his actions the night before would not go well.

Which left him with nothing more banal than a rather obvious dismissal. "Thanks for driving me back."

"You're welcome."

"I'm going to go in and check on things now."

"Sure. That works."

"I—" He realized there was something to say. Something that mattered. "After last night, it was the last thing I deserved, and you did it anyway. So thank you."

She smiled but didn't say anything, and he got the distinct sense that silence was costing her, but she didn't back down. Instead, she turned on her heel and walked back to her car.

Her outfit was similar to the one she'd worn the night before, a silky blouse tucked into another sexy skirt that hit at a respectable level just above her knee. It was professional attire, and on anyone else it would look conservative to the point of staid.

On Charlotte it was sexy as hell.

The way the material of her skirt hugged her hips. The long length of her calves. And those glorious heels that made his mouth water.

He still remembered what she looked like in pigtails and braces, and at the time, that look had held a strange power over him, too.

But this?

The feminine form that walked away left him raw and empty in a way that made him desperately want to call her back.

It made him wish he could do things different. Or maybe more to the point, that he could *be* different.

So he gathered up that feeling and buried it down deep. And headed back for the barn he'd willingly deserted an hour ago.

WHATEVER DISCOMFORT CONTINUED to linger after his half-finished evening with Charlotte, it couldn't, Chance knew, stand in the way of business. So with his boots firmly strapped on, he headed out to visit Zack Wayne.

And hoped like hell the man wasn't a mind reader for all the carnal images of his sister that Chance currently carried, stamped on every inch of his thoughts.

A highly uncomfortable thought that plagued him on the drive over.

And one that went nuclear when the only person to greet him from the inside of Zack's office was his father, Charlie.

Aka Charlotte's father.

A ribald *fuck* blazed through his mind as Chance doffed his hat for the elder statesman. "Sir. Hello."

"Chance. Hey there. Come on in." Charlie waved him in as he bustled his way around Zack's desk, taking a chair opposite the one he'd gestured Chance into after they shook hands.

"I hope I'm not disturbing you."

"Not at all. I was on the hunt for an instruction manual Zack claims is buried in a desk drawer. This is a welcome surprise and bound to be far more interesting."

They shared a few pleasantries, and Chance firmly put his evening with Charlotte out of his mind. He could be as uncomfortable as he wanted, but she was a fully grown woman, capable of making her own decisions in life.

Knowing her, she'd kick his ass for thinking otherwise.

"I came here, sir, looking for Zack, but you might be able to help me with some of my questions."

"Shoot."

Since Charlie looked happier than a pig in mud at the request, Chance felt a few more degrees of discomfort slip away. "I had some trouble overnight with hardware disease in one of my heifers. Nearly lost her if not for Gray and the quick thinking of his intern."

"He's got a bright crop this year." Charlie added, "Sameena is going to revolutionize the large-animal practice all on her own."

"Her quick thinking was one of the reasons the cow lived, in fact."

Charlie smiled at that. "Never fails to amaze me how much talent there is in the world. I love to see it put to good use."

"I came to see if Wayne and Sons had any other methods to manage the problem."

"You check the feed conveyors regularly? Make sure their magnets are all in place."

"We do a full equipment check at the end of each week. And we do a thorough ground check each time we bale hay or work fence line."

"Good, good." Charlie nodded, clearly pleased.

At the older man's obvious respect for his practices, Chance felt his own frustration over the incident improve. His father hadn't had much time for the additional labor involved in both steps, but Chance had insisted on it, doing it himself whenever he could and, once he had control over the ranch, implementing it as process.

"You check the magnets, too?" At Chance's obvious confusion, Charlie added, "When doing the equipment checks, it's an easy step, but it does catch a problem from time to time. Magnets sometimes get clogged up in their base, near the machine. You can't often see it, but you can get small bits of wire up in there that need clearing out."

"I'll do that right away."

"It's a small step, but it's one more practice you can put in place. The constant battle between nature and human progress."

"It's endless."

"That it is," Charlie agreed.

"Dad, did you—" Zack's holler faded away as he entered the office. "Chance. How are you?"

Chance stood and shook Zack's hand. "Good to see you."

"Chance has been shooting the shit with an old rancher. Which was a hell of a lot more fun than digging around for a baler manual."

"No doubt it is." Zack shot Chance a wry smile. "Talked to Gray earlier. He sounded like a zombie, but I heard he had a productive morning at your place."

The conversation moved from discussion of the heifer to the discussion Chance and Charlie had been having over husbandry practices when Zack shifted in a surprising direction. "I also heard from my sales team you had a fantastic meeting with the chain in Bozeman."

"News does travel." Chance could hardly be upset to be a point of discussion since Zack's same sales lead had helped get him the opportunity. "But I had to cancel my meeting because of the cow emergency."

"Come to the Trading Post tomorrow night. Hadley already extended an invite to the Hill family. We'd love to have you regardless, and I should have extended the invite sooner, but you can use the time to mingle and close the deal with them."

He said it so casually—made the offer as a matter of course, along with the assumption Beaumont Farms would get the deal—and once again, Chance was struck by the simplicity of it all. Where he'd spent a lifetime hearing his father talk about the evils of networking and giving anyone else a hand up or a break, the Waynes did it willingly. And unlike his father's misguided expectations, they managed a thriving business in spite of it.

"I'd appreciate that." Chance considered the invitation. "What's the Hill family doing in town?"

"Hadley's doing a special segment with an up-and-coming country singer for a sister network to hers. It's a bit of cross-promotion, and we've invited as many local contacts as we can. The lack of invite to this really is on me. I meant to reach out last week once we got it all finalized, and it kept slipping my mind."

"I'd like that, Zack. I'd like that a lot."

And just like that, Chance had to admit, his life took another sharp turn because of someone with the last name of Wayne.

CHARLOTTE APPLIED LIPSTICK one-handed and with an eye half on her rearview mirror as she snagged the last spot in the Trading Post lot. Damn, she was late. And she could lay the blame squarely on her nonagenarian grandmother.

"I told you I could drop you off."

"Why the hell would I want you to drop me off?" Mamma Wayne groused at her from the passenger seat. "I want to make an entrance on that stepper thing."

"The step and repeat?"

"Yeah. If we got here too early we'd look like them damn Kardashians."

"I think they're famous enough to be fashionably late."

"Then I *want* to be like them," her grandmother breezed on. "And if you dropped me off we'd have to make a big production of getting me outta this damn car since my knee's been acting up. This way, you and I can saunter up there like royalty."

Since there was no arguing with her grandmother when she got an idea in her head, Charlotte just nodded and finished applying her lipstick. Mamma Wayne loved being a part of anything having to do with Hadley's show. *And*, she'd informed Charlotte on the drive over, she wanted to fix her up with the country singer who was promoting his new album tonight.

"You do realize I'm more than a decade older than him. Why not one of the triplets?"

Mamma Wayne had bulldozed through that one. "All three of them are still young and having fun."

"And what am I?"

"Old enough to teach him a thing or two."

Charlotte had avoided any further questions—or the temptation to encourage more of Mamma Wayne's horny, homespun wisdom—for fear her grandmother would think to repeat her ideas to the poor, unsuspecting singer later. Something she'd be sure to do if she got any sort of response to her outrageous attitude.

Since a sigh would be tantamount to encouragement, Charlotte turned off the car and got out, coming around to help her grandmother. Mamma Wayne still had a lot of zip in her tank, but navigating the concrete parking area was a lot on her, and Charlotte wanted to keep a firm hand in place to guide her. Since their walk up had the added benefit of making that entrance her grandmother wanted, the two of them worked their way toward the crowd that centered around the front of the Trading Post, coming up to the step and repeat just as the last arrival moved past the posing area.

"Mamma Wayne!" The photographers hollered their excitement, further proof that her grandmother had become a bona fide star all on her own from her appearances on Hadley's show. Bea, Hadley's producer, had figured out the right mix of including Mamma Wayne in just the right number of episodes, all while keeping the audience hungry for more, and the woman had become a sensation all on her own.

One whose one-liners and sassy attitude were beloved by all.

Now, if I can only steer her clear of the country singer, Charlotte thought as they moved into the store.

She'd already spied her parents across the room and calculated how quickly she could get her grandmother to them when Charlotte's gaze came to a halt as she caught sight of Chance. She didn't know he was coming tonight but couldn't say she was surprised, either. Her brother and sister-in-law had invited a variety of friends and business acquaintances, and it stood to reason he'd be here.

But still, she couldn't slow her racing pulse and heated reaction.

Wasn't she supposed to be mad at him? Or, if not mad, at least still in a fine snit over their interrupted evening in Bozeman.

Yet here he was, clad head to toe in black, his broad shoulders absolute perfection in a well-fitted suit jacket, black jeans and black boots. The image of a well-dressed bandit immediately came to mind, filling her with a mix of heat and longing that set her knees to trembling.

It also gave her the abstract thought that she'd love to be tossed over his shoulder and dragged from the event out into the night. Especially when that dark gray gaze, like liquid silver, reached out and caught her in his thrall, daring her to look away.

Chapter 6

Equilibrium.

It was the lone thought that kept whispering through Chance's mind as he stared at Charlotte across the crowded Trading Post.

They'd had it. For a long time, they'd lived in a certain sort of balance. It manifested in their general swiping and hissing at each other, through high school and then on into adulthood, but it had always carried an air of good fun and basic congeniality underneath.

Only over the past six months had it tilted.

Oddly, just like it had when they were ten and they'd had the Valentine incident. It had taken them a while to get past it, but in the way of kids—hell, in the way of life—time had moved them forward.

Yet, here they were again. Harper's arrival

back in Rustlers Creek and her and Gray finding each other again had thrown Chance and Charlotte together more often than either of them had likely expected. It was more than a passing hello at the Branded Mark on a Saturday night or a few words at the annual Labor Day picnic in the town square. They were a common group of friends who spent time together.

And it was messing with his goddamn head.

Whatever mental bravado had carried Chance through his meeting the day before with Charlie and Zack, standing at a party staring at Charlotte erased it all. God, she was beautiful. In a way that never failed to stop him in his tracks.

He'd mingled with some folks he knew, was introduced to others, but the air in the room seemed to change when Charlotte arrived. Like some sixth sense, he'd instinctively known when she wasn't there.

And now she *was* here.

Her dress only added to the already-bright fire that was Charlotte. A vivid shade of red, the dress wrapped around her curves in a way that immediately made a man think of his hands doing the same.

Or maybe that was just him.

And the incredible sense memories that had imprinted on his palms from touching her.

All the reasons he'd left her behind in her hotel room—the complications and the distance it caused between them—surrounded him inside the Trading Post in human form. Her family.

Their collective friends. Even the business deal he'd discussed with the Hills—something that meant meaningful change to his business, yet was so small her family had no reason to even consider it.

The elements that separated their lives were real. Tangible.

It didn't make him feel any better about his decision, but it did reinforce why he'd instinctively pulled away.

Even as his unexpected visit with Charlie kept going through his mind.

The older man hadn't treated Chance's business as less-than. He'd spoken to him as one rancher to another. One who had experience and advice to give and who provided it willingly. Chance had only met the man a handful of times, but after each instance he'd come away with a mix of awe and a sort of quiet reverence that a man could provide that sort of example for his children.

That he could be that fair and honest and decent.

The exact opposite of Chance's own warped experience of a parent.

It was that realization that finally got him moving.

In every interaction in their past, Chance finally gave in and found some reason to go talk to Charlotte. She was the lodestone that tugged him toward her, irrevocably. Even as it happened, he'd hold out, playing some dumb game with himself before he gave in.

But tonight it was different.

Tonight, he realized he owed it to her and he owed it to that same family that both awed and inspired him to step forward and be a friend. It was the only way they'd get to that place of balance again.

The only way to get their equilibrium back.

CHARLOTTE FELT HIM before he spoke, coming up to the small conversational circle made up of her mother, her grandmother and Harper.

"Good evening, ladies." Chance tilted his head, greeting each with a soft kiss on the cheek before he came to her. "Charlotte," Chance said, his voice low before he pressed a chaste kiss to her cheek.

"Chance." Mamma Wayne leaned in before Charlotte could say anything. "You look like sin, young man. What bank did you rob on your way over here? And can I come on your next adventure?"

Since her grandmother's comment was practically a match for her earlier thoughts, Charlotte could do nothing but shoot her mother a helpless look and hope that Mamma Wayne would make some small attempt to behave.

Even though Charlotte knew that was about as likely an outcome as her suddenly sprouting wings and flying out the door.

"Chance, how'd your meeting go with the Hills?" Carlene Wayne cut in smoothly, ignoring her mother-in-law's antics, a skill she'd honed over a lifetime.

"Very well, thank you. Your husband and son were amazing to share the opportunity, and I appreciate the invitation tonight to close the deal."

"You closed it?" Charlotte asked, unable to hold back her excitement.

"Looks like," he said and grinned, and in that smile Charlotte was surprised to see the shimmering edges of the young boy she remembered.

"That deserves some champagne." Carlene clapped before nodding toward Charlotte. "We've settled in well here, but why don't you and Chance get some drinks at the bar for all of us and we can toast his success."

In a matter of moments she and Chance were in line at one of the open bars set up at various corners of the shop, Charlotte left with the subtle yet persistent sense her mother would have found a way to send them off regardless of the reason.

But since they did have a reason to celebrate, Charlotte opted to lean in.

"I'm so excited for you, Chance. This is fantastic news."

"We still need to finalize the paperwork, but they were pleased with my pitch and the ability to manage a ramp-up with them and build slowly."

"It's a fantastic strategy. You demonstrated that you can grow with them, yet didn't pressure them for capacity they're not yet ready to take. It's a good partnership."

Chance smiled at that, but Charlotte couldn't deny it didn't fully reach his eyes.

It was curious and reminded her, once more, that he was more comfortable celebrating others than himself.

And then there wasn't anything else to say as they gave the bartender their order, loading up the glasses of champagne. Since they'd already seen Gray join Harper in their conversational circle, each of them balanced handfuls of champagne flutes as they worked their way back to the table where they'd settled Mamma Wayne.

"I love a celebration," Harper said as she took a flute for herself and one for Gray. "And champagne makes it all the more festive."

The rest of the flutes were passed around, and everyone had them lifted high. Gray made the toast, and Charlotte was just about to take a sip of her drink when she caught a subtle gleam in her grandmother's eye, immediately followed by a small tumble forward at the table. The move was enough to toss Mamma Wayne's champagne from her glass all over Charlotte and Chance where they stood side by side at the table.

"Oh! I'm so clumsy!" Her grandmother looked vaguely contrite, that merry glint still hovering in her rheumy gaze. But it was Carlene who moved into action.

"Charlotte, Chance. We've got some wipes in the back office. Go ahead and get that cleaned off or it'll set in your clothes." Carlene shot a small side-eye toward her mother-in-law. "I'll see about getting refills."

Chance had already come around to hover over Mamma Wayne. "Are you sure you're okay?"

"I'm fine." Mamma waved him off. "Just clumsy is all."

Since Charlotte knew for a fact her grandmother could still fire one of her show pistols at a paper target and hit the bull's-eye, *clumsy* wasn't the first word that came to mind, but she took Chance's arm all the same. "Let's go get cleaned off. The champagne will set and will leave light marks on your suit coat if we don't get to it."

With one last concerned glance at her grandmother, Chance turned to follow Charlotte toward the back of the store. They wove through various people, nodding and smiling but not stopping. Charlotte used the clear, seeping stain over the shoulder of her red dress, along with a rueful smile, as her excuse to keep moving.

In moments they'd cleared the room and slipped into the back office of the Trading Post. Charlotte dug into the small desk her mother kept ruthlessly organized, hunting for wipes. She already had one in hand and was dabbing at Chance's suit jacket when she heard a low rumble start in his chest, followed by the shaking of his body as his arm jerked beneath her hands where she tried to dab at the setting champagne.

"What's so funny?"

"Other than the fact that we're both doused in champagne that was practically tossed at us? On purpose."

Charlotte stopped her dabbing and stared at him. "You got that?"

"Like a bullet to the brain."

"Sadly, subtlety isn't a trait my grandmother possesses."

"I'll give her credit, she's got great aim."

"God, please don't offer any words of encouragement."

Chance settled himself on the edge of her mother's spare, pristine desk and reached for the wipes. "Come here and let me offer you the same service. Some of the champagne got on your back."

Charlotte twisted to look over her shoulder, shocked to realize that her grandmother's aim had managed such a feat. "I didn't think a single flute could hold that much."

Since he already had her elbow in his grip and was turning her gently, Charlotte turned the rest of the way around and presented her shoulder, shocked to the core when her knees wobbled at his gentle strokes.

It should have been simple.

Realistically, it *was* simple.

Yet with each stroke of that small towelette she felt like her body was on fire.

Her mind was immediately transported to their stolen moments in her hotel room, when his strokes had been bolder. More forceful. And on a far more intimate place on her body. Even now she felt herself reacting to his touch, her skin heating as memories filled her.

And yet . . .

Charlotte couldn't deny there was a simple yet powerful intimacy in *this* act, in this instant.

A stolen moment between them, with the world at bay outside the door. One that was sweetly domestic, too. They could be any other couple, helping one another through a small mishap.

Only they were Charlotte and Chance, and they didn't do small mishaps, accidentally or otherwise. Oh no, they went for big and bold with a side of bad judgment tossed in.

And despite it all, it felt like so much more.

Just like he always felt like so much more.

Even if they'd somehow mess it up and head back to their respective corners until they faced off in another round.

"I'm sorry. For the other night. In Bozeman."

His voice was a deep murmur near her ear. She was a tall woman, and the addition of her heels and his seat on the top of the desk meant the sound sort of drifted up to her, the heat of his breath tickling the skin of her neck. He hadn't needed to clarify where they'd been, but Charlotte opted to leave it alone and simply nodded. "Thank you."

"I was careless with you. With what we shared. And I—"

She turned at that, pressing a finger to his lips. "It's not really a solid life moment to be apologized to for sex. Why don't you stop while we're ahead and not fighting with each other."

His gaze caught hers, so like that moment

across the Trading Post when she'd first walked in this evening. His eyelids had grown heavy, his gray eyes darkening with the intensity of the moment, and she wondered, certainly not for the first time, what this pull between them was.

It was a thread that had tethered them together since childhood, and she had no idea how to imagine her life without it.

Without him.

Even though there were moments the thread went slack and she managed to forget about him for a while, they always came back to each other. Life had always seemed to find a way to do that between them, and she'd grown surprisingly tired of the wondering.

The needing.

And the denial.

If she couldn't have him, why couldn't she stop wanting him? And why was she persistently left with the notion that things *could* be different if they could just find a way to flip the script?

She'd never considered herself a person who chased things not meant for her. Her life choices were her own, and she held a rock-solid belief that the things meant for you ultimately found you.

Yet Chance had never quite fit that mold.

Because with Chance, she could never quite give up on the hope that they fit.

It was that feeling—the one that said pushing for more would only dash those hopes once again—that had her stepping back.

"I think it's clean now." She smiled, her gaze

still on his even as she put a few more feet of distance between them. "And we'd better get back out there, or we'll only leave my grandmother with the impression she's succeeded."

"I suppose you're right."

"In fact"—she gestured to the small container of wipes still on the desk—"why don't you head back out. I'll put these away and join everyone in a minute."

He looked about to say something but seemed to think better of it. Charlotte was grateful since she wasn't sure she could make it through another apology.

Chance stared at her for one more moment before he pushed off the desk and headed for the door. It was only as he got there, his hand on the knob, that he turned to face her.

"You matter to me, Charlotte. I hope you know that."

"You matter to me, too, Chance."

He nodded at that before slipping out the door and back into the party. Since she could feel the telltale threat of tears in the tightening of her throat, Charlotte gave herself a moment to tidy up the already neat-as-a-pin office.

And felt a shot of triumph when only one lone tear slipped down her cheek.

CHARLOTTE HATED VALENTINE'S DAY with the passion of a thousand fiery suns. She'd rather walk naked through Rustlers Creek's town square in the middle of a Montana January than celebrate the holiday that suggested nearly naked babies could shoot arrows and somehow divine true love. And she most especially didn't care for the drippy, syrupy suggestion that having a Valentine solved all of life's problems.

Even if she refused to show any of that right here, smack in the middle of a lovely Saturday in late September, as Hadley shot the Valentine's Day episode of her wildly successful cooking show.

Instead, she'd pasted on a bright, sweet, *syrupy* smile and posed behind her sister-in-law's kitchen counter with her mother, her grandmother and Hadley, in full America's-sweetheart mode, all while Hadley demonstrated how to make some sort of dessert with crisped rice that had so much sugar and corn syrup in it Charlotte's teeth rotted just smelling it.

Which was what she got for committing to this in a weak moment nearly three months ago on a wine bender with Hadley and Harper in the backyard after a Fourth of July barbecue.

She was drunk on happiness for her friends, Harper and Gray together again, and Hadley and Zack making plans to renew their vows. It had felt like old times, she and the Allen sisters together laughing and talking.

If she hadn't had a man to go home with, well, that was what wine and one of Zack and Hadley's six bedrooms to sleep it off were for.

So she'd said yes in a weak moment. Besides, it wasn't like the rest of America actually *knew* how much Charlotte hated Valentine's Day. It might not be a secret in Rustlers Creek, but to the rest of the world she was just a smiling fool, caught in the glow of her sister-in-law's magnificent cooking.

But why did the Valentine's episode have to be such an extravaganza? And why did she have to join in?

Oh yeah, right.

Because Hadley was a force of nature.

And because her sister-in-law wanted her family around, all while giving Charlotte and her PR firm professional support and external recognition.

Damn smart bitch.

If she could have rolled her eyes at herself, Charlotte would have. Because she *was* appreciative. More than she could ever say.

"And cut!"

The director indicated they could all relax their big, wide smiles and too-close poses and Charlotte used the break to move away from the small crowd.

She knew this kitchen as well as her own, having spent several holidays, weekday nights and Sunday baking marathons in this very spot. Which always made it an odd juxtaposition to realize that homes across America could describe the kitchen, too, right down to the glass-fronted cabinets and marble countertops.

"I don't believe we're talking about Valentine's Day already." Hadley's producer, Bea Malone Jessup, came out of a small alcove off the kitchen, her baby daughter against her chest in an elaborate fabric carrier that strapped over and around her body.

Charlotte had already gotten in some snuggles with Penelope when Bea first arrived for the day's shoot but still couldn't resist tracing a light line down the baby's soft, downy head.

"You're always planning ahead."

Bea glanced down, her soppy smile both perfect and something none of them could have predicted even a year before. But Bea and the Wayne and Sons foreman, Carter, had unexpectedly found their way to love. The arrival of their daughter, Penelope, as well as their management of a relationship that spanned the distance from Montana to New York somehow worked, and Charlotte envied how easy the woman made it all look.

Even as she knew what it really took was a lot of love, a lot of hard work and a willingness to embrace a whole lot of chaos.

"I'm thankful for a calendar and an assistant who somehow manages to create thirty hours in every day."

Bea's success the prior holiday season, producing Hadley's Christmas special that hauled in a significant bonus for the network, had cemented her professional position, and the Cooking Network had given her a lot of leeway to manage her personal life as she wanted.

Bea continued on in the direction of the kitchen, Penelope's sweet baby-powder scent lingering in their wake, and Charlotte headed for the small alcove Bea had just exited. They used it for any number of things, usually as a production office when filming was in high gear, and she'd use it now to check her email.

She unlocked her phone, nearly into her email program when it rang, with Loretta Cox Hardwick's name coming up on the screen.

Charlotte answered and couldn't hold back the smile at Loretta's enthusiastic hello and immediate leap into the reason for her call. "I understand you saw my dad recently. And he gave me the very best idea in the entire world."

Charlotte doubted that, but she was well acquainted with how these pleasantries worked, even as she crossed her fingers behind her back for good measure. "It was a nice surprise to see him."

"You made his night giving him a bit of your time. But it also made me realize that I've been out of touch for much too long. When did you start dating Chance Beaumont?"

"Oh, I'm sorry if your father misinterpreted. Chance and I have been friends since grade school. We happened to be at the same restaurant for business dinners and met up in the hotel lobby. We caught up for a bit and then had a chance to visit with your dad."

To her determined credit, a bit of wind might have been knocked out of her sails, but Loretta wasn't done fishing. "It struck me like an exceptionally good idea, actually. Like the two of you fit."

"I hate to disappoint, but we're just friends."

"Oh. Well." Loretta let out a small sigh. Charlotte

would have laughed if she wasn't so curious as to the reason for the call. And since she really did like Loretta, she was willing to play along a bit more. "I guess what I'm about to ask you isn't such a good idea."

"Try me."

"I think you know I'm chairing the Cattle Baron's ball this December."

"I did know that. Congratulations. It's a huge honor."

"It is, and I was also just put on bed rest by my doctor. I'm four months pregnant and have been told in no uncertain terms that I cannot take this on."

"Oh no. Are you okay?"

And that was when Charlotte heard it. The overbright voice and the steady cadence of one-way questions had all been a coping mechanism. "I'm determined to be."

"Well, then, how can I help you?"

"I'd like you to take on the Cattle Baron's ball. And when I thought you and Chance were dating, I thought you two could cochair it and split the work."

"We can still cochair it as friends."

"Yes, of course. But it would be . . . well, it's just easier when a man's got that bit of a carrot-and-stick situation of a woman helping him." Loretta lowered her voice. "Withholding sex is such a powerful motivator, you know."

Charlotte mentally shook her head—perhaps Loretta had a bit more of her father's old-fashioned nature than she'd thought—but kept it professional. Chairing the ball would be a ton of work, but it would be a huge boon for her firm. And the additional contacts she'd make—through the ranching association, not just as a Wayne—were invaluable.

"Yes, well, even without that"—she cleared her throat—"motivation, I think we can get by. Of course, I can't speak for Chance, but there's no reason you shouldn't still ask him."

"I always hate to put that sort of burden on a man."

Charlotte glanced down at the small desk she currently perched on and mentally calculated how satisfying it might be to bang her head against it when Loretta rushed on. "But if you're taking it on, I know it'll be great. You'll keep it all running smoothly."

"Well, if Chance does say yes, I'm sure we can split duties and each play to our strengths."

Loretta laughed lightly, seemingly oblivious to Charlotte's frustration. "Of course. And one more thing. The committee always gives a prize bull to the chairs. Knowing my situation, they've offered to give you and Chance each one."

"Oh. Wow. Well, thank you." An image of a Black Angus bull standing in the middle of her living room struck Charlotte, and she smiled in spite of herself. But as she considered the generous prize, she recognized something else.

Two bulls could be a game changer for Chance and his ranch operations. Both for managing his own herd and for selling breeding services to other firms. She didn't know all the ins and outs, but she knew enough aspects of the business to understand what this could mean for him.

All she'd have to do was work with him for the next ten weeks.

Unbidden, the feel of his large body pressed against her back, his hand pressed to her most intimate flesh, assailed her.

Could she do that?

Could she afford not to? The bulls might make sense for his business, but taking this on would do a hell of a lot for hers, too.

She'd had more than a few difficult moments since Bozeman, thinking about that meeting with the Harveys. Her business wasn't new any longer, and while people recognized the value of good publicity in a conversation here or there, persuading them they needed to invest in it—with a small firm, no less—took a hell of a lot of convincing.

She'd started her PR firm determined to put a Western flair and sensibility on the ranching industry and businesses beyond it. Instead, there were weeks where she felt like she was just marking time, playing at owning a business.

"Does this mean you'll do it?" Loretta's question pulled Charlotte out of her job funk—Who was she kidding? Her life funk—and back to the conversation at hand.

"Yes, of course. And I really want you to take it easy. I don't want you worrying about this. Your only focus right now is the baby."

"I don't suppose you can convince my two-year-old of that?"

"I'm afraid my public relations skills don't quite work on toddlers."

"I'm not sure much of anything does," Loretta laughed.

She promised to send more details over, and in a matter of minutes after hanging up, Charlotte's phone was pinging with notice of an incoming email.

"You think she planned that one?" Charlotte muttered to herself, even as Loretta's efficiency had her smiling again.

After all, she knew what it was to put a strong pitch and proposal together. When you got a fish on the hook, you had to keep the line tight.

"Char!"

Hadley came around the corner of the small entryway, nearly colliding with where Charlotte leaned back on the desk.

"Where's the fire?"

"No fire, but an actual adult night out is in the works. Your mom and grandmother just convinced Bea to give them Penelope for the night, and she and Carter, Zack and I, and Harper and Gray are going out. Come with us."

Charlotte had never been a jealous person—it was a trait that caused far more grief in a person's life than benefit—but even she couldn't deny the small green monster that landed square on her shoulder at the list of couples. "Thanks, Hadley, for the offer. You guys go and have fun."

"It'll be more fun with you there." Before Charlotte could come up with another argument, Hadley turned on her full powers of persuasion. "I know why you're saying no, and I'm not buying it. We're all friends and family, and it's a chance to go out and have a fun time. Besides, Bea hasn't left Penelope alone yet, and even though that baby will be in the hands of two women who raised ten children between them, she's going to worry. The more girl power she has around her, the better off she'll be."

"How do you know why I'm saying no?"

"I'm guessing why you're saying no, and I'm trying to talk you out of it. We all want you there, and I know Bea could use the extra support."

Charlotte wanted to say yes, and she wanted to say no. Which not only wasn't like her but was indicative of the odd malaise that had gripped her of late.

"And we're not going to the Branded Mark, either."

Charlotte had assumed the town watering hole with the ever-fashionable peanut shells on the floor—their usual destination—was the plan, so damn it, now Hadley had her curious.

"Where are you going?"

"That new restaurant that opened at the end of town."

"Rafael's?"

"Yep. We're going out like adults and having a fine dining experience."

"You don't like the burgers at the Branded Mark?"

"I love them. But I'm interested in a less rowdy environment. Harper got a black eye after being elbowed in there six months ago."

"For the record, that cowboy was awfully sorry. And it was an accident."

Hadley waved a hand. "My point stands. And I think Bea will relax a bit more being away from Penelope if we ease her into an evening out."

Charlotte nearly gave in before one last thought rose up with as much force as a stampede. "You're not trying to set me up, are you?"

"Not really."

Hadley must have seen the same level of ire in Charlotte's gaze as one normally saw on a rushing herd because she rushed on. "Harper and Gray already had plans tonight with Chance. So of course we extended the invite. It would have been rude not to. And it's not a setup if we didn't intentionally do it."

"You've got to be kidding me."

"Come on, the two of you are friends now."

Friends who nearly had sex. One of whom had more of it than the other.

As if she needed that additional clarity.

"Yes, of course we are."

"So you'll go?"

Whether it was the hopeful expression on her sister-in-law's face or the opportunity to escape her own bad company for the evening, Charlotte didn't know.

But she had a sneaking suspicion the *actual* reason she said yes was tied to door number three.

Assuming Chance accepted the Cattle Baron's cochair, they'd be seeing a lot more of each other. Their brief interlude at the Trading Post had only reinforced to her that she needed to find a way to move past whatever feelings she had for him and put him firmly in the friend zone. Because if she didn't find a way to get past those heated moments in her hotel room—*and* the orgasm, her conscience taunted—it was going to be a very long ten weeks to the ball.

Chapter 7

Chance pulled into the large lot at the end of Main Street, put his truck in Park and eyed himself in the rearview mirror. He ran a hand over his recently cut hair and resisted the urge to tug—hard—on the short ends. How had he gotten roped into this? He thought he was having an evening out with Gray and Harper to discuss some business and mix it with a good steak and a few glasses of wine, and now he was on his way to a formal dinner with friends.

A formal dinner that Harper had reluctantly confessed included Charlotte.

Which meant he was equal parts excited and pissed that the two of them would be on display in front of the most eagle-eyed women in Rustlers Creek.

Not that he didn't adore Harper and Hadley, but

the sisters were . . . *intrigued*, Chance finally admitted, by him and Charlotte. Or what they imagined could be between him and Charlotte. All of which would be fine, if not slightly amusing, if it weren't for what happened in Bozeman.

He was still trying to figure out how he felt about it all, with wild swings between absolute certainty that he did the right thing by walking away to cursing himself a million times over for actually putting one foot in front of the other and walking away from the most intriguing woman he'd ever known.

And God help him if Harper and Hadley actually knew all of *that*.

A thought that started a dull ringing in his ears.

"Yo, Chance!"

The hard knock on the window pulled him hard out of his thoughts, and Chance glanced over to see Gray grinning at him through the window.

The man did that a lot lately.

Grinned.

Smiled.

Hell, Chance had actually heard Gray laugh recently.

His formerly stoic and gruff friend had fallen head-over-heels back in love with Harper—the woman he'd never really fallen *out* of love with—and had been whistling out his ass he was so happy.

"You coming?" Gray hitched a thumb over his shoulder, pointing toward Rafael's.

Determined to leave his bad mood in the truck, Chance nodded and in moments was walking on the other side of a physically entwined Gray and Harper.

"How's the cow doing?" Harper started right in.

"We've kept a close eye, but she's doing great. And her appetite seems undeterred by her brush with death."

Gray's laugh was hearty. "I'll make sure that's part of the paper Sameena is writing. Her professor already called me, excited she had real-world experience on her internship and asking if he could send a few more students out to the ranch."

"Send 'em," Chance said as noise and laughter spilled out of Rafael's, creating a warm welcome as they approached the restaurant. "Your interns and their quick thinking are incredibly good for business."

Chance waited for Gray to open the door for Harper and gesture her through, then followed his friend in. Bringing up the rear gave him a chance to scope things out, and it didn't take more than a blink to catch sight of Charlotte at the large table toward the back of the restaurant.

Something hard lodged beneath his breastbone, and he narrowly avoided rubbing away the ache. Why was he here?

Sure, he'd been in a social slump lately. Gray might have joked about being Miracle Max when it came to the now-healing heifer, but Chance felt like that was the role he'd taken on with respect to bringing Beaumont Farms back from the dead.

But since he'd looked at the bills today, he'd had to admit *mostly dead* would be an improvement over where things stood with his business.

The ranch's books had minimal red, which was better than they'd been, but every penny he managed to get to the positive went right back out the door to fix something, invest in something or pay off a lingering debt his father had run up.

When would it ease up a bit?

The table was already half-full with their dinner party and after shaking hands with Zack and Carter, giving a kiss to Hadley and to Bea, he and Charlotte came face-to-face.

"Chance. It's good to see you."

Her hands rested lightly on his shoulders as she leaned in for a kiss, and Chance gave himself that single moment of contact to breathe her in.

And instantly realized his mistake when his knees trembled at the reminder of having her in his arms. Her cheek was soft beneath his lips, and it would have been a simple slip to bend his head and brush his mouth over her jaw once more.

Well aware their audience had sharper eyes than most, he stepped back by sheer force of will— did he exert anything else around Charlotte?—and helped her into her seat.

And then took the one beside her, which he increasingly suspected was the intended plan for the evening.

Despite the scrutiny, things evened out pretty quickly as conversation sparked around the table. Charlotte and Bea fell into discussion about Bea and Carter's new baby, Penelope, and Chance was grateful when he had Carter next to him to talk shop.

"Heard you're riding high after closing a new deal with the Hills."

Chance couldn't quite hold back the smile or how good it felt to answer that comment in the affirmative. "Lawyers have been through all of it, and we're signing the papers on Monday."

"That's great news. And about time they expanded their offerings."

"That was part of the pitch, actually," Chance said. "We're doing some good work up here in our part of the world, and it'd be nice for more people to realize it. Part of the deal in putting beef in their stores is telling a sustainability story and why it matters."

Carter nodded his agreement, and Chance appreciated the opportunity to talk through the work. He'd spent a lot longer with his books just hovering in the red, but the sustainability work he'd implemented at Beaumont Farms was worth it.

It was all worth it.

"What in the ever-loving hell would we do that for? Land conservation?" Trevor spit a stream of tobacco juice on the ground. "We're in the cattle business, not some pussy attempts at that liberal bullshit they taught you at college."

Chance had no idea what any of it had to do with a political leaning, but he avoided saying anything, keeping his cool. If he had any chance of convincing his father, he needed to remain calm. "It's more than that, Dad. Come on, you know the science here. We can rotate the cattle and preserve the land and manage the biodiversity. The changes aren't impossible, they just take some commitment."

"Commitment? You think I don't have commitment?"

Chance avoided wincing at the tone, but it didn't matter anymore. His father was riled up now, and Trevor kept right on going, bulldozing through the conversation.

"Been ranching this land since I was a boy. Ain't no reason to change what I'm doing now."

"Then why am I here? Why'd I get a degree in all this? Why the hell do you keep me around if it's to keep everything the same damn way it's been for forty years?"

Trevor looked up then, and it was impossible to miss the darkness that crept into his old man's gaze. But it was the words that followed that put Chance on his back foot.

"Hell if I know."

"What's that supposed to mean?"

Something hovered there, and Chance held his breath. Whatever his father was debating in his mind, there was one thing for certain. It was the truth Trevor always buried way down deep when it came to his son.

But something obviously held him back, because when Trevor finally spoke, it was with the same snarky tone Chance had become used to long ago.

"You're young and cocky and you need the piss knocked outta ya is all I'm saying."

Chance pulled himself out of the odd memory, not entirely sure where it had come from.

"It's smart business," Carter said, oblivious to Chance's trip down memory lane. "And it's a great opportunity to tell the story of our work."

"What story?" Bea keyed back into the conversation, her producer's mind quickly narrowing in. "Is it something we can use on the show?"

"One-track mind." Carter hitched a thumb at his wife.

"And you love it. But really, what are you talking about?"

"The biodiversity work we're doing at Wayne and Sons and that Chance is doing over at Beaumont Farms."

"I love it when you talk business." Bea smiled at her husband, clear shots of adoration arcing between the two of them before she turned to the wider group. "It's far more fun to watch him in action than to be the recipient of Carter's pent-up worry and inability to concentrate on his job."

"You exaggerate."

"Hardly." Bea snorted before turning to Chance and Charlotte as she settled into her story. "He hovered around me for three weeks before I gave birth to Penelope. Followed me around convinced I'd collapse any minute."

A dull red flush crept up Carter's neck at his wife's description. "I wasn't that bad."

"You were too that bad." Bea leaned in and pressed a kiss to his cheek. "But it's inspiring me at this very moment."

"How's that?"

"You hovered over me, and I was just fine the

whole time. I'm keeping it in mind, even though all I want to do is check my phone every two minutes and text Carlene."

Charlotte smiled. "Go call her. My mom will understand."

"The woman's raised six kids." Bea waved it off, even as Chance saw a shot of longing in her face. "I know Penelope's fine."

"Of course she's fine." Charlotte pulled out her phone, and Chance saw her mother's name pop up on the screen as she hit the Call button. "Talk to her anyway so you'll be fine."

When the normally unflappable Bea reached for the phone like a lifeline, Chance leaned in close to whisper to Charlotte. "Nice move."

She smiled at the compliment even as something suspiciously like triumph lit deep in her gaze. "You give me too much credit."

"Oh?"

"My mother bet me she'd last an hour before calling."

Charlotte's tone was low enough that only he could hear her, and if they didn't have an audience he'd already be laughing. Instead, he battled the sudden heat that suffused his body at the intimacy of their position, heads bent toward each other.

"And you took the bet?"

"I told her double or nothing Bea wouldn't last twenty minutes."

"Jeez, first me falling asleep and now your

mother's babysitting. You're just a diabolical little gambler, Charlotte Wayne."

"Not really," Charlotte said, all that triumph morphing into a soft smile. "I just know people. Bea will make that call and then she can enjoy dinner."

Bea's shoulders relaxed immediately as she spoke to Carlene. That ease continued after she passed the phone back across the table. But it was when she ordered a glass of wine after claiming to only want iced tea when they'd first sat down that Chance had to admit Charlotte was onto something.

Maybe it was that lingering memory of his father that had settled in his gut like sour acid, but the contrast of being with someone who innately understood what someone else needed was, he had to admit, fascinating to observe.

The woman *knew* people. What made them tick. What made them happy.

What gave them ease.

And as he looked at Bea, smiling and happily chatting from the other side of the table, he realized Charlotte's ability to read people was more than a gift—it was a calling. One that was selfless.

Special.

And exceedingly rare.

CHARLOTTE TOOK IN the happy, animated faces around the table and couldn't help but think about how much had changed in a year. Her brother and sister-in-law had averted disaster in their marriage and had come out the other side stronger than ever.

Her friend had found her way back to her true love.

And a woman who'd believed her prospects for love had passed her by was now a mother and a wife.

Life turns on a dime.

It was one of Mamma Wayne's favorite sayings, and while Charlotte had never understood what a dime had to do with it, the underlying sentiment made sense.

Which made her earlier thoughts about marking time feel even more acute.

She hadn't been out in a while, and she didn't want to mar it with dour thoughts—nor did she begrudge her loved ones their happiness—but it suddenly all felt more overwhelming than she'd expected. Unwilling to let anyone see it, she excused herself with a bright smile and a murmured *Be right back.*

In minutes she was out the door and into the parking lot, rubbing her arms against the late-September chill.

God, what was wrong with her?

This maudlin behavior wasn't her. She didn't begrudge others, and she didn't measure her life against anyone else. So damn it, *why* was she getting choked up? Especially because she wasn't one of those lucky women who could cry over something and come back looking dewy and fresh. Not her. Oh no, she looked like a red-faced zombie with pink eye.

So why were the tears welling up all the same?

"Hey—"

Charlotte whirled, suddenly aware she was standing outside in a semidark parking lot all alone.

And found Chance standing there, her coat in hand. "Are you okay?"

"I'm fine."

"Okay."

"I am."

"I said *okay*. So now, humor me and put on your coat." He held it up, the edge of his knuckles brushing against her shoulder as he lifted the thin wool into place.

She shivered as she burrowed into her coat, that light contact spearing need through her as potently as if he'd kissed her.

"You want to talk about it?"

"Not really."

"Do you want to leave?"

"Not really."

"Do you want to go back inside?" He held up a hand, a small grin tugging at the corner of his mouth. "*Not really*, I know."

"I'm not usually like this."

"No, you're not. Which is why I followed you out here."

"Was I that obvious?"

He shook his head, and she tried not to notice

how the light, even breeze ruffled the very tips of his hair. Hair the color of chestnuts. Which was silly and stupid, but she'd always thought so.

Her mother had taken her to New York for a girls' weekend one Christmas season when the triplets were small. Charlotte hadn't fully recognized it, but she'd begun to feel like she was sort of invisible inside her now-large family. A family where she'd been the youngest of three and was now the middle of six.

Yet her mother had somehow understood that feeling of disappearing and instinctively sensed they needed the trip and the mother–daughter time alone.

Even now, Charlotte could remember stopping at a cart in New York, after she and her mother had taken an obligatory horse-drawn carriage ride through Central Park. The smell had been deep and sweet, wafting through the cold air, and Charlotte had wondered what made that wonderful scent. When Carlene had insisted on buying the roasted chestnuts—a treat both of them had ended up hating—Charlotte had looked at the deep brown color and thought of Chance's hair.

And how oddly appropriate it was that she hated those chestnuts as much as she did Chance Beaumont.

Even though, unlike the chestnuts, she didn't actually hate him at all.

Except for the moments when she did.

She hadn't felt that level of emotional confusion in a long time. Yet she did now.

"I'm happy for Harper. And Bea. And my brother. All of them. I'm really, really happy for them."

"I am, too." That grin expanded a bit. "Really, really."

"It's not lip service." She felt an answering tug of her own at the corner of her mouth. "Really."

"I don't think it is."

And then the smile vanished as the truth came spilling out. "So why do I feel so bitter and envious? Like I could rip all their faces off like something out of a horror movie?"

He seemed to give the question serious consideration before surprising her with his words. "I noticed something inside. With Bea and the phone. You knew what she needed. You truly noticed, and you helped her."

"She's just missing her baby."

"Yes, she is. And she also has guilt because she's out with her husband for the first time and can't stop worrying about the baby. And she's also out with her friends, and she can't stop worrying about her baby."

"She's a new mother."

"Yes, and she's adjusting to that. And you instinctively understood it and helped her feel better." He paused before continuing. "You did that with me the other morning with the pancakes, too."

"You hadn't eaten in hours. I had food, and I fed you."

Before she even realized it Chance had moved close enough she could feel the heat of his body.

"Don't dismiss it. That thing you do, when you put other people's needs first. You help them. But I wonder . . ." He moved even closer, his hand lifting to trace the line of her jaw.

"You wonder what?" She heard the breathy quality of her voice and marveled she'd even managed to make any sound at all. She felt as if all the air had left her lungs on a hard, heavy sigh.

"I wonder who puts *you* first."

"Nobody needs to put me first." She stared at him, completely still for fear of pulling him out of whatever seemed to have gripped him. Of whatever had made him move close so that he could touch her.

God, she loved his touch.

Loved being his sole focus. Loved feeling the rough calluses of his fingertips against her skin.

"It hardly seems fair," he finally said.

"Of course it's fair. I'm fine and capable, and I can handle myself."

Chance laid his hand against her cheek, his thumb brushing lightly over her lips. "What does capable have to do with it?"

"It has everything to do with it. I'm fine."

He dropped his hand then, and Charlotte felt that lack of warmth as if she'd just opened a freezer. "And that's why you're standing out here, berating yourself for feeling human emotions?"

It was one hundred percent true.

Which, Charlotte admitted, was why she came out swinging.

"That's awfully astute judgment coming from

a man who walked away from sex between the two of us."

"You going to hold that against me?"

"As long as it's true."

"You want truth? Then here's quite a bit." He didn't touch her again, but he moved in close.

So close she had to tilt her head to fully see his face.

So near his chest rose and fell against her body, even as his hands remained firmly at his sides.

So intimate she could *feel* his anger and frustration and determination to say whatever it was he needed to say pulsing in her own blood.

"I wanted you that night. I still want you. I want you like a drowning man who knows he'll never get another breath of air. But I can't have you."

He took a hard inhale, but the anger that painted his features in hard lines softened, replaced with a resignation that was palpable.

"You and me, Charlotte? It can't work. So could you please get out of your own way and recognize that?"

The words were harsh, the sentiment exacting. Was he right?

Were they really and truly that mismatched?

She didn't think so. She sure as hell had never *felt* so. And it was in that reality—one that she clung to as tightly as possible—that she recognized the truth.

The man who stood before her was six feet of virility and strength and charm, and none of it made a damn bit of difference. Nothing about the outward visage others saw and were even impressed by seemed to make a dent in the young boy still stuck inside.

She'd known that boy then, and she knew the man now. She knew his heart and knew his goodness. His work ethic. His determination.

She saw all those things, so why couldn't he?

"You seem awfully sure of that, cowboy."

"I know it. Trust me."

She shook her head at that. "No, I don't think I will."

With a sudden shot of moxie she wasn't quite sure she felt, Charlotte reached up, put a firm hand at the base of his neck and pulled him close. Heat and need and some of that self-denial Chance seemed so hung up on coalesced in their kiss—a wild, feral act of need between two people.

His hands covered the width of her back, pulling her close so she felt his galloping heartbeat—a match for hers—pressed to her breast. With that deft touch, his hands roaming a path over her spine, he managed to convey a strange sort of safety that promised he wouldn't drop her.

That he was as in this moment as she was.

Even though he kept telling her he wanted to be somewhere else.

And in the midst of lips and tongues and heated exhales and deep, chest-fueled groans that rose up in the quiet night, Charlotte got her answer.

Sometimes, like those burning days on the ranch, you had to destroy everything to get to the good stuff beneath the brush. You had to clear out the old and find a way to the new.

Rebirth.

Neither of them could change where they came from or what came before. But she'd be damned if she was willing to go down without a fight.

The two of them had been in a pattern—a way of behaving with and to each other—for far too long.

And it was time they stopped.

Both of them.

She'd burn through the old if she had to, but it was time to see where this led. She was tired of standing still. And who knew? Maybe they couldn't work, just like he said. Hell, maybe they'd destroy each other.

But as his mouth slid over hers, giving and taking in equal measure, Charlotte knew the truth.

It was a risk she was willing to take.

Chapter 8

Dessert arrived with a degree of fanfare usually reserved for heads of state. A fact the kitchen had seemingly recognized when word got back that Hadley Wayne was in the restaurant. Chance watched the parade of food come to their table and realized that it was a strange sort of metaphor for his whole damn evening.

A level of ridiculousness that bordered on unbelievability.

The heated words and even more heated kisses with Charlotte out in the parking lot had left him cratered inside. When they'd both finally come up for air, she'd excused herself, telling him she needed to get back inside. Chance might have followed her, but he realized it might behoove him to stay behind a few minutes and collect himself.

Because whatever he wanted to believe about

himself and his legendary self-control, something about Charlotte continued to feel inevitable.

He didn't like inevitability. He'd lived a lifetime of it with his father.

Trevor Beaumont was inevitable. In his behavior. His notions of masculinity and ownership. And his even more ridiculous determination to screw the world and everything in it, including his son.

Inevitability suggested you lost the power of your own choice, and that wasn't a place that sat well with him.

Even if Charlotte was the choice.

"Chance?" He glanced over to see Harper's smiling face, her cheeks bright with color. "You haven't tried any desserts yet."

Despite the heated interlude in the parking lot, he and Charlotte had both put on a good front once they got back inside.

That or their friends and family were too kind to say anything.

But the conversation had shifted to a series of topics, from funny stories to work discussions and back again. It had reminded him of the night about six months ago when he'd been part of an evening at Gray's with the same crew, minus Bea and Carter. The talk had been fun and lively and comfortable.

And damn it, wasn't that part of the strange disconnect, too?

He cared for these people, and he knew they cared for him. Their lives were intertwined and had been for years, and it made for the conversational

shorthand of old friends. One that, once their plates
were cleared and coffee ordered, had everyone re-
seating themselves around the table, the guys at one
end and the women at the other. In the reshuffle,
Harper had ended up on his other side.

"You look like you're trying to decide where to
make your move."

Chance looked over the table, laden with desserts. "That crème brûlée looks pretty good."

"So does Charlotte," Harper said, her voice so
low he might have missed it if she weren't sitting
right beside him, the soul of discretion.

He eyed her, but aside from it not being the
time or place, he wasn't interested in getting into
this now. "Crème brûlée it is."

"Chance."

"Harper." He said her name in the same drawn-
out, meaningful tone she'd used. "Relax and eat
some sugar. There's enough here."

Since it seemed to be a night for memories,
the one that always seemed so oddly acute, no
matter how many years passed, reared up in his
mind's eye.

*"You all need to sit down so we can open our Valen-
tines,"* Mrs. Gaines instructed her fourth-grade class.

*Chance would never admit it to anyone, but he loved
Valentine's Day in school. The shoeboxes they deco-
rated with different kinds of paper and ribbon. This
year Mrs. G. had even brought in these paper doily
things that they'd all cut into cool shapes. He'd made a
snowflake to add to the end of his box.*

Chance had worried that his Valentines were going

to be dumb because Mrs. Gaines had sent him home with extra paper and stuff so he could make homemade cards for the class. There was no way his old man was taking him to the drugstore to buy them, and he'd worried about what he was going to do about it. But she'd made sure that he had the supplies he needed and added a bag of Jolly Ranchers so he could tape some candy to each one. She even gave him a list of everyone's names so that no one was forgotten.

He'd worried about that even more than the cards, even though he knew every member of his class and could go through the list in his head.

But what if he missed someone?

He kept the Valentine-card project a secret in his room, working on the cards late at night. He'd been careful about it, too, not just in the hiding it from his father but in really thinking about each card he made for his classmates.

The guys all got red paper with black letters and black construction paper cutouts. For the girls, he specifically used pink. The hardest one was the Valentine for Charlotte Wayne. The decorating was okay, but then came the really hard part. He had to write something to her.

In the end he went with:

Charlotte
    You're a cool girl and can do a lot of sit-ups.
    Happy Valentine's Day.

                                    Your friend,
                                    Chance

He even drew a little figure of somebody doing a sit-up next to her name.

When he signed his name, though, he felt sort of funny. Like he'd wanted to write Love, Chance or make a few Xs and Os, but something stopped him. If one of the guys saw it they'd give him a hard time.

So he went with Your Friend.

Mrs. G. had all their boxes set up on the shelves near the classroom window, and he'd carefully placed each card in each person's box. He'd been surprised when a small group of girls over in the corner kept giggling and looking at him—it made him feel hot in his face—but he ignored them.

It was time for the Valentine's party.

Mrs. G. set out all of the food and punch on a table at the front of the room. She put a red tablecloth on it and had fancy heart napkins and paper plates, and then they were all allowed to come up to get their punch and snacks. She'd even made Rice Krispies Treats!

He walked over to get his box and was surprised when the lid seemed a little tilted. He didn't think anybody was allowed into the boxes, but what if somebody had gotten into his? What if somebody took his candy? He'd already heard the rumors that Cal Lockhart's mom had let him include Pop Rocks in everybody's cards. Chance vowed to keep an eye out for anybody who had two bags of Pop Rocks just in case his had been stolen.

Only when he got back to his desk did he realize why his box was askew. He opened the lid, and there was a card stuffed on top, and it was huge. It was from the actual card store, not those small drugstore Valentines with Star Wars or Power Rangers on the front. And it had his name on it and what looked like a whole Hershey bar stuffed inside.

A whole candy bar?

He tore into the card, excited about the candy before he realized that the room had gone quiet. And as he pulled out the pretty pink card with big hearts on it and a droopy-eared puppy that wished him Happy Valentine's Day, Chance realized that everyone was watching him.

The low rumble of giggles had started again, but they were quiet since Mrs. G. was standing at the front watching everyone.

As he opened the card, he saw neat printing down the blank left-hand page.

Chance,
    Will you be my Valentine?

If that weren't bad enough, there was a list of options with boxes beside the words.

Today?
Tomorrow?
Forever?

XO,
Charlotte

PS
Please check Forever.

Heat rose up in his face, and it wasn't the kind you got at gym from doing sit-ups or running around the *playground. It was the embarrassed kind. The sort he got when he was out in town with his dad, and Trevor got too loud and yelled at him for just touching a small bird statue in the feed store or for missing one nail when he was hammering up fence line.*

His dad was always doing stuff like that. Saying he was dumb and stupid and a burden no one wanted around.

Even if Charlotte's note seemed like she sort of did want him around. Forever?

He was paralyzed, not sure what to do about all of it. He liked Charlotte. A lot. And he sort of liked that whole forever *thing.*

Which didn't make any sense when mean words started falling out of his mouth faster than he could stop them.

"How about never?*" he joked as he waved the card to the people sitting next to him, allowing them to read what Charlotte had written to him. "Where's that checkbox?"*

Rafael's shimmered back to life around him, and Chance pressed down hard on the memory. Harper was still smiling, and he realized where he knew that look from.

It was the same one she'd given him all those years ago, the day after Valentine's Day when they all stood out on the playground at recess. Charlotte had ignored him all day, and he'd decided to go talk to her to find out why she'd embarrassed him so badly with the card.

Even if he had kept it and buried it in the bottom drawer of his dresser.

But instead of telling him, she'd gone on the defensive, quick to let him know she'd changed her mind and he could toss the card.

She'd seemed sincere. Convincing, too. And Harper had stood by Charlotte's side the whole time, that smile on her face and gentle understanding in her eyes.

He'd recognized it then, but he'd had a lot of years to understand it.

Part pity, part empathy, and all *way* too uncomfortably perceptive.

Do you ever get tired of all the attention, coming from a small hometown?

Maybe Charlotte had a point the other day. Rustlers Creek was his home, and these people were his friends, but it didn't mean he should have to fully give up his privacy.

His personal space.

Or the ability to regulate what he did and didn't want to remember.

Only, like the Beaumont Farms brand marks that sat on his steers, Chance Beaumont and Charlotte Wayne had both been branded that long-ago Valentine's Day.

Potential sweethearts.

Perpetual enemies.

And, if they handled themselves true to form, one of the town's favorite pastimes.

He suddenly recognized Charlotte's deep desire to get away earlier that evening.

And started counting down the minutes until he could escape.

CHARLOTTE WALKED INTO Zack and Hadley's kitchen and cursed herself for not just driving into town for dinner. But when Hadley had not only convinced Charlotte to go, she'd even talked her into getting ready at the ranch and enjoying a predinner cocktail with everyone.

Which now meant she had to do the nightcap niceties when all she really wanted was her PJs and her own bed.

Ultimately, Penelope's eating schedule had been the bell to end the evening, and Charlotte was more grateful for Bea's overfull breasts than she could ever explain.

Yes, dinner had been fun. She was even glad she'd gone.

But it had also been intermixed with enough weird moments that she was a special sort of exhausted. The emotional sort that had never sat well with her. The sort that, Charlotte admitted to herself, was too close to the surface for comfort if she was grateful for a friend's tits.

She'd been a good sport, and she'd managed to enjoy herself. But wow, the evening had been a lot.

Her mother came around the edge of the kitchen counter, her smile bright and eyes lit with a special sort of avarice. "Oh, that baby is precious! What a little doll."

"And you, softie, owe me fifty bucks."

"I will pay up." Carlene sighed. "And I didn't even tell you the bet was won even before dinner. Bea called me from the car on the way there. So drive me home, and I'll pay you from my kitchen stash."

Since her mother was a cash stasher—the woman hoarded bills in her dresser drawer, on the kitchen counter *and* in a small compartment in her purse—Charlotte sensed the ruse, but she was game for any excuse to get out of the house. After a few quick goodbyes, Charlotte and Carlene were back in the car and bumping over the property toward her parents' house.

"Did you have a fun evening?"

"Not nearly as fun as you."

"Oh, that baby is something special. And she's so good—" Carlene broke off laughing. "Until she's hungry. Then—oh wow—does that child have a set of lungs."

"I guess she doesn't need her mother's bull-horn to be heard?"

Carlene laughed at the joke, the bullhorn Bea used on outdoor shots around the ranch legendary. "No bullhorn needed, just an infant-size set of lungs that know exactly how to do their job."

"When did Mamma Wayne leave?"

"Your dad picked her up around nine. She claimed she was tired, but I think it was really that sweet little screaming dinner bell that did her in."

"Does it ever bother you that you don't have grandchildren?"

Charlotte wasn't sure where the question came from—especially knowing Zack and Hadley had lost a child when they'd tried for a family years ago—but she also didn't make it a habit to hold things back from her mother.

"I'll have them when it's time."

"Right, but does it bother you?"

"I look forward to the day when our family grows, however that happens. Spouses for my children. Children for my children. But it's not on my timetable, and I'm not interested in making any of my kids feel like there's some ticking clock to please me."

"Not everyone feels like you do."

"Then more's the pity. I was blessed with six wonderful children of my own. My sole goal in life is to know that you're happy and fulfilled in whatever you choose to do."

"I was thinking about something tonight. That trip you and I took when I was a kid. To New York."

"I loved that trip. All the walking around and the Broadway show and the shopping and the horse-and-carriage ride." Carlene stopped and Charlotte glanced over to see her mom's smile. "Why don't we do that more often?"

"I don't know."

"I think we should fix that. Maybe we should go around Christmas."

"It'll have to be after the Cattle Baron's ball. I'm cochairing it. Or chairing it," Charlotte amended, realizing she hadn't said anything to Chance, and he hadn't brought it up tonight. "With Loretta Cox on bed rest for her pregnancy."

"Oh, I'm sorry to hear that. I'll have to take

some food over to her. Something for her little one, too."

And just like that, Chance's compliment of her earlier took on a new dimension.

One she'd spent her life observing.

"Don't dismiss it. That thing you do, when you put other people's needs first. You help them . . . I wonder who puts you first."

"Nobody needs to put me first."

She'd been so sure of that, but now she realized that her mother had put her first.

Always.

Had Chance ever had that?

"The food for Loretta," she said, suddenly full of the knowledge of her mother's gifts. "You do that so effortlessly."

"Do what?"

"The things people need. You're so thoughtful and intuitive about it, too. It's special. And I wanted you to know that I know how special you are."

Charlotte pulled up into the driveway, the exterior lights filling the car as she turned to face Carlene.

"Those are very sweet and kind words, baby. And I know you mean them. Now, why don't you tell me what this is really all about."

"Can't I tell you I appreciate you?"

"Of course you can. And since you also make a point to show me every day in every way that you care, I'm less concerned with needing to be told." Carlene reached out and laid a hand over

Charlotte's where it rested in her lap. "Did something happen tonight?"

Charlotte let out a harsh laugh, the sound falling flat in the close confines of the car.

"Tonight. Last week. The fourth grade. Take your pick."

Carlene's hand pat was gentle. "Why don't you come inside, and we'll talk about it."

"There's nothing I'd like more than that, but do you mind if I take a rain check? I have some things I need to think through."

"I'll let you do that on one condition." Carlene's gaze was warm and tender, but steel threaded her words. "Whatever is going on between you and Chance, don't be quite so ready to take it all on the chin."

"How'd you know—"

Carlene held up a hand, cutting her off. "This has been a long time coming. Only more so now that Harper's back with Gray and they live on the portion of Beaumont property that Gray bought. You all see each other a lot more, and it's grown harder to ignore each other for long stretches. To put one another out of your minds for a while."

Her mother's keen eye struck again.

While she'd never fully put Chance out of her thoughts, no matter how much time they spent apart, they'd really only seen each other sporadically before Harper came back to Rustlers Creek. In that time, Charlotte had managed to date and try her hand at several relationships, some more successful than others.

But the point was, Chance wasn't an all-consuming part of her life.

He was a childhood regret and an adult nuisance and not much more.

Until he wasn't.

"But now it's make-or-break time, sweetie," Carlene added.

"Or it's nothing time. As in *nothing is happening* and *nothing can come of it.*"

"Don't lie to yourself, Charlotte. Your father and I didn't raise you that way, and I know you don't make it a practice to do so. You care for him. And he cares for you, even if he struggles to show you."

"I think he's scared."

She'd only just come to that conclusion, but the more she tried it out, the more right it felt.

"I think his father wore him down in ways I can't begin to imagine. In those places that affect how you see yourself. And even if he resents it, I think there's probably grief wrapped up in there, too."

"You may be right about the grief," her mother said, "even if it's more a steady sort of guilt. God knows the man has a right to it, based on how he was raised, and fear is a powerful motivator. And it can do some serious damage if it's not managed or, more importantly, overcome."

"I care for him. Most of the time I'd like to punch him, but when it's just the two of us, it's—" She stopped before pressing on. "It's magic. When we shut out everyone else and are just ourselves, he can forget whatever lives deep in his mind about our differences."

When they were just Chance and Charlotte.

When she wasn't a Wayne and he wasn't a Beaumont.

A fact that stared back at her through the windshield as she looked up at the large home she grew up in.

"Do you think people can change?"

"I think people can, yes."

Charlotte heard the hitch in her mother's words. "Then why do you sound so hesitant?"

"People have the capacity for change. We all do. But there's usually something that gets us into that stagnant place. The comfortable one that wraps us up in an emotional cocoon. It's hard to emerge from that."

"Butterflies emerge, transformed."

"They do. When they're left to struggle and fight for it on their own. Cut a butterfly out of that cocoon and it will wither and die because it didn't go through the struggle to change."

Was she doing that to Chance?

Their discussion in the parking lot had felt pretty damn transformative to her. And she *had* pressed him, forcing him to acknowledge what was between them. Moreover, she'd walked back into the restaurant resolved to break through his lack of belief in the two of them.

His unwillingness to even try.

Was that the right move?

A human wasn't a butterfly, but the analogy

wasn't totally off the mark, either. And when you added in a lifetime of conditioning and stubborn male pride, well . . .

You got Chance Beaumont.

"You should go after what you want, baby. I will always support you one hundred percent on that. But when what you want is another person, you have to go in with your eyes open. And you have to recognize there may be limits on what they can give."

"I know."

Carlene took her hand and gave it a tight squeeze. "I know you think you do. But our hearts have a way of pushing forward anyway."

Chapter 9

Chance walked around the northern edge of his property, the air crisp and cold as the sun worked its way up out of the eastern skyline. With a sleepless night spent full of thoughts of Charlotte, he'd finally reasoned around five in the morning that if he wasn't going to get any rest, he might as well channel his restless energy into his business.

He hadn't been out here to this part of the ranch in a while, but the near loss of the heifer and the risks of hardware disease had gotten him thinking about what was needed to rotate the herd. He was careful about the rotations, well aware he needed to keep them moving into fresh pasture, all while managing the land itself.

The last few times he'd run the numbers on contracting a few more hands to make the rotations a bit easier, he just wasn't solvent enough to make the hires he needed. With the new deal with the Hills, he figured he could finally invest.

You gotta spend money to make money.

It was a tune his father had sung through the years, usually when he was itching to make an investment in something, and it had become Trevor Beaumont's mantra when he wanted to excuse a bad business deal or a whim he'd decided to indulge.

Shaking off the memory, Chance rode the land, making note of the things that he would need to handle. Although it wasn't ideal to start burning in the fall, there were a few patches of land he would probably address. There was also a line of fence that needed some serious work and attention.

What he couldn't quite shake was the lingering—and slightly fanciful—idea that his father was a ghost. Whether it was some sort of outsize influence or just the leftover feelings that stemmed from a lifetime with an emotionally abusive parent, he wasn't sure.

But it surprised him to realize how true it was, all the same. How much he *felt* the old man's presence, breathing down the back of his neck.

"Not much value in the north pasture." Trevor coughed. *"When my daddy bought this land up after the war, he didn't give a lot of thought to exactly what he was buying. He just wanted a place to call his own. That north pasture's never done well for me."*

"What's the problem with it?" Chance asked. "I've been up there a few times. The land doesn't look that much different from the rest of the ranch."

Trevor shook his head and spat a stream of tobacco on the ground. "It's no good. Bad stuff happens up there, and I'm superstitious enough to keep my stock off it."

Chance wanted to argue, but he recognized that look. He'd seen it since childhood, and despite being in his late twenties and well away from those days, nothing much had changed. When his father got something stuck in his head—and that was often—there wasn't a whole lot that could dislodge it.

If Trevor thought that land was bad, or cursed, or whatever the hell else had gotten its hooks in him, there wasn't a whole lot of convincing him otherwise.

And still, the memory gnawed at Chance.

His father had been diagnosed with cancer not too long after that, and he'd gone quickly. They'd only had one appointment in Missoula with an oncologist when the diagnosis of a fast-growing, fast-moving cancer was revealed, and his father was gone in a matter of weeks. With Trevor's quickly declining health and constant orders of what needed to be done around the ranch, Chance hadn't given it much more thought.

But now it was time to think about it again.

He didn't have any hands still on the ranch from that time, but he thought old Jack Sampson might still remember a bad season or two years ago. He made a mental note to give their former foreman a call and see what the man might recall. Perhaps they'd had a bad winter or a tough run during calving season.

None of it meant the land was cursed.

Chance shook his head, willing away the small chill that skimmed his back.

What did the old man know, anyway?

The shame of it all, Chance thought, was that his dad had actually known quite a bit. Despite his bad investment choices, Trevor hadn't been a bad rancher. Although he had done it with rough words and even tougher expectations, he had taught Chance how to work the land, how to manage stock, how to live a rancher's life. He might not have given a care for evolving his practices or had a head for making good investments, but he knew the mechanics of ranching.

It was the one thing that held him here now, and it was the one lingering bond that couldn't be broken.

Was it the notion of ghosts? Or was it the simple reality of fathers and sons and the bonds that forged them? Bonds that, when forged in difficulty and resentment, kept them trapped there, too.

Not everyone had a relationship like his and Trevor's. He'd now seen that over at Wayne and Sons a few times. The way Charlie interacted with Zack, the way the two men worked together.

And in the way Charlie shared his knowledge as easily as he shared his affection.

It had been one more thing to cement Chance's feelings about Charlotte. She came from a family that loved, trusted and encouraged one another.

And he did not.

Refusing to feel so defeated, especially this early in the morning, Chance climbed off his mount, holding Squash's lead in his hand. He had named the horse Sasquatch on a whim, and somehow the pretty bay had morphed into Squash a long time ago.

"Come on, let's walk a bit."

Chance dug out a few sugar cubes and fed them to Squash as they ambled over the land. In the quiet of the early morning and the easy companionship of his horse, he felt his equilibrium slowly return.

He *could* do this. And he would do this. There was no other acceptable outcome.

He would just have to work harder. Get more out of every day.

If he could make something out of this part of the ranch, that would help. In the short term it would help with the herd rotation, and in the longer term, herd expansion. All of which were big things. Good, productive things.

He moved around a craggy patch and felt his boot catch on a rock. Slowing down, unwilling to risk Squash losing a shoe, Chance looked down to the ground and saw something dark and slick glinting in the early-morning sun.

He dropped down to his knee, touching that small patch, surprised when his fingertips came away coated with a black oily sludge.

"What the hell?" Chance held his fingertips to his nose and breathed deep.

And in that moment, he knew exactly what he had.

With even more striking clarity, he understood

why Trevor had warned him off the north pasture.

The old man hadn't been sitting on a curse at all. With every last dollar he owned, Chance would bet that Trevor Beaumont had simply been biding his time to get his son out of his will and untethered from the property.

Property that held oil.

CHANCE SPENT MUCH of the morning in a trance, a million thoughts racing through his mind on what needed to be done. And chief among them all was who he was going to talk to for advice.

Because once he acted on this, life was going to move fast.

He'd effectively won the land lottery, and no one's life stayed the same once that happened. He'd diligently avoided singing the *Beverly Hillbillies* theme song all morning—barely—but another thought weighed on him.

Who could he trust?

And no matter how he sliced it, he kept coming back to the one person he could talk to about all of this.

Charlotte.

After cooling down Squash and giving him an extra pail of oats for breakfast, Chance had headed back to the main house and scoured whatever he could find. He'd diligently avoided living in the old man's house—content to stay in the foreman's cabin on the ranch—but he now realized how shortsighted that had been. Beyond a cursory glance, he'd pretty much ignored everything in his father's office that didn't immediately pertain to the running of ranch business.

Their housekeeper, Kate, still came in and cleaned the house every two weeks, and she always made him food that she stored in the ranch freezer in the garage, but other than coming for his meals, he'd avoided the place like the plague.

One more haunted part of the property he'd avoided.

To his detriment, Chance now admitted.

Because when he finally dug through a box of papers stored in the small credenza in the office, Chance found all he needed to confirm the truth.

A geologist's survey report on the north pasture.

Copies of the original deed of sale to his grandfather with the confirmation that the entire property was owned by the Beaumont family— inclusive of those precious mineral rights.

And several scrawled notes in his father's handwriting of how to manage mineral rights, with one last note at the bottom.

Confirm inheritance rights.

Chance was secretly glad that was all he'd found. Even a drafted but unexecuted will could have given him problems.

But that note confirmed all he needed to know.

Trevor had been determined to remove him from the ranch and all the benefits that came with his inheritance. All that he'd worked for and believed in.

None of Chance's goals and dreams had meant a damn fucking thing to his father.

Every time in the past he'd convinced himself his father wasn't that bad—that their relationship had glimmers of hope in it—he'd been disappointed.

But never like today.

Never like this desperate emptiness that suggested he'd mattered even less than he'd been made to feel.

Which probably meant he should stay away from Charlotte and all the impossible dreams she wove inside of him.

A reality that came a tad too late—since here he was, knocking on her door—in a small neighborhood off the main thoroughfare into downtown Rustlers Creek.

"Chance. Hi."

She had on a pair of yoga pants that covered her long legs in a shade of peacock blue that should have been ridiculous but instead looked as sweet as a cone of cotton candy. Her oversize University of Montana sweatshirt couldn't fully hide the curvy frame beneath. And her upswept hair made his fingers itch to trail along the column of her throat.

Instead he shoved his hands in his pockets.

"Good morning. I know it's early, but—"

"I've been up since six working, so I could use a break. Come on in. I actually wanted to talk to you anyway."

"Oh?"

He followed her down the long hallway, a woven rug muting the sound of his work boots on the aged hardwood floors.

"Has Loretta Hardwick called you?"

He vaguely remembered an unknown number popping up on his phone that had gone to voice mail. "I'm not sure."

"Check your phone, and I'll pour you a cup of coffee and refresh mine. Then I'll tell you what I'm working on."

He wasn't sure what he'd done to get this nononsense version of Charlotte, but it was a bit of a relief in the midst of all they'd shared the night before.

Even if something did tug on him low in the gut that he wouldn't have minded a sweet hello or a welcome kiss.

All more of the ridiculous knots this woman seemed able to tie him in.

The voice mail he'd ignored was from Loretta Hardwick, and in her message he finally understood what had Charlotte so focused. He shoved his phone back into his jeans. "She wants us to cochair the Cattle Baron's ball."

"She does. And with it we both get some smelly bulls as a thank-you as well as all that publicity and access to the organization."

"You want a smelly bull?"

"No, I want to give you my smelly bull. And I want to use this opportunity to expand my PR business and make some contacts. Which you and I are going to do, assuming you take this stellar, albeit smelly, opportunity and run with it."

More of that strange hazy trance that had gripped him all morning seemed to dull his senses.

The offer to cochair the ball was exceptionally rare and, while a lot of work, came with serious benefits. Not just the gift of the livestock but the contacts and the prestige, which couldn't be underestimated.

He'd have jumped at it in a heartbeat.

But now, with all he'd discovered this morning?

Had he woken up in a parallel universe? One where his business issues had seemingly vanished overnight?

"Why us?"

"I don't know. Loretta called me first the other day. She started in all friendly and said that since you and I were dating she thought it would be something we could do together." He didn't miss her grimace as she turned to the fridge after setting his coffee on the table. "Or that I could do it and you could be pretty window dressing while I did it all."

Chance was offended on Charlotte's behalf and, frankly, for himself, too. Not about the dating, but the work part? Hell yes. "Why did she think we were dating? Or that I'd make you do it all?"

Charlotte came back with a container of creamer. "Clearly her father wasn't so drunk while having cocktails with us that he couldn't remember to gossip to his daughter."

"But why'd he think that? We were clear we'd met up after both being in town."

"Because we were two single adults having drinks together." She poured a small splash of cream into her own coffee before pushing it back to him. "And to be fair, if we were attached adults having drinks people likely would have thought the same."

"And you're not insulted?"

"About the dating part?" She shrugged. "It's not like we haven't done some of those things people already suspect we're doing."

Since those things they'd done hadn't been far from his thoughts for a week, he couldn't quite argue with her point, but it still chafed. Emotions he'd need to get over because there was no way he was turning this down.

But it did give him an idea.

If the two of them were going to live with all this antiquated thinking, the least they could do was their level best to turn it all on its ear and really make something of the event. Something that wasn't the staid, old, boring event of the past, full of flowing booze and rubber chicken.

A few ideas started to brew as Charlotte continued. "I *was* insulted at the idea I could do all the work and you'd be some arm candy at the end of it."

"If I take this on, I'll do my part." Which he would do regardless, but he couldn't resist poking her a bit. "But let it go on the record that you're the one who called me *arm candy*."

"A figure of speech."

Her back remained prim, but that no-nonsense attitude she'd worn like a shield since he'd walked in relaxed a bit. "And I know that you will do your part. I never doubted it, either. I just don't know why other people, women my own age *especially*, don't get that."

"People are way too trapped in their own ideas of what life should look like. And you and I are going to figure out a way to upend that in whatever it is that we plan for the event."

"I like that." She smiled at him over the top of her coffee mug. "You really want to do this?"

"I do."

Her gaze turned thoughtful. "But if you didn't know about Loretta, why are you here?"

"Something happened this morning. I was up early, too. Couldn't sleep. So I saddled up and rode out to the north pasture on my ranch."

She was clearly intrigued, but she didn't say anything, so he used a few extra moments to make his coffee, heavy on the cream and sugar, before glancing back up into her incredulous face.

"You want some coffee with that cream?"

"It hides the flavor."

"I guessed as much. Forgive me for pointing out the obvious, but why drink it, then?"

"I like it this way."

"It's a hot, coffee-flavored milkshake."

"Which I'll gladly argue with you on later. But

right now I need—" The morning flashed through his mind from the oil slick to the papers from his father to the unmistakable proof in those papers that the oil was his.

"What's going on, Chance?"

"I think I'm sitting on a gold mine."

CHARLOTTE LISTENED TO Chance's tale—twice—and was still fumbling, trying to organize her thoughts.

"And your father's lawyer didn't tell you about this when he read the will and worked through the transfer of the estate."

"No." Chance got up and got the pot of coffee, both of their first cups long gone. "I'm starting to wonder if he knew. Even if my old man had sworn him to secrecy, there'd have been no reason to keep it from me after he was dead."

"And the geologist?"

"I did a quick search on the firm. They're legitimate and very well respected. The one thing my father did right, apparently. That was confidential business, and if they found anything they were honor-bound to keep it to the person who paid for the appraisal."

Although he'd been measured in his telling, Charlotte figured this was her time to go for broke. "And your father? He did this without telling you."

"That would be correct."

"When?"

"About a week before his cancer diagnosis."

"I'm sorry about that."

"The cancer or the geology report?"

"Both."

When he didn't respond, she figured he couldn't quite say the same about the cancer, and she wasn't sure she could blame him. She knew she was fortunate for the relationship she had with her parents and had understood a long time ago that not every child was raised with the same good fortune.

That reality only made the conversation with her mother the night before that much more relevant.

Carlene was her biggest and fiercest champion, and Charlotte knew nothing could change that. But for as much as her mother liked Chance, her reservations had been clear.

When what you want is another person, you have to go in with your eyes open. And you have to recognize there may be limits on what they can give.

Charlotte had tossed and turned on those words all night. Because if her mother were right, it meant that she and Chance might have more than a bumpy road ahead. They might not have a road at all. Not for the long haul, anyway.

Could she live with that?

And why had it suddenly begun to matter so much?

"Can I ask you something?" When he only nodded, she pressed on before the urge to be direct faded. "Why me? Since this happened this morning, I'm assuming I'm the first person you've told."

"You are."

"Why?" she asked again, softer this time, even as she felt her own urgency in that lone word.

"I'm not sure. But I knew I needed to tell someone, and each time I thought that, you're the person I kept coming back to."

"What if we hadn't seen each other last week in Bozeman?"

He seemed to consider it, a rally of emotions flying across his face. "I'm not sure I'd be here. But I'm not sure I'd have been in the north pasture this morning, either, if I hadn't seen you in Bozeman last week." His grin amped up. "Arm candy like me needs his beauty rest, you know."

She swatted him on the arm. "I'm not going to live that down, am I?"

"Not anytime soon, no."

His humor faded, replaced with something more serious. He reached out a hand and placed his palm over hers, linking their fingers. "I'm not sure why Bozeman happened. It'd be easy enough to say *Right place, right time*, but I'm not so sure. It didn't feel that way then, and it still doesn't."

"You think there's something more woo-woo going on?"

"I think something's been put into motion. I don't know why or how, but I think it has. The dinner in Bozeman. And before that, Harper coming home, and her and Gray finding their way back to each other. He's my best friend, and she's yours. It's put us in each other's way."

Since it had done exactly that—and matched the same path her own thoughts had traveled—Charlotte just nodded.

And stared down at their linked fingers, her mother's gentle guidance from the night before echoing in her ears.

Our hearts have a way of pushing forward anyway.

Was she pushing forward on blind faith? Or sheer folly?

And how did anyone ever know the difference?

Chapter 10

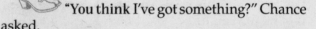

"You think I've got something?" Chance asked.

Charlie stared at him across the small patch of oil in the north pasture, his dark gaze direct. "You've got more than a little something here."

Chance wasn't sure why he'd been holding his breath—between his own oil-slicked hands that morning and the geologist's paperwork he'd discovered—he knew what he had.

But something in Charlie's acknowledgment dislodged the fist in Chance's midsection that had gripped tight all morning.

Charlotte had offered to take his secret to the grave if that was what he'd wanted, but in her gentle way, she'd also encouraged him to get help with this. And the first person she named—who also happened to be the one other person he'd trust with this confidence—was her father.

"They've talked and rumored about oil in Rustlers Creek for decades," Charlie said. "And I've always wondered, since very little of it's ever been found."

"You never had your property surveyed, sir?" Chance asked.

"Years ago my father did. Didn't turn up much beyond a few pockets of natural gas. That's great, but I figured on leaving it there until we needed it. Cattle operations have always been what I cared about anyway."

They were what Chance cared most about as well, but he also knew what this finding meant. He could run his cattle operation the exact way that he wanted to.

"I have a feeling things are about to change around here."

Charlie grinned at that. "You could say that again, son. Things are about to change for you in a big way."

"Please tell me I'm not the only one who can't stop humming the *Beverly Hillbillies* theme?" Charlotte said.

Chance started laughing. "Been trying to ignore that earworm myself. Though I'm not quite sure I want to be compared to Jed Clampett."

She batted her eyelashes. "How about Jethro, then?"

"Let me toss a wet blanket on it all and be as honest as Granny," Charlie said. "You'd better get your house in order. Add onto your security at the front entrance, and I'd get the house and stables locked down, too."

"This is really happening." Chance had thought the same thing to himself over and over, but each and every word out of Charlie's mouth only reinforced it.

"That it is." Charlie smiled before making a full turn to look at the vista all around. "But I tell you what. If you're game for it—and I'll make sure we keep it small—why don't you come over for dinner tonight. We'll toast your good fortune and eat some good food. There's plenty of time tomorrow morning for all these details."

"I'd like that, sir."

"Excellent. I'd offer my home, but the moment my daughter-in-law gets wind of this, she's going to cook her ass off in that huge kitchen of hers."

"Either place is fine with me. It's time with people I trust."

Charlie extended his hand. "You've got my word on that. My family knows how to keep things to themselves."

Chance shook his hand in return and knew those words for truth. Charlie had shot straight with him since they'd headed over to the pasture and had given good, sound advice. Advice that ensured Chance would be successful in managing this sudden discovery.

The older man nodded and tilted his head toward his truck. "Charlotte, I'm going to head over to Zack's and get to party-planning. Why don't you walk the house and grounds with Chance and help him make a list of those things he'll need to look at. And you should probably work him up a PR plan while you're at it. He's sure as hell going to need one."

At those slightly ominous instructions, Chance waved to Charlie and watched his large truck bump its way back toward the main entrance. It was only when he turned to find Charlotte, a bemused expression on her face, that he stilled. "What?"

"You. A hurricane has just blown through your life, and I can see you making lists in your head."

"Right back at you. In all of ninety seconds, standing between you and your father, I could see where genetics and ambition meet. Although," he added with a smile, "I do expect it takes a bit longer than a walk around the ranch to work up a PR plan."

"Aww." A light blush colored her cheeks, just like he remembered from grade school. "That's one of the nicest things anyone has ever said to me."

"Because it's true. It's obvious where you get your no-nonsense style. Is there anything about anything your father doesn't know?"

"Not much. And when it comes to ranching, it's even less than not much. But please don't tell him I told you that."

"Because he'll be insufferable?"

"Hell yes. That man loves to know things, and he loves to share his wisdom." She paused, her gaze growing distant as she looked out over the direction where her father had just driven off. "You gave him a gift today. Calling him here. Asking for his advice."

"Your father's an amazing man. He's what a father should actually be like." Chance wasn't sure why he'd shared that. His relationship with his own father wasn't a big secret, but it wasn't like he went around telling other people he thought their fathers were great.

But Charlie Wayne really was.

If Charlotte sensed his awe—or the mental comparisons he made to his own father—she left him to those private thoughts.

"He went through a hard time last year. When Zack asked him to stop working the ranch day to day."

"This was what Johnny Cox asked you about over drinks last week?"

"Yep. He really struggled with the inevitable changes life demands of us. He hurt my mother in the process, yet she stuck around. She didn't put up with his shit, but she stuck around." Charlotte sighed before turning her attention fully back to him. "I guess that's what more than forty years of commitment looks like."

What would that be like? Chance wondered.

To look at your parents and see them as people you liked. People you actually wanted to spend time with. People who'd built a relationship you recognized for its commitment and effort.

People you admired.

His memories of his mother were so limited,

and he had always assumed that her dying so young was what had set his father off on such an unpleasant path. Trevor—or Chance's memories of him—were of a man who saw no joy in life. A man who thought anything he wanted should simply be his for the taking.

And with that greed, a man who never appreciated the child he had.

Would that have been different if his mother had lived? Or would Trevor have simply brought her down, too?

They were questions without answers, because life made its inevitable marks, the years ebbing and flowing as it did.

But with what he had learned today, Chance couldn't help but wonder.

He had always thought that losing his mother had set his father on a very dark path. But perhaps that way had been set all along.

CHARLOTTE SENSED SOMETHING profound had happened to Chance today. It wasn't just finding the oil, though that would change anybody's life in any number of ways. But it was what the discovery of that oil stood for.

Both an answer to his dreams and a very dark reality of his relationship with his father.

He didn't have to say it.

She could see it. *Hear* it, rather, as he'd recounted his discovery—and all that had followed in finding the paperwork—over coffee in her kitchen.

All the things he said as well as all the things he held back.

She couldn't begin to understand what he was going through and knew her own family relationships meant she could empathize but she could never really know. But it also meant that her normal, bullheaded way of pushing through any obstacle to her goal likely wasn't going to be the right approach here.

Chance wasn't a goal.

And for the first time since he walked out of her hotel room in Bozeman, she was grateful they hadn't slept together.

Not yet, at least.

"Do you ride much?" Seemingly blessedly unaware of the direction of her thoughts, Chance interrupted her.

"Not as much as I used to. I get out from time to time with Zack, but those outings have been few and far between since I started my own business."

"You up for a ride now?"

"I'd like that. You want to get a head start on that list?"

"I actually would like to ride a bit and get some fresh air with a pretty girl."

"But if I want to make a list, you won't stop me?"

A hard laugh rumbled out of his chest as he pulled her close, side-arming her in a hug. "Far be it from me to stop you."

They walked like that back to his truck, and Charlotte wondered at the change. He'd held her hand over her kitchen table and now his affection extended to touching, albeit more like the platonic touching between friends.

Should she press him on it?

Or take the moment for what it was? A momentous day she'd been invited to share.

Those vacillating thoughts occupied her through their drive back toward the stables and the mounting of two horses for their ride. He'd put her on a sweet mare named Dusty Rose, and he sat a large white quarter horse named Elvis.

"You named your horse Elvis?"

"I can't take credit. His former owner did it, and I thought the name suited him. His white coat reminded me of Elvis in his Vegas years."

"I'll give you that."

"He also happens to like Elvis's music, which is fun to watch when we get some tunes going in the barn. He's crazy about 'Burning Love.'"

"You're making that up."

Chance raised his hand. "Swear to God."

They moved out of the barn and farther onto the property. Things were quiet, the stillness of a Sunday afternoon ensuring minimal activity was happening. He spent some time showing her the cattle out in the pasture and pointed out a few funny details about some of the calves.

From there they moved on toward the outer stretches of the property and a small stream that ran down the western end. The sun was high, turning the September afternoon exceptionally warm, and Charlotte finally gave in, stripping off her sweatshirt to the tank top underneath.

Dismounting, she led Dusty Rose to the creek to drink her fill. Chance did the same with Elvis, looking at her from over the top of the horse's back. "It's gotten hot this afternoon."

"Which is weird since they're calling for snow by Friday."

"Life in Montana."

Although his conversation was casual, she didn't miss the way his gaze roamed over her shoulders, dipping slightly to her breasts before turning to focus on his horse.

And in that small moment of acknowledgment, Charlotte felt the sweetest victory.

Side-armed hugs be damned.

Which now left her with an odd dilemma.

He'd backed away again, from the physical between them. And while she'd pushed over the past week on that front, something now had her backing off.

For as much as there was mutual attraction, there was now hesitation, too.

They were working together on the ball for the next few months. His life had just been upended, and they were about to have dinner with her parents.

With all those things happening, she suddenly found herself reticent, and that wasn't her normal MO. It also felt like mixed messages, which only added to the deep-seated feelings of being off-kilter that he seemed uniquely able to create in her.

"Those are some serious thoughts for a pretty fall afternoon."

"I'm frustrated."

"By me?"

"Yes." She played with the reins in her hand. "And no. And yes, sort of, because it all revolves around you."

"Why don't you take me through it, then."

It was inane, but if she and Chance had proven anything over the past week, it was that they could talk about things. It was one area of intimacy they seemed to have mastered, even if all the other areas were giving them fits and starts.

"*Yes* because you're you, and we have this weird thing spinning between us that's not been there before. Or hasn't been there before like this," she said as an afterthought.

When he only nodded, she kept on. "And *no* because it's not your fault our friends and family watched us like bugs under a microscope last night."

"Fair." He reached for some bottled waters he'd stowed in a pack on Elvis's back, tossing her one. "And the *yes, sort of*?"

"You look at me like you want me, and if pressed, you even say it. And then you do weird-ass brother shit like side-arm hug me. And then you look at my chest when you don't think I'm looking, and it pisses me off."

She took a deep breath and twisted the cap off her water, drinking deep. "And it all pisses me off because I'm nearly thirty-three years old, and I shouldn't feel so damned confused. But I get around you, and it's like I'm ten again, which only just adds to the frustration because I am so *not* ten anymore."

"You're most certainly not ten. Trust me, I've noticed."

"This isn't funny, Chance."

"Maybe not, but it doesn't mean we can't laugh at ourselves. At least a little bit."

He crossed to a small copse of trees and wrapped Elvis's lead around a low branch before walking back and doing the same with Dusty Rose's. Charlotte was thankful for the silence, desperate to come up with a pithy response that would get her out of this juvenile, petulant place where it seemed all she needed to do was add a stamp of the foot to punctuate her words.

Which made it a surprise when he walked back over to her and wrapped his arms around her, settling his hands low on her back.

"For starters, I'm not laughing at you. And I have a *yes* and a *no* and a *yes, sort of* myself."

She raised her eyebrows at him in a move her brother Jackson had taught her when she was a teenager. It had done her well through the years, defusing any number of situations, but it only seemed to make Chance smile more.

"Yes, we do have a weird thing spinning between us. One that has only spun longer because I was too chickenshit to take my shot on the Fourth of July. And then the window closed completely when you went off with your boozehound friends and got drunk in the backyard at the Waynes'." He teased her lower back with his thumb. "Confession. I always call that place Wayne Manor in my mind."

"As in *Batman*?"

"Yep. It sort of stuck one day, and I can't get it out of my head."

"Since you're the one who discovered oil, you'd better get used to having a manor, too."

"I don't—" He shook his head. "That one's going to need a lot of time to settle. Besides, I like my foreman's cabin."

"You don't live in the main house?"

"No."

"Oh."

One more revelation in a line of them this week, Charlotte had to admit to herself. It was like each and every time she thought she had a handle on him, the sands shifted.

More like fell away from beneath her feet, she corrected.

Sensing a probe on the main house was out of his comfort zone, she kept on with their odd conversation. "And the *no*?"

"I agree on the bug under a microscope bit. That's not your fault, nor is it mine. And to be fair, I'm not even sure I'd say our friends are at fault so much as they're just not . . . subtle."

"Not in the least."

They weren't subtle, and Charlotte struggled to understand why it bothered her quite so much. She'd certainly been interested in Harper and Gray's relationship and hadn't attempted to hide it. And while her brother and sister-in-law had kept their marital troubles to themselves, she'd admittedly felt a bit slighted to not have known anything was going on.

So really, she had no leg to stand on.

Which only added to the emotional swirl when it came to her and Chance.

Because she wasn't a hypocrite. Yet, she wasn't willing to let her friends in, either.

Why?

A question even harder to answer as she stared up at him, the firm strength of his arms wrapped around her.

"And the *yes, sort of*?"

"I do want you. The timing sucks, but it doesn't change the fact that you do something to me, Charlotte Wayne. You always have. And I've done without you for a damn long time. So long that I'm not sure what I'd do if I caught you."

"Is that what this is about? Catching each other?"

"What would you call it?"

In his question she recognized there wasn't an easy answer. Was it as simple as a matter of timing? Or had they gone this long living separate lives expressly *because* they didn't belong together?

How did you know?

"Maybe we're finally in the same place in life where we can give it a try."

"And if it falls apart?"

Why was that his default expectation? Especially because the past few weeks had proven, yet again, that when you peeled away the world around them, and they were simply Charlotte and Chance, things *worked*.

"Last week, over drinks in Bozeman, you and I really talked to each other. And it mattered. It mattered a lot."

"It did."

"When we get to that place, when no one else is around, we do okay."

"We do."

"So how do we find that place?"

He looked somewhere over her shoulder, considering the land, but Charlotte suspected he was more focused on something only he could see.

When his gaze came back to her, there was a level of certainty lining his jaw and setting his face in deeply grooved lines she'd never seen before. "Maybe we can't find it because there *are* always people around. People who've known us, our families and our lives forever."

His reasonable arguments empirically made sense, but she believed deep in her heart there was more to both situations than was simply explainable.

"So that's it? We don't even try to see what we could have? We let the world around us, a world that really isn't part of the intimate details of our life, make the decision?"

Confused and not sure if she even had an argument to make beyond disappointment in their conflicted views, she slipped from his arms.

"I have a question. A legitimate one, not steeped in what I believe but what I am afraid you believe."

Charlotte had rolled the idea of him being afraid over and over in her mind, and while she didn't expect full-on agreement, she wanted to see if she'd at least gotten inside the ballpark. "Why do you measure your life by mine?"

Those gray eyes narrowed immediately, storms rising up in the depths. "What's that supposed to mean?"

"The whole lady-of-the-manor bullshit I seem to inspire in you. You're my friend. You're friends with my friends. You're professional colleagues with my brother. What gap do you see when you look at us? Because it feels pretty damn unfair to me every time you toss out the *You're a Wayne and I'm a Beaumont* bullshit."

He swallowed a few times, clearly fighting the rising anger that was evident in his eyes. "You asked me a question, so I'll ask one of my own. Why are you so quick to ignore that aspect of who we are?"

"Our last names?"

"Where we come from, Charlotte. What made us. What do we really have to build on? A fourth-grade crush and a lifetime after full of ill-advised and barely concealed fury with one another."

His words put her on her back foot, and she wasn't sure what to make of it.

"We were kids, Chance. And we've had a lifetime since to build on. We have attraction and interest to build on. We have common goals and a future to build on. That's what I see when I look at you. That's all I ever see."

"And all I see is a life that, until this morning, felt like an endless slog of one problem to the next. An endless *Fuck you* from my father that continued to screw me, no matter how hard I worked."

"But it is changing," she pressed him, not sure why he couldn't see that. "And hanging on to an idea that wasn't even true to begin with, and is less true now with the oil discovery, is blatantly ridiculous."

Charlotte sensed it even before he spoke. The words that had spilled out, sincerity lacing every one, had the exact opposite effect as intended.

"*Ridiculous?* Did you somehow miss this morning's discovery? That I've been up to my eyeballs in debt, digging out of it one fucking cow at a time, and all this time it was because my father wanted to fuck me out of my inheritance?"

He flung a hand wide. "That he wanted to screw me so bad that even *after* he'd been diagnosed with cancer and had no hope of living through it, he still made sure I didn't know? That I wasn't going to know?"

"And now he's gone. And you're still acting like he's here. That all the work you have done, one fucking cow after another"—she tossed his words back with relish—"means nothing. That you mean nothing!"

"You don't understand. And you don't actually know anything about it."

"Then tell me! Tell me what I don't understand."

"If a man can't love his son, if he sees supporting him as nothing more than a frustrating duty, if he tries to screw him over even in death, what does that actually say, Charlotte? About me? What value am I going to bring to a relationship? To living a life with someone? To *making* a life with someone?"

How did you argue with that? Charlotte realized. With any of it? With wounds that went so deep they barely made sense anymore?

Even if, standing there under that great big sky, she finally saw something she'd never really fully understood before this moment.

Trevor Beaumont hadn't simply damaged his son with emotional abuse and a vague sort of neglect. He'd actively poisoned him with a lifetime of actions designed to reduce and wear down and belittle.

That was the real difference between them, and no amount of talking could make it change.

It wasn't the whole Wayne–Beaumont bullshit he'd somehow wrapped around himself. It was the belief that her family unit—one steeped in strong bonds and a deep respect—made her better. More valuable.

And at risk for ruin.

With tears tightening her throat, she marched off toward Dusty Rose, careful not to spook the animal but unwilling to stand there one minute more and take the layers and layers of excuses about who they were and what they wanted.

All in service to some absurd notion of why he wasn't worthy.

And wasn't that just the part that hurt worst of all?

If he didn't want her, she'd accept it. Lack of interest—and a requirement to walk away when that was clear—went both ways, and she wasn't going to chase after a man who didn't want her.

More, she wasn't interested in a man who didn't want to be with her.

Yet, here she was.

With a man who *did* want her but who refused to think he even had a right to fight for it.

For them.

A man who was so wrapped in the past he had zero vision for the future.

Chapter 11

Chance watched the heavy rise and fall of Charlotte's shoulders and struggled to come up with the right words. Which was likely the last thing he needed to do since anything he picked usually came out wrong.

Or, worse, came out in a way that suggested he wasn't mindless with need for her.

Which he was.

God, he so fucking was.

Oh, he'd done his level best to manage it.

To lie to himself that he didn't want her *that* badly.

To keep his distance and hope he'd finally fall for someone else or just move the hell on with his life so that the image of Charlotte Wayne didn't haunt him at odd moments, both while awake and in the vivid, fiery dreams he'd always had of her.

Because he hadn't lied to her. Even as he shared the shameful truth that crept in when he thought of his father, he couldn't shake off those feelings. Nothing he did could eradicate that bone-deep fear that he meant nothing.

And hadn't the oil discovery proven that?

What sort of man cons his own kid out of a life? A future? Especially when it was evident he had none, being at the mercy of a cancer that ravaged his body so fast he'd barely had time to take a breath.

What did Trevor see when he looked at his son that disgusted him so much?

He'd never worried that he'd be like his father. He made the choice every day to view people as valuable and to live an honorable life. But none of it meant there still wasn't something fundamentally broken inside of him.

Something deeply flawed that could ruin something real and lasting at any time.

He'd done it with that damn Valentine's card at ten, and he'd done it in that hotel room in Bozeman at thirty-two.

When things got too serious, he ran.

Because nothing was half measure with Charlotte. She wasn't raised to expect it, and she sure as hell wouldn't accept it.

But damn it, she wanted more than he could give. More than he *knew* he could give.

And that wasn't a place he could live in.

Which gave him no right to approach her now. Even as he marched toward her and reached for her hand, just as she was about to unwrap Dusty Rose's lead from the tree.

"Come here a minute."

"What?"

"With me. Please."

He took her hand and pulled her toward the creek, her long legs easily able to keep stride with him.

"Chance, what is this about? Why are you—"

He got far enough away from the horses that any further arguments couldn't upset them when he dragged her close and crushed his mouth to hers.

Need—hot and blinding—consumed him as he fought to show her all she meant to him. All the things he couldn't be or have were bound up in that kiss along with everything he so desperately fought to be. And since he had nothing else to offer, he tried to convince her with his body what his words never seemed quite able to do.

That she mattered.

That he cared for her.

That he wanted better for her.

Although he sensed her hesitation—more from anger than actual resistance—she gave in quickly, her mouth open beneath his, hot and enticing, welcoming him.

Encouraging him.

And, in ways he couldn't describe, believing in him.

So he gave and took in equal measure, the kiss like a tether that kept them coming back for each other, again and again.

His hands moved over her, the delicate skin of her arms, warmed by the sun, like silk beneath his work-roughened fingers. He trailed his fingertips over her biceps and then back up to her shoulders, before moving one hand to tease at the collar of her tank top. He traced the neckline before moving down to cup her breast through the cotton.

"Chance." His name was a moan against his mouth, exhaled on a light rush of air.

And just like the week before, he again felt the glorious response of this woman to his touch.

Why couldn't it be different?

It was that truth that finally had him pulling away.

And it was that truth that had him staring down at her with an ocean of regret that he couldn't separate wanting her from not wanting to hurt her.

"Why did you do that?"

"To remind us both that walking away isn't about desire."

Where he'd have expected a tart response or another difficult conversation, she surprised him. In that way she had, of never being quite who he expected, she nodded, her face gravely serious.

"Maybe you're right. Today was big, Chance. Important. And it's going to change your life."

"I—" He stilled, not sure why he was suddenly at a loss for words. Especially when her response was so reasonable.

Eminently so.

Frustratingly so.

Agreeably so.

She still stood close but didn't touch him or lean in for another kiss. "And you said something before, and I was too fired up to listen."

He mentally cycled back through what he'd said in the heat of their argument and quickly realized a new type of fire had scrambled his mind.

What the hell had he said?

"Your life did change. Literally, this morning. Between the work ahead of you with the oil and the ball and the fact that we're both playing a lot of push-pull with our hormones, maybe we should back off. Take some time to take sex out of the equation."

"Sure. I mean, yeah. It makes sense." It did?

"Then we're agreed? We'll put this behind us, and we'll be friends and collaborators on the work."

Friends? Why did that suddenly sound like the equivalent of jumping into the creek in January? A thought that seemed particularly comical as his hands itched to close over her breasts once more.

"Yeah. Sure."

"Good." She slipped away and headed back to where the horses were tied up, mounted up onto Dusty Rose's back with practiced ease. "We'd better get back to the house, then. I need to get cleaned up and head over to Hadley's. And I'll see you there later."

"Maybe after—" He walked toward Elvis. "Maybe I should cancel."

"Maybe after what?"

"I'm not rejecting you, Charlotte. Whatever you might think, please don't walk away thinking that."

Some of that cheerfulness—and he wouldn't quite call it forced—dimmed a bit. "Thank you for the clarification." She seemed to consider something before obviously deciding it was worth continuing. "I'm not rejecting you, either. Nor am I playing a game. But I really do think a lot changed today. Give it a bit of time to settle."

"I get it. Which is why maybe it's better if I don't come over to see your family tonight."

Her eyebrows shot up at that. "After my sister-in-law has no doubt begun a feast? I hate to break it to you, but you'd need to have broken both legs and knocked out a few teeth for her to even hear of it."

"Why do I always forget Hadley's love language is food?"

"I really don't know." She reached out for his hand, squeezing it when he took hold of hers. "We're okay, Chance. Really, we are."

He climbed back up on Elvis and followed her back to the stables. The ride was more subdued than when they'd headed out, but it wasn't unpleasant. Which was an odd surprise since he'd braced for the cold shoulder.

Only, it never came. And, strangely, they *were* fine.

It really had been a hell of a day, he thought as he followed Charlotte back to the stables, her light chatter keeping pace the whole way.

He'd somehow managed to strike oil *and* talk himself out of what he suspected could be the best sex of his life, all in the same day.

"WE'RE WORKING TOGETHER. Neither of us has time for fooling around."

"You practice that one in the mirror?" Harper asked her as she helped Charlotte carry several plates out to the back porch.

Although the summery day had turned colder as the sun set, Zack and Hadley had set up big propane heaters on the long porch that ran the length of the kitchen and living room. Between the heat and the pretty white lights strung over the space, they were more than comfortable eating outside.

"I don't need to practice anything."

Charlotte kept her focus on navigating through the house with eight pounds of barbecue on a serving platter and not on her friend. It also kept her from considering if her nose was actually growing as she confessed to Harper some of what had happened earlier.

"You keep telling yourself that."

Charlotte settled the platter on the table Hadley had designated for serving, and Harper added plates on one side and rolls on the other.

"I don't have to tell myself anything. We've fooled around a bit, and it's not going anywhere, Harper. What am I supposed to do? Attack the man?"

Her friend's face fell at that. "Oh, Char, I'm sorry. I mean, I just thought—" Harper glanced toward the house, satisfied no one was coming, before leaning in closer. "He's really not interested?"

"Interest doesn't seem to be our problem."

Confusion stamped itself in her friend's pretty hazel eyes. "What is your problem?"

"A loving family who raised me and runs one of the most successful ranches in the entire state versus a motherless child whose father was a royal shit. In a nutshell."

"That's just dumb. And—" Harper stilled. "And more proof that relationships between fathers and sons, especially the bad ones, can do a significant amount of damage."

Harper had lived with that damage herself. Gray's deeply troubled relationship with his own father had been the catalyst to break up with Harper when they were young, which had been the further driving force to send her to Seattle.

What would have happened if she hadn't come back to Rustlers Creek earlier this year?

Would Harper and Gray still be struggling along, separate and alone?

Was this really all about timing, like she'd thought? Or did it go far deeper, the effects of his father's abuse too damaging to really recover from?

"Let me ask you a question," Harper said.

Since she and Harper were still alone on the porch, Charlotte nodded. She'd opened the door on this, and to be honest, it felt good to talk to her friend. Even if the mixture of amusement and subtle teasing was a bit more than she'd bargained for. "Okay."

"If the two of you stayed friends, if you got through the planning of the ball, and he got his ranch up and running, and you kept this really great friendship you have, despite the fact that you both do your level best to screw it up as often as possible—"

"We don't do that." She didn't even need Harper's side-eye to give in. "Okay, yes, we do that."

Harper plowed on. "Could you live with that?"

"With a friendship?"

"Yes." Harper nodded. "With just something platonic coming out the other side of the next few months. After whatever this thing is that you claim is a friendship but which seems a lot like a friendship-plus runs its course."

Why was that thought so oddly bleak? Yet even as she struggled against the cold feeling that settled in her chest, Charlotte also knew the simple truth.

"Well, yeah. I mean yes, of course. I care about him, and I'd rather have him in my life, no matter what."

Harper's smile was indulgent, even though Charlotte got the distinct sense her friend was barely holding back from throwing a dinner roll at her.

"You do have something special between you. He came to you first, Charlotte. Today. About his discovery. He came to *you*. That means something."

"He needed help."

"There were a lot of places to go for help, including his lawyer. Think about that."

Harper patted her on the shoulder, leaving her to arrange the basket of silverware they'd brought out earlier.

Could she live with that? Charlotte wondered. Just a friendship?

And with startling clarity, she realized that yes, she could. She'd done it for nearly her entire life.

That friendship had changed and morphed, and yeah, they spent a lot of time swiping at each other, but if she'd had to describe her relationship with Chance, she'd have always said he was her friend.

Even in the moments he'd felt like her fiercest enemy, he'd been her friend.

Was that why this was so complicated?

It didn't make sense to compare her relationship—or lack of one—to others, but if she used Harper and Gray as a model, they had ended their relationship and hadn't even had a friendship to show for it. They'd simply cratered, each heading to their respective corners of the world.

She'd missed her friend terribly in the decade that Harper had lived in Seattle, but in looking at her and Gray with fresh eyes, Charlotte had to acknowledge something else.

She couldn't have walked away from someone she loved like that. No matter what the pain of ending the relationship was, the thought of fully losing that person in her life would have been untenable.

Not that Harper was wrong.

But if she modeled the exact same behavior with respect to Chance, Charlotte just couldn't picture herself walking away.

"OIL." ZACK SHOOK his head. "I just don't believe it."

He'd broken out some good bourbon for their evening as Zack, Charlie and Chance had settled into the Wayne library to catch up.

Despite the generosity, Chance had found himself gravitating to a beer. He had an early morning tomorrow—when didn't he?—but something else had lingered in the back of his mind since his afternoon ride with Charlotte.

Since you're the one who discovered oil, you'd better get used to having a manor, too.

To be fair, a lot of their conversation—and even more, the moments when they *weren't* talking—had lingered in his mind, but she'd managed to sum up the entire unreality of his day with that one statement.

A manor?

And all that went with it, including the truth that this discovery was going to make him quite wealthy.

For all his mental gymnastics about his finances, Chance had always known that selling the property and walking away would set him up comfortably. There was a big life outside of Montana, and he could go after a piece of that bigger world if he'd wanted to.

But he'd never wanted anything other than Beaumont Farms.

So he'd scraped and managed and got by because he was in the exact place in the entire world he wanted to be.

"Believe it." Charlie nodded. "I saw it myself."

"I nearly fell on my ass because of it." Chance took a long pull of his beer. "I'd've slipped in it if I hadn't slowed down for my horse."

"Let me cry a river of tears over your checkbook."

In that moment, Chance realized *this* was why he'd come tonight. For all the teasing—and there'd been quite a bit—the Waynes were genuinely happy for him. It was a testament to the type of people they were and the fact that while their own success sat comfortably on their shoulders, the success of others wasn't seen as a threat.

And maybe that was true wealth, Chance realized.

The revelation felt a little like the moral at the end of a Christmas special, but it didn't make it any less true.

"Do you know who you're going to contact first?" Zack asked.

"I put a call in to my security company and got lucky with an opening in their schedule tomorrow. Your father suggested I beef up some things around the ranch, and he's right. That oil's sat there a long time. A few more days won't change anything."

"Security was one of the first things we had to do once Hadley's show hit. One day we had some fence around the property to keep the cows in, and the next we had to worry about people sneaking onto the grounds."

While not exactly the same, Hadley's meteoric rise did have a lot of parallels to what he was dealing with. "Was that hard? That sudden upheaval of your life?"

"It had its moments." Zack considered the amber liquid in his glass before setting it down on the small coffee table in the library. "And I know it's not a secret, but Hadley and I had some things we had to work past in our marriage late last year. Not directly tied to that success, but all of it sort of snowballed into a bigger deal. Especially with all the activity on the ranch all the time."

"I can imagine."

"It's good, right? Success and the money that comes with it. More, the comfort and ease that money brings. It's what you work so hard for, so even as you're telling yourself not to be an asshole and to just be grateful, you end up being a dick anyway."

"Last fall was a shitty season for all of us," Charlie added. "But if even old cowboys can get their heads out of their asses, I have a lot of faith in the next generation not to get stuck quite as long as I did." The older man smiled at that. "Which also reminds me I promised Carlene I'd help her get a few things out of the car."

As excuses went, it was as fair as any other, but Chance got the distinct sense Charlie wanted to give him and Zack a bit of privacy.

It was only after the older man had left, promising that they'd pick up where they left off because he had a few ideas Chance could talk about with his lawyer, that Chance turned to Zack.

"Your father's a special man."

"He is, and I know I'm lucky to have him. Ornery as a rattlesnake when he decides to be, but I suppose that's what keeps life interesting."

"I suppose it does."

Zack poured himself another glass of bourbon before settling back in his chair. "So what's going on with you and my sister?"

Chance should've been expecting it. On some level he *was* expecting it. So why the hell was he still caught off guard? "We're spending time together working on Cattle Baron's. We're getting to know each other better."

"You don't know each other?"

"Come on, Zack. I get she's your sister, but are we really having a discussion about this?"

Zack's grin was rueful. "I'm not gonna lie. I was curious, but I also have been getting an endless stream of theories from my wife. And I have no doubt Hadley and Harper are giving Charlotte the full-court press, too."

"Theories?"

Zack ticked a list off his fingers. "Just friends.

Enemies putting on a good front since your collective group of friends got together. Two people playing a joke on all of us. Or two people falling in love." Zack stared him dead in the eye on that last one. "That's Hadley's favorite."

Jesus, how had the conversation gone this direction?

And love?

Whatever his thoughts—and he'd had a hell of a lot of them flying at him from a lot of different directions over the past few months when it came to Charlotte—love was another matter entirely.

He cared for her, of course. And in the way of the people in his life he cared about, he could say he loved her.

But *in love*?

Had he ever been in love?

Since the idea didn't sit nearly as uncomfortably as he'd have expected, Chance shifted tack. "Look, Zack, you and Hadley both have eyes. I can't believe it's escaped your notice that your sister is a beautiful woman. And she's my friend. Which is probably why this isn't simple. In any way."

Although he hadn't exactly looked comfortable since launching into this line of conversation, for the first time Zack looked genuinely unsettled.

"I recognize this is between you and Charlotte. But I'd be lying if I didn't tell you that she's different when she's with you."

Different?

If he got beyond the idea that talking about his feelings for a woman with her brother was the height of uncomfortable, Chance couldn't deny that Zack now had him interested.

"Different how?"

"She's more settled when she's with you. Which makes no sense, since the two of you swipe at each other like two pissed-off wet cats most of the time." Zack shrugged. "But I don't know. Something seems different."

"Something *is* different. A lot of things are different, actually. Isn't that what we've been in here talking about?"

"We've all seen a change, Chance, even before your discovery this morning. Last night at the restaurant, things were different between the two of you, and that was before your life got upended."

"All I can tell you is that I think your sister is an amazing woman. And even though I know what you mean about acting like a pissed-off cat, I also consider her my friend. On top of it all, I admire the hell out of her."

Chance searched for the words—the right ones—to explain to her brother how he felt about the woman. "She's special, and it's not just because she's absolutely gorgeous. Her heart is big, her ambition is big, and her willingness to go after what she wants is bigger than all of it."

"She's always been a go-getter."

"But it's more. Her ambition has heart to it. And I don't even know how to explain what I mean, other than the fact that most people seem driven because of money or status. But Charlotte is all fired up and excited about what she's doing. That enthusiasm rolls off her and pulls other people in. It's why her talents are wasted on some of the dumbasses in our business."

He was still pissed at how Tom and Merrill Harvey had dismissed her and her work in Bozeman. And while there wasn't much he could do about it—nor would he presume to fight Charlotte's battles for her—it had been one more piece of evidence that she was facing an uphill battle in her chosen profession.

Especially with her determination to stay in Montana.

"Not much deters my sister, but I know she's been discouraged of late."

"The Cattle Baron's ball should go a long way toward changing perceptions."

"Will it?" Zack's question invited discussion, yet Chance heard there was a clear opinion underneath.

"You don't think so?"

"I think that environment's full of the same people Charlotte's been pitching for business. And while I don't want to prejudge the situation, I don't think they're suddenly going to give her the professional time and attention she craves because she's taking this on."

Was Zack right?

He'd understood the professional benefits of cochairing the ball for himself—the two promised bulls would go a long way toward his own livestock program—but Charlotte had been focused on her own professional growth.

And on the opportunity to make new connections through the event.

For all that Chance saw the Wayne name as something of a boon, putting the family and their reputation somewhere in the stratosphere, he had to admit that same attention could work against you.

Especially in a male-driven business like ranching. One where her father's reputation far overshadowed her own. But maybe there was something he could do about that, helping her secure the professional opportunities she craved.

He still didn't believe he had it in him to give her forever, but he'd always been her friend.

It was time to double down and be the very best version of one.

Chapter 12

⋖ৎᎧৎ⋗

Charlotte took in the normal ruckus of the diner as she considered the points she wanted to build into her email to the fundraising committee. She wanted to sound both collaborative and accommodating, but since stepping into Loretta's role she'd also found the committee needed a firm hand, and she hadn't struck quite the right tone yet.

"What are you working on?"

Charlotte glanced up from her laptop as Chance slid into the booth opposite her.

"Politics."

"The good kind or the bad kind?"

"Is there any version of that word that implies *good*?"

The snow promised the prior Friday had arrived just as expected, and she'd finally accepted four days later that she had a raging case of cabin fever. She and Chance had done Zoom calls during that time—him giving her updates on the oil discovery before they'd settle down to work on the various aspects of the ball—but it hadn't done a thing to eradicate her restlessness.

So today she'd finally put a stop to it. She *had* to get out of the house.

"Here, I'll show you."

Although she'd intended on turning her laptop toward him, he came around and took the seat beside her, his large body crowding her so that she had to move over or risk being singed by all that heat.

God, how did she never fully manage to remember just how big he was?

Or how good he smelled, that light mix of earth and very subtle aftershave doing something to every nerve ending in her body.

Friends, Wayne, she reminded herself. *You're working on being just friends.*

The waitress who'd barely given Charlotte the time to order a cup of coffee and cinnamon roll beelined for the table, falling over Chance in a rush to put a coffee cup down and pour him some. "What can I get you for breakfast, cowboy?"

When he'd ordered roughly half the kitchen, he offered a respectful smile and went back to focus on Charlotte's laptop, even as she didn't miss the moue of frustration painting the waitress's lips.

Breaking hearts wherever he goes, she mused, before turning back to the screen.

"Tell me what I'm looking at here. I see very impressive words like *return on investment* and *prioritization of our industry*, but I don't know what that means."

Charlotte felt vaguely offended before she registered that he both was serious and looked genuinely interested in learning.

"That doesn't make sense?"

"I mean, I get it in broad strokes, but what do you actually mean? It feels like a lot of big words without a lot of meaning behind it."

"But there is a lot of meaning. For every dollar spent on publicity, the ranching community will see more than one hundred back."

"Then say that." He tapped the screen. "Right there."

"But it's *return on investment*."

"If you went to business school. If you're focused on your bank account, it's *a hundred to one*."

Charlotte sat back and reached for her coffee, taking a large sip of the now-cooled brew. "You don't like it? This was my whole sales pitch to the sponsors we're courting for the ball."

"I love what you're saying. I just think you have to say it differently."

Their waitress came back with their breakfast and a big smile for Chance, and he used the arrival of the food to swing back around to the other side of the table. He waited until they'd also gotten a refill on their coffees before he started back in.

"I am not trying to offend you with this."

"I'm not offended." She heard the prim stiffness in her words and wondered why her back was up.

Even as she realized that her back was, in fact, way up.

With that realization, she waved a hand. "Hold on a minute. I'm getting stuck at the corner of Chance-and-Charlotte-Swipe-at-Each-Other, and I don't mean it. What caught you here?"

"I think you're losing your audience before you even have a chance to win them over."

"Even though it's a business note?"

"It might be a business note, but it's in a language no one understands, coming out of the mouth of a woman who intimidates her audience."

Whatever she was about to say fled on swift wings at that assessment.

"Excuse me?"

"You're gorgeous, Charlotte. And then you start talking like you walked out of Harvard, and that combination is terribly intimidating."

"So I should bat my eyelashes and hike up my skirt?"

"No."

"Then what are you suggesting?"

"I'm suggesting you use English. I'm also suggesting you use words that actually mean what you're talking about instead of some business jargon."

"But ROI is an accepted method of performance."

He grinned at her, and Charlotte found herself oddly unsettled. Because he *wasn't* baiting her. In fact, he was helping her.

"You think I'm intimidating?"

"As all hell." He quickly nodded. "I totally do."

"But that's bad!" The last word came out on a screech so she forcibly tried to calm down, lowering her voice. "I don't want to come off that way. I'm just me."

"You can't control what other people think or take away. But I am telling you so you're aware of it, and then you can stack the deck in your favor."

"By using small words?"

"By considering ahead of time where your audience is coming from. Most of these guys—and most of them *are* guys—sit on a horse ten hours a day. They're not reading marketing magazines or trying to come up with the best way to position themselves. They're worried about the weather and their herd and if they've covered off vaccinations and what possible shitstorm Mother Nature is going to throw at them."

"I suppose." Working to swallow back her hurt pride, she added, "Actually, I do suppose. And I can see what you're saying."

Hadn't she grown up watching her father worry about those very things? And wasn't that a big part of why, when it was time for her and her siblings to get their share of the ranch, she'd ultimately opted out, selling Zack her share?

She wasn't a rancher, but she'd been raised by one. And somewhere along the way she'd forgotten all of those lessons.

"Come on. Eat your cinnamon roll, and we'll

figure out your spiel. I got us a dinner meeting tomorrow with a buddy of mine, Gage Warner."

"Warner Ranch is the one with the new drone program?"

"The very one. Gage has also done some amazing work on herd management and overall well-being of cattle."

"His research programs on herd health and avoiding stress on the livestock were really well done." Charlotte picked at her cinnamon roll. "And he got to use big words."

"He's also very much in favor of your ideas and how we need to be bringing all the work the industry is doing into the mainstream. The beef industry gets a bad rap from a lot of people, and it's not entirely unwarranted. But there's good work being done to change that. You're going to wow him with your PR brilliance and, knowing you, will lock up a sponsorship for the ball in the process."

Excited about the possibility of the meeting, she gave Chance his due. "That was smooth, by the way. Ignoring my petulance."

Those big shoulders lifted up and down, and God, how was it the man could even make a shrug look sexy?

Oblivious to her discomfort, Chance kept on. "You're entitled to it. I dropped a bomb on your carefully ordered work. Work I have no doubt you spent a lot of time on. I did it to help, but I get how it might not have felt like it."

"That doesn't change the fact that I needed to hear it."

He grinned at her. "Look at us. Just a couple of mature adults handling our disagreements."

The urge to smile overtook her as something sweet and unbelievably real settled in her chest. The same something that always got its hooks in her when she looked at him.

Fully looked at him, like he was the only person in the world. In *her* world.

"You know, I think we are."

Pushing against the longing, she kept herself focused on next steps. Work. Business. This new footing where they seemed able to collaborate.

That was good, too.

Better than good, she admitted to herself.

"Let's talk to Gage tomorrow night. He invited us out to his ranch to see his program in action. Plus, he's got great ideas, and he's got his ear to the ground. It'll be an evening well spent."

"I'm in."

"Then I'll pick you up tomorrow at four. I want you to get there early enough to see his program in the light."

CHANCE RODE ELVIS back through the property, their late-morning jaunt focused on a survey of the north pasture. He'd wanted to get out early so he could cut his day a bit short to head out for his business dinner with Charlotte. He'd had two good meetings now with the geologist, the second one that morning reaffirming all the details in the survey report his father had commissioned.

There was oil beneath his land.

A meeting with his lawyer the prior Monday had also given him the confirmation that the mineral rights were one hundred percent his. Every last piece of his father's will had gone through probate since Trevor's passing more than two years ago, and Chance was the full and sole owner of Beaumont Farms.

Which meant those mineral rights were fully and solely his.

There were times his head spun with the reality of it all.

Or *un*reality, he thought as he rode up to the stables.

Elvis had been tireless today, so as he dismounted and headed into the stables Chance considered what special treats he'd give his boon companion.

And found Gray in front of one of the stalls, feeding sugar cubes over the door.

"Hey, man. What are you doing here?"

"I came to do a quick check on Minnie. She's looking good, and her mud fever is barely even visible any longer except for a very small area on her right foreleg. I'd say she'll be fully back to health in another week or so."

He'd been keeping a solid eye on the mare since Gray had diagnosed the bacterial infection a few weeks ago, and careful and continuous application of medicine and a focus on keeping the area dry had worked its magic.

That and the incredibly keen eye of his vet.

"You caught that early."

Gray shook his head. "You caught it early. You knew something wasn't right. Diagnoses are easy, it's getting them in time. The healing goes a lot smoother when the animal has good handlers and people watching out for them."

"Since you're here and giving my horse the full bedside-manner show, can I at least get you a beer?"

"I'd love one."

Chance kept a small fridge in the postage-stamp office in the back of the stables, and he pointed in that direction. "I'm going to cool down Elvis and feed him, and I'll join you in a few minutes."

By the time he got back to the office Gray had his long, jean-clad legs stretched out, and he was half dozing in the guest chair. Chance almost left him to it, figuring the beer could wait, when Gray's eyes popped open. "Sorry. Long day."

"You've been working hard."

"Takes one to know one," Gray shot back. "You've been nonstop for months now. And you've just gotten busier with all the news buzzing around here."

Chance popped the top off his beer and took a seat. "It's been quite a week."

"Congratulations." Gray leaned forward and tapped his bottle to Chance's. "It's news well worth celebrating."

Chance stared down at his bottle, all the things he'd been struggling to put into words suddenly filling up his chest. "It's a game changer. I mean, it literally changes every single thing about my life. The money I need for the ranch. The overall solvency of Beaumont Farms. Even the hiring I need to do. I can run this place the way I've always dreamed."

"Hot damn, I love it when good things happen to good people."

"It's not real. Or I tell myself that and then look around or get another text message or a call from the lawyer, and I know that it is."

Gray stared down at his beer, edging his nail along the label before he looked back up. "You doing okay with it?"

"I'd be a fool not to be."

"I know, but it's a lot to take in. The way you found out. And the reality that it's been here all along."

Chance considered trying to brazen his way through just how fine he was.

All of which was unnecessary, even as it felt very necessary to the image he projected to the outside world.

But this was Gray. Probably his best friend in the world, and the one who knew all about the baggage because he'd lived his own version. His father, Burt, had run with Chance's father much of their lives. It had put Gray and Chance together, the tag-along children on their fathers' often misguided adventures.

"*A lot* is probably the best description. I mean, it's hard to be sad about it, for starters. But it's a complicated sort of happy. Knowing if he'd lived, the old man would have screwed me out of it?" Chance took a drink of his beer. "Complicated."

"It seems pithy to say things work out for a reason, but I'm not sure that's the right card here, either."

"Probably not. But you could say it another way. The bastard got what was coming to him."

With uncharacteristic anger, Chance stood and tossed his bottle against the wall, the smashing of the glass a punctuation to his words.

Even if it wasn't nearly as satisfying as he'd believed it would be.

Gray didn't say anything, just got up and crossed to the small fridge, snagging two fresh beers. It was only after he'd twisted the caps off on both, handing one to Chance, that Gray spoke.

"You don't have to have it all figured out, you know."

"You mean striking oil doesn't come with an instruction manual?"

"I've yet to find anything in life comes with an instruction manual. But this is from a man who actually got amnesia, so what do I know?"

It shouldn't have been funny, but as Chance considered his friend—and all Gray had lived through six months before, when he'd sustained a head injury from an out-of-control horse—he couldn't hold back the laugh bubbling up in his chest.

"You actually did have amnesia. Like some woebegone doctor on a soap opera."

"If we're keeping with the soap analogy, it did reunite me with the love of my life."

Before Chance could say anything, Gray rushed on, his tone growing serious. "And because Harper and I went through that, I understand what you mean about being happy. I'm happier than I've ever been, to be with her, but we've had our fights, too."

"You guys okay?"

"We're great. And that's not bullshit. We are really and truly solid. But being solid doesn't mean those ten years apart just vanished. We've had to address that. Talk about it and work through it."

Maybe, Chance realized, that was the real point of this conversation. He'd looked at Gray and Harper as this miracle love story. And while they had found their way back to each other, there was still a lot of healing to do, too.

Necessary work to get to a solid and productive relationship.

"But you're finding a way forward?"

Gray grinned at that, a lightness in his friend Chance had never seen before. Not even when Gray and Harper had dated years ago. "Yeah, we are." Gray waited a beat before adding, "What about you and Charlotte?"

What about him and Charlotte? Their meeting the day before at the diner had been a good one and, after he got over fumbling through his criticism of her work, highly productive. They'd hashed out an approach to their visit with Gage Warner, Charlotte's inspired PR strategy about how to highlight the man's technology something to behold.

One more thing in a long line of what was amazing about Charlotte.

"I think she friend-zoned me. Which was what I told her I wanted."

"Why the hell would you want that?"

"Something's missing, Gray."

Gray nearly fumbled his beer as he stared at Chance across the small space of the office. "Between you and Charlotte?"

"In me."

"Bullshit. Complete, utter, absolute bullshit." Gray settled his beer on the desk before leaning forward, his forearms on his thighs. "But I get it."

Chance had had a few days to think about all he'd said to Charlotte when they were walking the property, and he still wasn't entirely sure why he'd shared those details about his father. Was he really convinced his old man's attitude toward him was his fault?

That he was damaged and had been since he was a little kid?

"I get it because no matter what you do, no matter how hard you work or how many years pass, it's there, man. It's in your head. It talks at you in ways you can't always fight. And it's especially hard, and that voice gets extra loud, when the world around you is changing."

"Charlotte doesn't have anything to do with the oil find."

Gray looked up at him from where he'd focused on something on the floor, his gaze unyieldingly direct. "She's one more element of change in your life."

"Sure, she's back in my life, more now than before. You and Harper are partially to blame for that, by the way." Chance took a long pull on his beer, trying to settle his thoughts. "She's got nothing to do with the oil."

"Good God." Gray shook his head. "There's a reason I work with animals and not people."

Chance wanted to be irritated, but Gray's look was so comical—that sappy grin he'd worn shifting to such frustration and pure disgust—that Chance couldn't quite find the mad. So he offered him a half-hearted *Fuck you* instead.

"Come on, Chance. Everything's changing. You've had feelings for Charlotte for a hell of a long time, and now you have a shot at them. You've wanted to make a real go of Beaumont Farms for a long time, and now you're going to have the cash flow to do it. Even without the oil, you got the Complete Grocer deal. The hard work's paying off, pal. Good things coming to a damn good person."

"Yeah, but Charlotte is—"

"She lights you up, man. We all see it."

Chance considered Gray's words and had to admit there was a hell of a lot of truth there. Truth from someone who knew.

Who understood.

And who'd lived a similar version of the same nightmare.

"From one asshole to another, let me give you a piece of advice. Your old man's ruined enough. Don't let the prick have any more satisfaction."

"God, the man was a rotten bastard. I just never expected that'd be as true alive or dead."

"That's one truth I can't argue with." Gray's smile faded. "Give yourself time, Chance. You're entitled to it. It doesn't all have to be perfect to know that it's good. Lean into that while you give yourself the time to process it all."

Gray's advice still lingered in his mind an hour later as he finished up with the horses and shut down the stables before his night out.

He could have multiple emotions at once. And while he hadn't been raised in an environment that gave much credence to anything that smacked of feelings, it didn't make all of it any less true.

His future was bright, and he was excited about it.

Those feelings didn't mean he couldn't still be bone-deep hurt by the one person in the world who knew what Beaumont Farms meant to him.

And who in that knowing had still set out to take it all away.

Chapter 13

Chance drove the last mile into town, scanning the length of Main Street as he went. The snow had pretty well vanished, but the cold snap had kick-started fall in a big way. The wind had a blustery bite to it, and the leaves had solidly started to change.

Just like his life.

It doesn't all have to be perfect to know that it's good. Lean into that while you give yourself the time to process it all.

Gray had a point. One Chance hadn't gotten out of his mind since their talk.

Life *was* changing. His attitude included.

And top of that list was the increasing temptation to pursue Charlotte, imagined consequences be damned.

Because they were imagined. The belief they

couldn't have a solid future only lived in his mind.

He made the turn for Charlotte's street and tried to keep his uncharacteristically optimistic thoughts in check. Sure, things might be changing, but what gave him the right to change the rules now?

His conversation with Gray over beers had gone a long way toward allowing him to confront his grief over his father's betrayal, but it had also jump-started all those other feelings he'd been trying so hard to avoid.

The ones that suggested he could pursue something with Charlotte and, maybe, have it all work out. Why did that feel entirely possible and entirely impossible, all at once?

Even if a fresh-faced Charlotte, sitting opposite him at the diner with the sun haloing her through the window, had damn near killed him with all the possibility he saw.

That he always saw.

He pulled into her driveway and quickly cut the engine on his truck. They were heading to a business dinner, one that was important to her work. He'd worry about friend zones and the future and all the freaking emotions in his gut later.

Tonight was about her.

He knocked on the door and heard her muffled holler of *Coming!* and saw her hazy silhouette through the paneled glass.

She opened the door on a rush, a lone curler hanging haphazardly from the side of her head. "I'm almost ready. I had an idea for the proposal, and I got distracted. But I *am* almost ready. Come on in."

She rushed off, leaving him in the foyer, yet he got the distinct impression he should make himself at home.

A small living room was off the front hallway, but instead of holding a couch and chairs, an office space had been created. He'd somehow missed it the other day when he'd come over, likely because he was so focused on the curve of her ass in those cotton-candy yoga pants.

But he was curious enough now that he walked in and looked at her setup.

The cherrywood desk was elegant and immediately reminded him of Charlotte. That same laptop she'd brought to the diner sat next to an elaborate setup with an additional monitor. But it was the shocking amount of mess covering the desk that was as surprising as it was unexpected.

Who knew the polished and put-together Ms. Wayne was a messy-desker?

Especially since her mother's desk at the Trading Post had been so neat?

He continued moving around the small space, intrigued by the mix of the professional and personal. A large bookcase spanned the interior wall, and he saw the obligatory business books—Wonder if there were chapters devoted to ROI in there? he thought with a smile—as well as thrillers, mysteries and a set of clearly well-loved romance novels.

More proof the woman was dynamic, interesting and *engaged* in the world around her.

"I'm ready." Charlotte stood in the open framed entrance to the room, her keys in hand. Any lingering curlers were gone, and she had slipped into one of her multitude of pairs of heels. She had dressed casually for the evening, or as casual as Charlotte got, in a pale lavender cashmere sweater and dark slacks.

She was gorgeous.

The swirling thoughts that had accompanied him on the drive over—hell, which had accompanied him for years—had him moving forward.

No, this wasn't a date.

But hell if it didn't *feel* like a date. And with that last rational thought, he let the consequences be damned.

He pulled her into his arms, his mouth finding hers with unerring precision. Silently, he gave thanks for the heels that put them at a nearly even height and then forgot everything as she kissed him back.

Something fierce and needy rose up in his chest, a thundering, desperate sort of desire he didn't fully know what to do with.

No, no, his body screamed. He knew exactly what to do with it, but it was his mind that kept holding him back.

She was as eager as he was, her tongue meeting his stroke for stroke, and Chance, despite looking forward to the evening with Gage Warner, was increasingly tempted to cancel on his friend and stay right here.

Which was the thing that finally pulled him back.

The woman staring back at him had a hazy expression in her gaze and a thoroughly kissed look on her face, which had smudged all of her freshly applied lipstick.

"That shade looks good on you," she teased.

He was already reaching for his mouth when she beat him to it. Her thumb spread over his lower lip, the move practical yet eminently sensual. He felt her gaze on him and the touch of the pad of her thumb and recognized he was about to be in for a very long night.

"I'm glad we got that out of the way."

"Out of—" He was stunned by her amused expression.

"Yes, *the way.*"

"Why?"

"I was thinking about kissing you, too. Now we can go focus on business."

"Right. Yeah. Business."

She jingled her keys and pointed toward the hallway.

But it was when she grinned at him—that hazy look now replaced with innate feminine knowing—that Chance realized he was very likely done for.

SOMETHING HAS CHANGED, Charlotte thought as she walked out of her living room and into the foyer.

What wasn't as clear was why. Especially not after that haunting confession he'd shared about his father.

About feeling unworthy.

God, she'd gone over it and over it in her mind. The bleakness of living that way. Feeling that way.

Worse, of believing it was at all true.

But what had changed? Because that kiss in her office? There was an urgency there and a promise she hadn't felt before.

Or maybe that's just you, her conscience taunted.

He looked good tonight. And while she usually thought that, the white button-down shirt and charcoal gray slacks suited him. Casual, yet professional. And well fitted to his physique.

In fact, she admitted to herself, the cut of the shirt reminded her, as it always did, that he had something of a boxer's build. The slim hips, broad shoulders and a certain compactness to his muscles that suggested strength.

"Let me just get my coat," she said, stopping in the foyer. "I knew that heat wave we had last weekend wasn't going to last."

"Welcome to Montana in October."

After she locked up, they walked to his truck. It was sweet how he opened the door for her, helping her up into the cab.

They were both quiet on the drive out of town toward the highway, a subtle tension that wasn't awkward so much as unbroken. That strange waiting you had while blowing up a balloon, wondering if it would get bigger or simply pop in a loud burst.

"You said you were working on the proposal?" Chance started in.

"I had a breakthrough earlier." His honesty at the diner had helped tremendously, and once she had a chance to look at it through his perspective, she'd seen how to make the work better. "In fact, I'd say you did me a major favor when you suggested I stop using business-book logic to make my points."

"You had a lot of good stuff when we left the diner yesterday."

"And now it's better."

"Oh God, I don't want you to think Loretta was right. That you get stuck doing all the work on this."

Charlotte considered his profile as he navigated around a slower driver on the highway. "You pointed out some really smart things to me yesterday. Your point about featuring cow-calf operations as the centerpiece, then building our story off that is perfect. Those operations are what our audience does, and it's silly to bury the lede. Besides, I think you're doing very good work since you got us this meeting with Gage Warner," she couldn't resist teasing, "and now it's my turn to play arm candy."

The joke was enough to get a laugh out of him, and she took it as a good sign. Especially since the conversation she'd had with Harper—about remaining friends with Chance no matter what—had stuck with her.

"Even if this isn't a date."

"Of course not."

She heard the lightly wistful note and figured she'd go for broke. They had kissed each other, and her breezy attitude had seen it through.

Maybe it was time to lay her cards on the table.

"I've been thinking about something. About our friendship."

"You mean our recently discovered friendship."

"Just because we swipe at each other, and have done so for more than twenty years, doesn't mean we don't have a friendship. We know each other. We grew up together. There's something solid there, and it matters to me."

"It matters to me, too."

It did matter. Wasn't that part of what she'd finally acknowledged to herself?

Dancing around a relationship wasn't going to be the end of their friendship. No matter how the dance turned out.

"It's just that I had this realization last week. About Harper and Gray. They spent ten years apart from each other. And while I can't begin to understand their pain or either of their personal reasons, it doesn't change the fact that they've lived that way. They had something together, something more than a friendship, but it was also steeped in a good and solid foundation. And then when it went sideways, they lost all of it. For ten years, they walked away from it, Harper most of all."

"They did."

"I don't want to be that person." She blew out another breath. "God, I know I sound so judgy and wrong about my friend, and I don't mean it that way. But all I'm saying is that I don't want to lose the good already here. I don't want that for us."

"I don't want that, either."

"Okay."

"I have something to tell you, too. I guess a realization of my own."

She kept her gaze on his profile, his meeting hers before he returned it to the road. "I have to work on some of that stuff I told you about. About my father."

A lightness settled in her chest at his decision. One that knew, absolutely, that this man deserved better in life than to spend one more minute thinking he was unworthy in any way.

"I'm really glad, Chance. I want that for you."

"I also don't want to kiss my other friends. So I really need to work on figuring out what to do about that."

His words hung there, even as a small grin edged his lips. Charlotte recognized the look and suspected she'd worn something similar before they'd left the house.

That subtle sense that he'd gotten the upper hand.

Especially when a shot of something deliciously dark and lusty swirled low in her belly.

"I can't say I want to do that, either."

"Good." He nodded as if the matter was settled.

And it nearly was, before one of those small, sneaky grins tugged the corner of her lips.

"So if we do decide to sleep together, we're not going to let all the good sex get in the way of being two assholes who somehow found a friendship underneath all the bickering?"

She kept her gaze on his profile, taking in the way the cords of his neck tightened before he let out a semistrangled, "Nope."

"We won't let sex ruin our friendship."

"Not us."

She crossed her arms and sat back in her seat, satisfied she'd made her point. "Damn straight it won't."

CHANCE STARED UP at the sky, watching the drone head back toward them, and focused on counting backward from one hundred. This was his seventh try, and he'd yet to get past ninety-two without having Charlotte's words come into his head and fuck his concentration once more.

We won't let sex ruin our friendship.

For all his attraction and carnal awareness of her, nothing yet—not even that night in Bozeman—had turned him inside out like that simple promise.

What had also become clear in that slightly silly, meandering conversation on the drive was that she was not only deeply aware of the consequences of taking their attraction to the physical, but she'd thought through it, processed it and come to a conclusion.

Yet, here he was, the dumb lug who still battled a painful erection at the word *sex*.

Good sex.

All while Charlotte had arrived at the ranch, immediately befriended Gage and his wife, and even now was talking about all the various aspects of Gage's drone technology.

"Gage, this is amazing." Charlotte sat in a director's chair behind an extensive setup of screens about ten yards away, utterly oblivious to Chance's inner turmoil.

Gage Warner smiled, his grin toothy, and his skinny chest puffed up good and high at the receptive audience. "We're able to keep an eye on the herd no matter where they are. I can manage a small team on the tech and deploy ranch hands wherever I need them to go."

"So you save time, money, effort, all while maintaining the needed attention on the livestock. How soon are you rolling this out?"

"I've tried a few places. The setup costs are a bit steep, but once in place the benefits are immediately clear."

She nodded, her attention focused and serious. "You've just described my life's work. But as I've been told"—she shot Chance a saucy wink—"cowboys aren't always interested in a discussion on cost–benefit analysis."

"I'm not going to argue with you there." Gage

picked up the drone and did a quick check over the equipment before flipping a switch to turn it off. He nestled it into precut foam in a large case before closing the lid. "I've tried a few ways in, talking to some friends about this. Nothing's quite getting through."

"You know . . ." Charlotte trailed off, her eyes suddenly set somewhere on the horizon as the sun dropped low in the sky.

"What?"

"This might be the way in for the opening of the ball." She stood, her eyes bright. "We use the drone footage to capture the vast openness and then descend onto the herd. I know Bea will help us."

"Who's Bea?"

"My sister-in-law's producer." Charlotte's eyes were still unfocused when she spoke. "She'll know exactly what to do with this."

Chance immediately saw where she was going with it all and attempted to translate for Gage.

"Let me catch you up on the shorthand. Bea is the TV producer of Charlotte's sister-in-law's cooking show. We've been a bit besieged by Hollywood in Rustlers Creek and sometimes forget not everyone walks around imagining TV sets in their head."

Gage smiled, clearly pleased to have an audience. "I figured it would all make sense eventually. Why don't we go inside, and we can talk about a few ideas over dinner."

"You've given my husband a birthday gift and Christmas morning all rolled into one." Selma Warner smiled as she finished making a tortilla at the long counter in the ranch house's kitchen.

"How's that?" Charlotte asked as she set up the fixings for a taco bar at the opposite end of the counter.

"He's my cowboy geek, as I've always teased him. And it's rare he gets someone who wants to talk the geek part of that equation. The cowboy part, all the time. The tech part," Selma said with a frown, "not so much."

"It's amazing what he's built. It's a game-changing approach to ranch management."

"I know." Selma smiled, the frown now nowhere in sight. "He's so excited about it and can see all the possibilities and several more that are only in his head."

"I've been holding off on texting my brother, but I know Zack will be beating down your door the moment he sees some of this. He's going to want this for Wayne and Sons, our family ranch."

They worked in companionable silence, Selma finishing up the tortillas while Charlotte laid out the grated cheese, chopped tomatoes and bowls of sour cream and fresh guacamole. "This is a feast, Selma. There's no way the four of us will finish it all."

The other woman waved a hand. "I always send some home with Chance when he visits."

"You sound like my sister-in-law."

"She's the one with the TV show, yes?"

"She is. Hadley's the Cowgirl Gourmet."

"I love that show. She did an episode recently on sticky buns. I made them and swear my husband fell a little more in love with me." Selma winked. "A few of the ranch hands, too."

"Her love language is food."

"Mine, too. I've tried to cultivate other interests but come back to this one over and over as my true love." She rolled another ball of dough for the tortilla maker. "Although, Gage has gotten me into operating the drone. It's like playing a video game. One afternoon of training and I was hooked."

"How long have you been married?"

"Five years. But we were interested in each other a lot longer than that."

"Oh, I love a romance story." Charlotte pulled out a chair that fronted the long counter and sat down. "Tell me more."

"My mother was the housekeeper here, and I grew up on the ranch. Gage and I ran wild over the property when we were kids." Selma shrugged, but Charlotte didn't miss the flashes of sorrow, so similar to the frown from before. "Then for a long time we didn't. When it wasn't seemly any longer. When he realized I was a woman, and I realized he was a man. And when people thought I was a gold digger who wanted the ranch owner's son."

"I'm sorry," Charlotte said. "I'm sorry people can be so narrow-minded and cruel."

"We found our way past it in the end. But it took a while to get there. I had to move away. I worked in a restaurant in Spokane for several years. And then one day I looked up and he was standing there, right in the middle of the restaurant. He had his hat in his hands, curling the brim he was so nervous, and telling me he loved me and that he wanted me to come home."

Charlotte pictured it all in her mind, the earnest man she'd met today and the woman who stood opposite her at the counter.

"What did you do?"

"Oh, I denied him at first, even though my heart was bursting from it all. Told him we couldn't make it work. That no one would support us and he'd be disinherited. He didn't care about any of it, but I did. This place matters to him. It's in his blood."

"What changed your mind?"

"It was really simple, in the end. Gage told me that no one would ever love me like he did. And that there was nothing else on earth worth more than that. So I could throw it away for what other people thought or even for what I couldn't get over in my own mind, but nothing else would ever matter more."

Selma smiled, her gaze hazed with the memory. "And smart man that he is, he was right."

"It sounds like something out of a movie."

"Oh, I didn't go right away. I sat and stewed and suffered for several weeks, long after he'd gone home and I figured I could make amends."

"What changed your mind?"

"A woman came into the restaurant. I was off

that night, but I had offered to fill in for a wait-ress who was off sick. She had come in for a blind date, and I talked to her for a few minutes as I took her drink order. She was so hopeful. So de-termined to believe the evening might end up with that elusive outcome of someone she would fall in love with."

"What was her date like?"

Selma expertly flipped the last tortilla off the griddle. "An asshole who never showed up."

"Oh."

"*Oh* is right. I watched her leave, dejected by the experience, and I realized I had that—that elusive person that she was waiting and hoping for. I had that. And I'd thrown it away." She shook her head. "Or was throwing it away by being so stubborn and stuck in my ways.

"I left that night and drove straight here. Ar-rived around seven in the morning looking like I'd walked out of a horror show. But I found Gage, and I told him I loved him, and we've been to-gether ever since."

"That's so romantic. And I'm a sucker for a happy ending, especially one for two good people."

And she was.

Which also meant some of that equilibrium she'd lost—that had her sad in the Rafael's park-ing lot even as she was happy for her loved ones—might be returning a bit.

Thank God.

Her life was her own.

That was a gift her parents had given her and continued to give her every day. They were proud of her and wanted her happiness. On whatever terms that meant for her.

And maybe what it also meant was that she'd come to a place in her heart where she'd accepted that whatever happened with Chance, she'd come out the other side.

Because something wonderful or something good was the outcome.

They were either going to find that same happiness her loved ones had, the same sort of happiness Gage and Selma Warner had, or they'd be left with something good.

A deep and lasting friendship that had survived whatever the two of them managed to throw at it.

What was increasingly evident, she realized with startling clarity, was that it was time they found out.

Chapter 14

"Holy shit on toast, those were some amazing margaritas."

Even as the words tripped out of her mouth, Charlotte recognized the solid buzz she had going off Gage Warner's pitcher of bliss.

"I'm going to piss Hadley off so bad when I tell her they were better than hers."

"I'd like to be there when you tell her."

"I think I'll tell her right now." Charlotte reached down to her purse at her feet to dig out her phone. It was only Chance's words that stilled her.

"Put the phone away. No drunk texting or dialing."

"I'm not drunk."

"You're not Fourth of July drunk, but you're not sober, either."

"Spoilsport."

"No, I'm the unlucky bastard who had to drive tonight and only got one glass out of that pitcher of magnificence."

"So you agree!" She realized her words had come out as more of a triumphant shout than an agreement and figured he had a point about the phone. "Then you have to back me up and tell Hadley, too."

She could already imagine the conversation when another thought jackrabbited into her mind. "Oh! Oh! Hadley needs to have Selma on her show, and they can make that amazing food, and then they can do Gage's margaritas at the end to wrap it all up. And Selma can tell her all about their love story."

"You sure have the Hollywood bug tonight. Getting Bea's help with the drone, which I agree with by the way. And now having Selma Warner guest on Hadley's show. That PR machine in your head never stops, does it?"

She'd laid her head back against the seat, battling the gently swaying motion of the car, and turned toward him. "Does that bother you?"

"Why would it bother me?"

"Because it's like you told me. All that PR stuff is intimidating. I'm intimidating."

"I didn't mean that to insult you."

"I'm not insulted," she rushed on before amending, "or not exactly. But I'm surprised."

"By what?"

"That you see me that way. That anyone would see me that way."

"Why?"

"Because I'm just me. I have five brothers and sisters who will all tell you the same thing. I'm just the oldest girl, which means I sort of come in and take over. It's genetics or birth order or some weird freak of nature. *Intimidating* makes it sound like I lord stuff over people."

"You don't do that. And *intimidating* isn't about what you do. It's about how others feel, which is entirely their own problem."

"Oh."

Well, when he put it that way . . .

"You can't control what other people think or do." He reached out and grabbed her hand, giving it a quick squeeze. "Even if being the oldest girl means you have an opinion on it all the same."

"I do that, don't I?"

"It's all part of your charm."

Although the margarita buzz wasn't going anywhere, the darkness outside the car and their conversation was enough to keep her focused and in the moment.

The large bottle of water Selma had pressed on her before leaving the house was helping, too.

"I do think you had a point about the marketing stuff. And the people I'm trying to sell my PR services to. It's like the Harveys a few weeks ago. I sent them this huge proposal, and all I wanted to do was talk about it. But if I'm being fair, I didn't talk to them. I talked at them."

"Yeah, well, I wouldn't lose any sleep over those two."

"Especially since Tom ended up being a raging asshat. But still, I can take a lesson and do things differently next time."

"I think you're already doing things differently. And your ideas for the drone footage to kick off the Cattle Baron's ball is incredible."

They talked like that for the rest of the drive, bouncing ideas off each other about the ball and their work, and Charlotte was surprised to realize that she was nearly sober when they rolled back into Rustlers Creek.

"I'm sorry you got screwed out of the elixir of life tonight."

"I'll survive. And I'll likely be a hell of a lot happier about it at five o'clock tomorrow morning when Squash and I start out over the ranch."

"Squash? And you also have an Elvis? Who names your horses, Chance Beaumont?"

"I like a bit of whimsy in my stable. And Squash is the shorthand for Sasquatch since he had enormous feet, even as a foal."

She shook her head. "Men and their horses."

"What's better? Going through the annual list of most popular baby names and ending up with a stable of Liams and Noahs and Olivias?"

"Those are good names."

"For people. A horse needs something more distinctive."

"Which is why the racing community comes up with things like Millionaire's Run and MacDougal's Pride or some such nonsense."

He pulled into the driveway and turned to her.

"Tell you what. Next horse I get, you can name whatever you want."

"I already know the name."

That was enough to surprise him, and she smiled at the speculation in his gaze. "You do?"

"Yep. Next horse you get should be named Beaumont's Strike."

"For the oil?"

"Yep. It's the strike that changed your life."

"Since it shortens to BS, that sounds a lot like my life."

Chance turned off the engine and abruptly jumped out of the truck. Charlotte was stunned still, his quick movements at odds with the gentle, even conversation they'd shared.

Why had he—

She stopped herself.

It was the discussion of the oil. A topic that hadn't been far from her thoughts since last week, but which he'd only glossed over each time she'd asked.

He came around the front of the truck toward her door, pulling it open. His smile was unfailingly kind, but it never reached his gray eyes.

She allowed him to help her out of the truck and knew he'd follow her to her front door. He might be doing his gentlemanly duty to see her inside, but she was done running.

Done doing this ridiculous dance.

Done hiding behind whatever walls they each retreated to when things got strange or awkward or cut a little too close to the truths they both knew yet stubbornly tried to hide.

Her keys jangled as she dug them out of her purse. She felt his large physical form behind her, but he didn't touch her or make any move closer.

And then she had the door unlocked and open, turning toward him.

"Why don't you come in."

"Like I said, I have an early morning. I'd better get going. Thanks for coming with me tonight."

"Of course. Right." She nodded, stepping closer and laying a hand on his shoulder. "What was that you mentioned in the car? *BS*, I believe you said? How about if we dispense with it and you come inside with me."

"Charlotte, come on, you know that's not a good idea."

"Maybe not." She tilted her head, her gaze unerringly locked onto his. "But it's time you and I made a decision."

INEVITABLE.

That lone word kept going through his mind, its steady refrain catching him at odd moments for the past few weeks.

Why did it feel that way? Why was it so damned clear there was no other outcome for him and Charlotte?

Because you know she's the one, Beaumont. You can keep running, but you can't actually run away from it.

And wasn't that the God's honest truth of it all?

There was nowhere left to go.

Was that what Gray had meant? When he talked about all the things changing in Chance's life? This wasn't about the oil, even though it was an easy excuse.

It was about them.

And instead of getting tetchy when a topic that made him uncomfortable came up, he needed to come clean.

"Before. In the car. I haven't worked out exactly how I feel about the oil. I'm sorry my first reaction was to be an ass about it."

"Thank you. I also realize that I keep pushing it, and I'll back off a little, too. It's life-changing, which means it's a lot."

"You're not at fault. Hell, it's not just big for me, it's going to be huge news in Rustlers Creek, so I'd better get used to talking about it."

"And the rest?" She stood opposite him in the foyer, her head cocked slightly to the side.

"What rest?"

"You staying the night."

His stomach cratered with need, all that want and the stubborn hope he kept fighting adding to the moment.

So he tried once more.

One more shot of reason before he tossed it all to hell and leaped into the flames after every one of his good intentions.

"You're tipsy, and it's not a good time to talk about this. Or do this, as the case may be."

She turned from where she hung her coat up

in the hall closet and simply extended her hand for his jacket. "Why don't you let me hang that up for you?"

When his hands acted of their own accord, stripping his jacket off and handing it to her, Chance had his first inkling this had moved past inevitable and straight on to inescapable.

And he'd never been happier to be caught.

"I'm not tipsy. I was when I got into the car, but a forty-five-minute car ride and a bottle of water have sobered me right up."

"So that means we should leap into bed together?"

"Do you have a better idea?"

She still hadn't moved closer—still hadn't touched him other than the barest brushing of fingers when she'd taken his coat—yet he felt her as if she were draped over him.

Felt the rising need heating up his blood and that desperate craving low in the belly that smacked of arousal and desire and promise.

The sweet, sweet promise that was Charlotte.

That had always been Charlotte.

Even from the earliest days, when he couldn't come up with the reasons, he'd just known he wanted to be near her, it had been Charlotte.

She was his lodestone and had been for as long as he could remember.

And in that acknowledgment he finally understood what she was trying to tell him and why she'd invited him in.

"It's always been leading here, hasn't it?"

She stared up at him, right there in the middle of her small hallway, and nodded. "I think it has."

And then there was no more waiting.

No more wondering.

There was just the two of them.

He pulled her close, their mouths meeting. And Chance gave himself up to the reality of her.

Of them.

He'd sidestepped long enough. Now it was time to take.

With that new reality filling him, he pulled her close, his hands tracing a path down her spine to cup her ass. He fitted her to his body, the insistent press of his erection against her belly. She smiled as her hand snaked between them, pressing the front of his slacks.

"I sure am glad I invited you both in."

His body reacted to that tempting touch, fireworks shooting a blazing path through his system as he fought to stay in the moment.

Fully present in the moment and in control.

Because there was far too much exploring of one another to end it all now.

"Where's your bedroom?"

"Upstairs," she whispered against his lips.

With quick motions he had her up in his arms and was striding toward the stairs he'd seen off the hallway.

"Chance! You can't carry me."

"Looks like I just did."

"But I'm too—" He cut off her protests with a kiss before focusing on the walk up the stairs.

And once they were at the top he kissed her again, giving himself the moment to savor her.

The upstairs hallway was small, and he easily found the bedroom that was hers. The still-unmade bed and messy heap of throw pillows beside it were his first clue.

"I really did expect you to be a lot neater than you are."

"I'm not messy, I'm just . . ." She sighed. "Yeah, I'm messy. It's not like I try to be, but there's always something to do other than make the bed. Or dust. Or fold laundry."

A feisty look filled her gaze as he settled her on her feet. "I can clean up now if you prefer."

She turned to do just that, moving toward the heap of pillows before he snagged her arm. "Don't you dare."

They fell onto the bed, a tangle of arms and legs, and he let himself drink his fill.

He might have been deprived of margaritas tonight, but he wouldn't say the same about Charlotte.

Long, languid, drugging kisses dragged out between the two of them as they lazily stripped one another bare. First her sweater, then his belt. One of her heels went flying across the room, and a button popped as she dragged his shirt out of the waistband of his slacks.

And through it all there was laughter.

Secret smiles.

Erotic touches.

And joy.

Whatever Chance had expected when he finally gave in to this need, he'd never expected that odd juxtaposition of carnal need and sheer, buoyant happiness.

Charlotte's hands pressed on his shoulders, pushing him back against the pillows that smelled of her. It was heady and mind-bending, that feeling of having her literally surrounding him. She straddled his hips, her hair curtaining over him as she kissed a path over his jaw, his neck, the thick bones of his clavicle before she worked her way over his chest. Flames struck his skin wherever her tongue lapped, an unerring path over his body that was as pleasurable as it was torturous.

"Chance?" She whispered his name before she blew a breath over the ridges of his abdomen, wet from where she'd pressed her mouth. Gooseflesh prickled his skin, even as he recognized that he owed her an answer.

"Hmmm?"

"Remember how you asked me if I was tipsy?"

Tipsy? When? Why?

He fought to surface from the haze she'd woven around and over him but finally gave a half-hearted, "Um, sure."

She lifted her head and stared up at him, the erotic image of her spread over his body, her lips bee-stung from their kisses and her dark eyes wide with arousal doing something inside of him.

But it was her voice—that deep, sexy, temptress's voice—that strung him up even tighter.

"When you think about me tomorrow morning, and you *will* think about me, remember that I am stone-cold sober right now. And everything I'm about to do to you was done with a very sound, very willing, very dirty mind."

And then her mouth was on his cock, her tongue firm and hot and wet against his flesh, and nothing in his life prepared him for the experience. Pleasure, so intense it blinded him, shot from the center of his body to radiate out in steady waves, his hips moving in unconscious rhythm to match the motions of her tongue.

Helpless, he gave himself up to her and simply took, unable to do anything but give in to the mindless needs of his body.

"Charlotte," he moaned as she doubled down by placing her hands at the base of his erection. He was nearly done for right then and there until he managed to still her motions, his hands firm on her shoulders. "Let's do this together. Please."

She moved sinuously up his body, teasing his skin with her lips, until he had her near enough to drag her the rest of the way. "Temptress."

"I'm doing my best."

He pressed his lips to her ear as his hand shot down between their bodies, finding the wet warmth between her legs. "I'd like to do my best, too," he whispered as he made a beckoning motion with the tip of his finger against her inner muscles.

A hard cry escaped her lips and he forgot his own needs as the overwhelming urge to make her come flowed through him, tightening the muscles of his forearms as he plied her body with his hands. When he was rewarded with a scream, Chance kept up the pressure, riding her through the storm yet unwilling to let her go easy.

Unwilling to break this feral madness that gripped them both.

"Inside of me. Now." She practically sobbed the words. "I need you now."

"But we—"

Anticipating his thoughts, she leaned over and dragged a new box of condoms out of the bedside table, the box crushing in her hands as she fumbled with it.

"Let me." His voice was gentle as he took the box from her fist before he tore it open and ripped off one of the packets inside. He made quick work of the condom, fitting it over himself mere seconds before she followed, her body welcoming him home.

He could still feel the aftershocks of her release, milking his body even more effectively than her beautiful mouth, and in that moment he knew he was lost.

Their hands linked, she settled herself into a rhythm over him, and he matched her, thrusting up as she came down over him, his gorgeous goddess taking her pleasure. Like magic, he felt those tremors increase, coming to life once more as they gave and took in equal measure.

Somewhere inside he kept telling himself to slow down. To take his time. To make her come again. But all of it faded down to nothing as his own release came over him, dragged fully from him as her body tightened and clenched around his.

On a hard shout, he pressed up into her once more, the feel of her surrounding him exquisite and raw and so fucking life-affirming he saw stars.

And when she fell against him, her lips pressed against his neck, her body still wrapped over and around him, Chance felt the world shift away.

For the moment, there was only the two of them.

Nothing in his life had ever felt better.

Chapter 15

This was what he'd been running away from?

A bright, vivid, vibrant woman who fell apart in his arms and who managed to do the exact same thing to him in return?

Somewhere deep inside, that small thought caught fire and grew rapidly out of control. Because nothing in his life had ever felt this good or this soul-destroyingly right.

And two more bouts of the best sex of his life had only reinforced it all.

Chance let those thoughts dance behind his eyes as he lay on his back, sated so thoroughly it ought to be criminal.

It was only as he slowly came back to himself, conscious of his surroundings, that he realized Charlotte was no longer in the room.

He sat up and glanced at the clock. It wasn't quite four, which gave him a bit of time before he had to get home and get out to manage his early-morning chores.

When you think about me tomorrow morning, and you will *think about me, remember that I am stone-cold sober right now. And everything I'm about to do to you was done with a very sound, very willing, very dirty mind.*

Think about her?

He could get hit on the head, fall out of the saddle and lose consciousness and he'd still be thinking of her. She was imprinted on every nerve ending of his body; she flowed through each and every synapse.

She'd destroyed him, body and soul.

There was no way a man forgot that.

But he still wondered where she was. Climbing out of bed, he reached for his discarded clothes. It seemed ridiculous to put on a pair of slacks and nothing else like he was some suave lothario out of a sixties sex comedy, but he wasn't going to roam around her home naked, either. So he slipped into the thin gray wool and padded off to find her.

She'd left a few small lights on downstairs so he followed the glow and headed that way. The kitchen was empty, which left only one more place to look: her office.

And he found her there highlighted by the glow of her computer screen as well as a small desk lamp, her fingers flying over the keyboard.

Standing still, Chance gave himself a moment just to watch her. That nearly fierce set of her jaw, the way her gaze remained so focused on the screen and the slight bend of her neck where her hair was pulled up into a messy topknot.

She made quite the picture.

Sexy ambition.

As he realized how well that moniker fit, he couldn't help smiling to himself.

"I think I just got my horse name."

"What?" She looked up, her gaze unfocused from where she'd stared at the screen, before coming to land on him. "What horse name?"

"Earlier. You told me I needed to get better at naming my horses. I've got a name."

"What's that?"

"Sexy Ambition."

"You can't name a horse that."

"Of course I can. And since those two words will never leave my lips without the deepest level of appreciation behind them, my horse will know it's special."

She picked up a wadded-up piece of notepaper from beside her and tossed it at him. "You're a goof."

"And you're working. After sex. It wounds a man's pride to be so easily forgotten."

Her eyebrows lifted at that. "You made me scream. There's nothing wounded about your pride at all."

She might have been right, but that wasn't going to deter him. "Oh, I don't know. You might have to prove it to me. Clearly I've been cast off and forgotten, just a boy toy discarded in your bed after you took your amusement."

A hard laugh escaped her, but that did get her moving out of the chair. "Discarded boy toy? How about that for your horse name?"

"Nope. It doesn't have the same ring as Sexy Ambition."

She moved into his arms and lifted her face for a kiss, the lazy meeting of tongues changing something immediately between them. He reached for the clip that held her hair, releasing the messy knot and fisting his hands in the lush strands.

How could need rise up so quickly? And how did it have such sharp teeth, even after they'd sated each other so thoroughly already?

His hands roamed over her body, slipping beneath the thin robe she wore and parting the material, baring her body to him. Chance broke off the kiss and looked down at her, awed by the soft skin and the round fullness of her breasts, the blond hair a few shades darker than her natural color at the apex of her thighs.

She was beautiful.

Lush.

And now that he knew the secrets of her body, he realized that having her wasn't enough. It would never be enough, this snapping, jarring need that felt endless.

Timeless.

And necessary in a way that scared him.

He'd believed that he knew what wanting was. His whole life he'd wanted—nay, *craved*—certain things.

A different existence, one that mattered outside of the shadow of his father.

The respect of others that he'd never seemed to find at home.

And the ranch that was as much a part of him as the A positive that pumped through his veins.

But never had he wanted like this. A sort of eager, necessary neediness that made all the rest fall away.

This was what she did to him.

Suddenly impatient, he turned and swiped the stacks of papers off the desk.

Before he could check himself—or even think to apologize for messing up her space—she leaned around him, tossing several more stacks before grabbing a few folders that she set on a credenza behind them.

"I really do need to clean up in here."

"I've got a better idea."

He picked her up and settled her on the desk before sitting down in her chair. It was still warm from her body heat, and Chance felt it against the bare skin of his back.

The desk was large and sturdy, and he took full advantage as he pressed her back before dragging her legs up over his shoulders, positioning himself at the juncture of her thighs.

"Chance."

"I believe you made me a promise earlier," he

said as he stared up at her, running the tip of his index finger down over that sexy seam, watching the way her stomach muscles contracted at his touch.

"What was that"—she fought to keep her voice level, but he heard the cracks around the edges as he added his thumb to the top of her mons, pressing against her flesh—"that I promised?"

"You said I'd be thinking of you this morning."

"I did say that."

"Right back at ya, baby."

Without giving her another moment to even take a breath, he gripped her hips and pulled her to him, pressing his mouth to the most intimate part of her, devouring her with his tongue.

Her response was immediate, a deep resounding moan of pleasure that seemed to echo through him in great, shattering waves as he stroked her with his tongue.

Whether it was the simple magic of what was between them or the fact that they'd spent a night already making love, he had no idea, but her response was nearly instantaneous. He felt her inner muscles tighten against his mouth, and still he kept up that relentless steady pressure with his tongue.

In all his life, he'd never imagined anything so sweet or lush as Charlotte Wayne.

And as she shattered beneath him, screaming his name, Chance accepted the truth.

He'd never tasted anything as sweet because he'd never been in love before.

He'd spent his whole life running from the truth. And it had only been in the running *to* that it had finally caught up with him.

It wasn't about hearts and Valentines.

It wasn't a name or a reputation.

It was Charlotte.

The woman he loved.

CHARLOTTE CAUGHT HERSELF humming around one o'clock that afternoon and realized that she'd spent enough of the day puttering around and that perhaps it was time to throw in the towel on being productive.

She'd tried to go back to sleep after Chance had headed to the ranch to work, but that had been elusive.

After a shower, she'd gone back downstairs to her office and tried to do some work of her own, but she'd only ended up organizing her papers in between remembering exactly what he'd done to her on the top of her desk.

Which meant she needed something else to do.

Something that involved getting out of the house before she did something really sappy like go smell the pillowcase where he'd laid his head.

Which was how she'd found herself standing at her grandmother's front door a half hour later.

"Charlotte, baby!" Mamma Wayne said as she opened the door. Her outstretched arms dropped as her eyes narrowed. "You had sex."

"Mamma Wayne!"

"Get in here." Her grandmother's grip was surprisingly strong as she grabbed her hand and dragged her in the door. "Get yourself in my kitchen, and you'd better be prepared to share details."

Whatever she'd been expecting—and Mamma Wayne was unpredictable on the best of days—telling her grandmother about her world-class orgasms hadn't been on the list.

But she was here now so she'd better come up with something that would satisfy her grandmother, because there was no way she was escaping with an enigmatic—albeit besotted—smile and a zipped lip.

Her grandmother's house was small, her acquiescence to age and the frustrating limitations of her mobility. But it was also hers to live in alone, and it seemed to make her happy.

A question that suddenly seemed important to ask.

"Are you happy here?"

"You mean, am I happy being an old lady with not much but my soap operas and my memories to keep me company?" Mamma Wayne waved a hand, her smile going wicked. "They're some damn good memories, so yeah, I do okay."

"This from a woman who had three husbands."

"I could've had four if Deke Coltrain hadn't died on me."

"He was eighty-two."

"Loser." Mamma shook her head, her curls bobbing in the shade of red she still religiously dyed it the third Thursday of every month.

"Some just aren't lucky enough to have your constitution."

"Speaking of which, I was just about to make myself some lunch. Want some chili with me?"

"It's nearly two."

"I didn't wake up until eleven. Besides, I'd say you've worked up quite an appetite, and I'm working up one waiting on this story. So spill."

"I'm not sure—"

Her grandmother turned from where she leaned down in the fridge, wagging a finger. "And don't leave anything out. That Chance Beaumont is a looker, and I want to hear every last detail."

Charlotte got up and took the covered glass dish, gesturing to the table. "I'll tell you if you sit down and let me fix lunch."

"Don't be skimpy. You're skinny and pretty and all that, but I'm old and I need my strength."

"So noted."

"And there's corn bread in the pantry. Get some of that, too."

"Will do."

In the end it didn't take long to warm their chili feast in the microwave, and Charlotte sat down opposite her grandmother, two steaming bowls between them.

At her grandmother's expectant stare, she started talking. "Okay, yes, you're right. He's a very attractive man."

"He's hot as sin."

"Well, yes. That, too."

"I bet he's good at it, too." Mamma Wayne set her spoon down from where she was blowing on her chili. "Good Lord, do I miss those days. A big, broad-shouldered man. Slim hips that knew how to pump and grind just right." She stuck out her tongue and blew a raspberry. "My vibrator just doesn't work the damn same."

Charlotte made the mistake of taking a bite and the still-scalding temperature along with her grandmother's casual reference to sex toys nearly had her choking.

Mamma Wayne's rheumy brown eyes were wide, but Charlotte didn't buy the faux innocence in them for a minute. "Don't be looking at me like that. I've got a bedside table, too, and it's got a drawer in easy reach."

"I'll keep that in mind." *And ensure when you do finally pass on—and I hope it's a million years from now—Daddy isn't the one to clean out your room.*

"Now, spill. You and that boy have danced around each other for so many years, I thought I'd die before I saw this day."

"We've been spending a lot more time together. Since Harper got back to town and now that we're working on the Cattle Baron's ball together. Things just . . . happened."

"Things have a way of happening around a man like that." Her grandmother took a bite of chili before sitting back in her chair, a thoughtful expression riding the worn grooves in her face. "Why haven't they happened sooner?"

"It wasn't the right time."

"Why's now the right time?"

"I'm not sure. Maybe I just got my head out of my ass. Maybe he did, too."

The response got the cackle she was expecting, and it was only when her grandmother's face grew sober that Charlotte saw something else there.

"Are you okay?"

"Just remembering your grandfather."

"Daddy has always said what a special man Poppy was. Mom, too."

"He was the best." Mamma Wayne's eyes closed for a minute, and Charlotte had the sudden sense she might have fallen asleep when her eyes popped back open. "Nobody before or since has ever come close, even though I tried. That man loved me to the moon and back. Thought I hung the stars, too, but that was just the side benefits of all the sex we had."

"And we're back to that."

For all her wiliness, her grandmother wasn't nearly as silly as she pretended. And it was that version who reached over and laid a hand over Charlotte's.

Charlotte took in the tissue-paper-thin skin over hands that had done so much. That worked and sweat and had put a lot of years into living a big, bold life out in the Western wilderness.

She'd traveled in Wild West shows as a child, becoming a crack shot and a stage presence to boot. That sort of thing was waning in popularity, but she'd managed to draw a crowd. One that, on a blazing hot Sunday in August, had included Charlotte's grandfather.

"When you find a man who thinks you hang the stars, and you feel the same? That's when you do two things, Charlotte."

"What's that?"

"You love him through thick and thin, and you don't let him go. Not ever."

Charlotte laid a hand over her grandmother's, and the two of them sat there a long time, just like that, connected by a unique thread.

Mamma Wayne, with seventy-five-year-old memories that still kept her warm. And Charlotte with memories of her own, fresh from that very morning, that she knew would never dim, even if she was still thinking of them seventy-five years from today.

"My GRANDMOTHER ASKED me all about the sex we're having," Charlotte said as she wrapped her arms around him from behind. "Just before she told me about the vibrator in her bedside table."

"Charlotte Wayne!" Chance turned around to look at the woman who had him in a vise grip in the middle of his kitchen, ignoring how her breasts rubbed against his chest. "Why in the ever-loving hell did you just tell me that?"

"If it has to live in my brain, it's got to live in yours."

"It's like spiders have invaded." He lifted his

hands and gripped the sides of his head. "Big hairy ones."

"Are you suggesting we stop taking sexual pleasure because we get old?"

"I'm suggesting I don't need to hear about your grandmother's vibr—" He shook his head and could have sworn those mental spiders just scampered across the top of his head. "I don't need to know about those things. And I sure as hell don't need to talk about those things. Ever."

"Well, then." She turned her mouth down in a small moue before dropping her arms and taking a few steps back. "I won't tell you all about my vibrator and this really great thing it can do when I turn it just—"

He grabbed her then, dragging her close and kissing her before whispering against her lips, "Vixen."

"Horny bastard." The insult was barely out when she snapped her fingers. "That's a good horse name!"

"No, it most certainly is not."

They stood like that, in the middle of the kitchen staring at each other with goofy smiles on their faces, and he was so caught up in the moment, it took Chance a few beats to even realize it.

What had happened to him?

Because twenty-four hours ago, the thought of having sex with Charlotte was just a fantasy that had always lived somewhere in the back of his mind.

And now?

Now it was a living, breathing entity between them.

And, he had to concede, it was the *knowledge* in *carnal knowledge* that made all the difference.

Which he didn't dare tell Charlotte, or she'd be off on another horse name.

"I'll win you over on that one. It's all part of my charm."

She slipped out of his arms to get the bottle of wine she'd brought in with her, along with what looked like half a fridge of food in a cooler she'd dragged in.

"Where'd you get all that?"

"Hadley sent me with spoils. It was a filming day, and she made six casseroles, six chicken pot-pies and about four full racks of ribs."

"Wow."

"What we don't eat I figured we could run over to the bunkhouse."

"I can give some to Gray."

"Harper took her share home, too."

"Again, all I can say is wow." Chance considered their choices for dinner. "How'd you end up at Hadley's?"

"I headed over to the main house after my grandmother and I finished our visit. I had forgotten they were shooting today. I wanted to talk to Bea about our visit to the Warners' and ask her opinion on the opening video piece I want to do for the ball."

The conversation shifted to their talk of the ball, and they mapped out what they wanted for the opening montage over a truly spectacular chicken potpie and a good bottle of merlot.

"I keep thinking about what you said, about instead of talking about ROI saying something would make one hundred dollars for every dollar spent, and it gave me an idea."

"What's that?" Chance poured what was left in the bottle between their two glasses before settling back in his chair.

God, he could listen to her talk all day.

That sexy timbre of her voice. Her ideas. Her intermittent bursts of humor. It all added up to a heady sort of fascination that had him hooked.

"What if we talked about all the people employed by the industry? We could then talk about the extended jobs, how they ripple off the main. It's like Hadley's show."

Caught up, he let her go, seeing her ideas come to life as she spoke.

"It's like us going to Rafael's the other week. A restaurant like that would never have existed in Rustlers Creek if the population around here hadn't gotten more interested in our town. But now we have all the Cooking Network people coming in and the reporters and now the tourists who come to see Hadley's Trading Post. All of it builds on itself."

"Those ripples you were talking about."

"Exactly! No one's buying my PR ideas because they don't think beyond the fence rails that surround their property lines. And that's not being jerky about them, but no one's helped them understand that they're part of something."

"You want to use the ball to help everyone see they're a part of something."

"That's my plan. If you agree and think it's the right way to go. I realize I'm a bit keyed up about this, but it's *our* project. You need to agree with it."

"I do agree with it. Even if I did think I was playing arm candy."

"I thought that was my job." She stopped, her eyes lighting up. "Wait, another horse name!"

"God, I've created a monster. My stables aren't big enough for all the names you keep coming up with."

"Details, details. You're rich now. Add on."

She was already reaching for her wine when something in his expression must have stopped her, her motion stilling with the glass halfway to her mouth.

"I'm not going to just waste money or be frivolous."

"I wasn't suggesting you were."

"Then what were you suggesting?"

"Chance. What part of *You struck oil* still hasn't penetrated your thoughts? You can do some of the things you want. And you sure as hell can make jokes and fantasize a bit about the money that's going to roll into your bank account."

She was right. *Of course* she was right.

"It takes some getting used to."

"Well, yeah, sure." Charlotte stopped, her gaze

considering. "And just like yesterday, I tumbled into that one. But come on," she said, her natural enthusiasm spilling out over the conciliatory comments. "It's like you won the lottery. Doesn't it feel a little exciting?"

That flash of anger that had twisted his gut faded as he considered it from her point of view. This wasn't about money, but it *was* about opportunity. And in his haste he kept forgetting that.

"For the last several years, everyone's avoided talking to me about anything financial."

"I don't mean to speak ill of your father, but people knew what you went through. What challenges he had before he died. The community understood you inherited all of that. You got a ranch with great bones and little else."

"I think that's part of the problem."

"What is?"

The realities hit in a torrent, and Chance finally had the words for what he was feeling.

"I have worked hard. So hard that fixing this ranch has been all I could see for years now. And now there's money, at a snap of the fingers. All that work, all that effort. I can just throw money at it now."

"It doesn't negate all the work you've done."

"No, but it does change things." Why was he upset about that?

"I guess it does."

"Is that what your life has been like?"

He didn't ask the question to be an asshole, yet as the words filled the space between them, he couldn't deny it likely wouldn't land well.

To Charlotte's credit, her expression was wary, but her tone was even when she spoke.

"Is my life like what?"

"You're Charlotte Wayne. That has to open doors."

"Not as many as you'd think."

Since he'd seen that for himself with the Harveys, Chance realized she wasn't wrong. And yet . . .

"Your brother has an easy time of it. Your father. They're ranching royalty. Doors open for them. So many doors open they spread them around and give some of them to others."

"Where are you going with this?"

"It just suddenly dawned on me that the people I've come to for help, while deeply well-meaning, don't have any frame of reference to match mine."

She carefully set her drink down, her features strangely blank. It was odd, knowing how expressive she always was.

And it should have been his first clue that she was royally pissed.

"I'm quite sure neither I nor my family deserve however you're processing this situation, Chance. But I'm damn fucking *certain* none of us are living *easy* lives."

He wasn't upset, Chance realized. All the anger

at his father he'd carried for so many years was completely absent.

Yet he was furious at himself.

He'd gotten a gift beyond measure—two, if he included the oil strike in addition to Charlotte—and he seemed unable to well and truly accept either of them.

Not all the way down, where that small voice still whispered he wasn't worthy.

So the words—the one thing he always seemed to have an abundance of—kept right on flowing, spilling out in spite of every clamoring warning inside to just stay quiet.

"You want to sit here and tell me it isn't the truth? That what I've said isn't how it really is?"

And it all suddenly seemed like some play he was acting in instead of his life.

That surreal state that had seemingly descended around him the moment he'd realized his father's betrayal. More, the deeper understanding that through that discovery he'd also found his way forward in life.

Fucked over, yet flourishing. Wasn't that how it all went?

"I'm not sure what bug just crawled up your ass, but let me assure you I have no interest in sitting around as you try to get it out." She stood, crossing to where her purse sat on the counter near the fridge. "When you decide you can act like a decent human being, give me a call, and we can pick up the planning for the ball where we left off."

"Charlotte—" He stood, his chair scraping the kitchen floor, and he caught it just before it toppled back.

She didn't even turn around as she headed into the open living room off his kitchen, hollering as she went. "Don't follow me."

Chapter 16

"Who had the over-under on less than twenty-four hours?" Charlotte looked around the table at her friends—Harper, Hadley and Bea—and tried to pretend she was enjoying herself in the rowdy Thursday-night crowd of the Branded Mark.

At least they'd gotten a table.

"Why didn't you tell us the other day?" Harper asked. "When it happened? We'd have been there for you."

"I know that, but I wasn't ready to."

"I can understand that," Hadley offered. "Those fights. The ones that cut you down at the knees? They're hard to talk about."

"Thank you." Charlotte nodded at her sister-in-law and not for the first time realized just how much her brother and his wife had been through with their marital problems. And how close they'd come to losing each other.

"I just don't understand it." Bea reached for a handful of peanuts from middle of the table. "Chance is such a good guy."

"A good guy with a view of the world that doesn't match a single bit of that goodness."

And that was the part that Charlotte couldn't stand. And hell, she'd lived with it since she was ten fucking years old.

"What exactly happened?" Hadley's frown was a match for her confusion. "I saw you at the house after our shooting day wrapped up. I sent you off with food, and that was nearly five o'clock. When did this happen?"

"That night. I brought all the leftovers over to his place, along with a bottle of wine. We sat and had a nice dinner, talked about our ideas for the ball and some of our evolving plans for it. He was doing fine. Until the oil strike came up."

"That bothers him?" Harper asked.

Charlotte glanced at her friend and considered how to play it, before just opting for what was simple. "Yes."

Hadley shot her sister a sharp look before she and Bea made a rather unsubtle sort of eye contact across the table.

"I can see you both, you know." Charlotte shot dark looks at both of her friends. "Just say what you're thinking."

"Sometimes it's hard to get everything you want in life," Bea finally said. "We're wired to want everything, but we don't always know what to do when we get it."

"So striking oil is to blame?"

"Oil. The opportunity that comes with taking on the ball. Sex and a growing relationship with you." Harper let that last item on her list hang there. "It's big, Char."

"But I know him. He knows me. We're supposed to be figuring this out together." Charlotte shook her head, trying to explain her frustration and well aware she was likely failing miserably. "It's not that I don't understand what you're saying. I do. And we both recognize that taking the step, particularly after knowing each other for so long, has . . . *baggage* is the wrong word, but it's got weight. You know?"

"It does." Hadley nodded. "It really does."

"So the answer is fighting about something as dumb as suddenly taking the pressure off day-to-day life?"

"But there's more pressure now than before," Hadley said. "There's just *more*. More of everything."

There was more, Charlotte realized. But she couldn't say that. No matter how badly she felt, the situation with the oil was his business. And since that business was also wrapped up in his relationship with his father, well . . .

Charlotte instinctively knew she needed to hold that piece back.

"Maybe it's best to give him space right now," Bea said. When she clearly got daggers out of three sets of eyes, she quickly doubled down. "Come on, hear me out."

"Okay." Charlotte nodded. "I'm open to all perspectives. Shoot."

"I know we use that word *baggage* very freely. And it's not that I don't believe in it, but it suggests that it's something that you can set down. That it's an object that you can make go away instead of something that lives with us. That lives inside of us."

Charlotte nodded again, Bea's words making a lot of sense.

"I went through it with Carter. To be honest, I still go through it some days. There I was, thirty-nine years old and falling in love with a man after I got accidentally pregnant with his child."

She waved her hands in the air. "Not that I'm not wildly happy with how things worked out and with marrying him and us having Penelope, but I was so scared about it. And all those things that made me worried. Being older. Not having been in a relationship for a long time. Not living anywhere near the father of my child. It all weighed on me. Carter bore the brunt of that." Bea gave her a gentle smile. "You have every right to be pissed, and we will be your loyal girlfriends who think he should go fuck himself. And if it makes you feel any better, he's probably horribly miserable."

"I can get on board with that."

And she could, even as she had the abstract thought that Horribly Miserable might make an interesting horse name.

"Come on." Hadley moved her chair closer and put her arm around her. "Let's order another round, and you can tell us about the good part before the fight."

"You're not serious?"

"Well, to be honest, I came here expecting a sexy story, and so far you've disappointed."

"Hadley," Harper hissed beside her. "Now is not the time."

"All I'm saying is she might be miserable, but her cheeks still have a decidedly rosy glow. That doesn't just happen."

Charlotte wasn't sure if she should laugh or cry, but at her sister-in-law's expectant smile she couldn't quite find it in herself to stay mad.

"You're as bad as Mamma Wayne."

"You told Mamma Wayne!" Hadley's shout had people at the next table turning around. "Sorry," she said with her voice lowered, "but why her and not us?"

"She figured out I slept with Chance before he pulled the asshole routine. She got it in one, actually, and called me out the moment she opened the door. Only instead of a lot of sexy stories about me and Chance, we actually spent much of the time talking about her sex toys, so I'm not sure it's actually a story you want to hear."

"Your grandmother has sex toys?" Harper's eyebrows shot up. "But she's in her nineties."

Bea ran her hand over the table, clearing off her discarded peanut shells. "Hey. If the playground's still there, you might as well ride the equipment."

CHANCE WASN'T SURE why he was out, what day it was or if he even wanted a beer. But when Gray had come over and practically dragged him out of the house, Chance hadn't figured out a way to say no.

Especially since he was dead on his feet but hadn't managed more than about four hours of sleep in the past two days. Maybe a beer would mellow him out enough to finally sleep a bit.

His fight with Charlotte played over and over in his mind, an unerring film loop of what an ass he was.

Chance walked into the bar behind Gray, the sound of happy people all around him, and nearly turned right back around. The fact that he'd allowed Gray to drive suddenly seemed like a bad idea.

"What am I doing here?" he hollered to his friend over the din.

"You're out to have a beer and shoot the shit with a friend. People call it *socializing.*"

Although he hadn't told Gray about the fight with Charlotte, Gray had figured it out, his oh-so-stellar attitude along with the bags under his eyes to rival a bloodhound's likely giving him away.

"You want a draft or a bottle?"

"A draft is fine."

Gray nodded and headed for the bar, leaving Chance to find a table. Only, when he turned to scan the room for an empty one, his gaze landed on Charlotte. She didn't see him right away because she was huddled over a four-top laughing with her friends.

God, she looked beautiful.

Luminescent.

And hell and damn, what had he done?

Why had he picked that ridiculous fight? Because it was a fight, even if they hadn't shouted words across the kitchen, red-faced and angry. If anything, this had cut deeper because the emotion covered him like a wet blanket, suffocating and heavy.

It was Bea who looked up and saw him first. Her soft smile was oddly encouraging, and she lifted a hand to wave him over. He considered shaking her off or flat out ignoring her, but that wasn't his style.

So he'd go over, say hi and then leave Charlotte and her friends to enjoy their evening.

Bea's wave was enough that the rest of the women stopped their conversation to see what had caught her attention, and he snagged Charlotte's gaze when she turned around.

A world of communication arced between them before she turned back to the table. Once again, he questioned his idiot decision to let Gray drive, then questioned his own idiocy in coming in the first place, before he put one foot in front of the other and walked over to the table.

"Hey there."

"Hi, Chance." A series of hellos flowed from the table, but it was Charlotte who was the last to speak.

"I'm sorry I haven't followed up with you this week. I owe you a few details about the planning for the ball."

The ball?

So that's how they'd play it. All business. Fine, he could do that, too, and maybe get them onto solid footing.

"Sure, I actually owe you a few emails, too. I got some quotes on several local production people with the know-how to take drone footage."

Bea looked up at that. "We can cover that for you, you know. The network. I can do it at cost, and I may even be able to get some of it covered by the show if we can keep the rights as well."

"You don't need to do that," Charlotte rushed on. "That's an awful lot to ask. When I came to you, I just wanted to get your expertise."

"I know." Bea smiled. "But if I can contribute to the cause, please know that I'm in. In fact, maybe we can work it into my upcoming production meeting in a few weeks."

Although he considered himself a fairly hardy soul, the stilted conversation and the varying degrees from pity to disgust radiating at him from the women at the table was finally enough.

"Charlotte, do you have a few minutes? I'd like to talk to you."

She didn't say anything, just nodded and stood before following him through the bar. They passed by Gray, two beers in hand, and Chance tilted his head in the direction of the table. "They're back there."

He kept on going, following Charlotte as she wended her way through the throng of people, well aware his friend could find his way.

The same, Chance thought, likely couldn't be said for him.

Charlotte slipped out the front door and walked to the end of the building, out of earshot from anybody who might be coming in. It was cold and her breath puffed out when she finally spoke.

"What did you want to talk about, Chance?"

"There's a lot to say, and I figured I might as well get to it." She just stared at him so he continued on with an apology that was sorely overdue. "I'm sorry for the other night. Sorry for what I said."

"Okay."

That lone word was about as much as he deserved, so he pressed on. "Look, I know it sounds empty. And I know I don't deserve your forgiveness. But I am sorry."

She shrugged, a resigned look in her eyes that bothered him more than her quiet.

"You deserve better. A lot better, actually. Not giving it to you is one hundred percent on me. I'm sorry."

"Right. I get it. You're sorry. Remorseful, even. But what I really want to know is why do you keep doing it when you're really not a dick in real life, no matter how much you try to pretend you are?"

He dragged a hand through his hair before scrubbing at the back of his neck with the tips of his fingers.

"I don't know, okay? I really don't know. But you do something to me. I think things are good and we can be good together. And then something happens, and it gets all fucked up in my head."

As excuses went it was a whopper, and he hated himself for even saying it. But how did he explain it? Because it might be an excuse, but it was also the truth.

Hell, he *felt* it happening. The way that panic and fear swirled in his chest, building up until he forced her away.

Every. Damn. Time.

"What happened the other night? I know the subject of the oil strike bothers you. We've said as much. But why are you so determined to let it ruin everything?"

"I don't like the insinuation. The one that says that yesterday I was poor and today I'm rich. That suddenly—poof!—my problems all went away."

His whole life had changed in that moment. The very foundation, from his roots to his future, was all wrapped up in that crazy, unbelievable, wild discovery of oil.

"Why does it have to be about anything? About problems or solutions or anything in between? Why can't it just be the start of the next phase of your life?"

It was a novel idea. If there wasn't so much emotion wrapped up in it all, he might even be able to consider it.

"My father warned me off the north pasture,

telling me fucking ghost stories. He said bad things happened up there and the land was cursed."

She shook her head, the indifference she'd worn since walking out of the bar fading away. "He did that?"

"He knew about the oil, that we had a way out from all that debt. He knew we were rich. And he not only didn't tell me but he made up stories to keep me away from there. Because he was waiting for the goddamn day he could screw me on my inheritance, write me out of his will, get me off the fucking property. He'd have done all of it if Mother Nature hadn't intervened. And the worst part is I can't even say any of this. The very discovery of what has changed my life means I can't get a damn answer from his mouth."

He wanted to move in. Wanted to just hold on to her until everything faded away. All of this clanging in his head and the constant ghost of his father that haunted him mercilessly.

"That's what I come from, Charlotte. That's what made me. A rat bastard who didn't give one single shit about me up to the very end."

CHARLOTTE'S MIND SWIRLED with the implications of it all. Since the day he'd brought her out to Beaumont Farms to see the oil, she'd understood it was tied to his father. But each element he revealed was worse than the last.

"I'm sorry you can't get closure. Worse, I'm

sorry that after his diagnosis, your father just left it all to rot. The ranch. The business. You."

Whatever she'd thought about Trevor Beaumont, and her impressions were extremely limited to a few occasions growing up when she'd seen the man around town, this was a level of terrible she'd never have imagined.

And it reinforced every single thing she kept saying wasn't real or didn't matter. All his talk of what it meant to be a Wayne and what it meant to be a Beaumont. She didn't believe he was right, but she began to understand what *he* saw when he looked at his life.

What he thought about who he came from.

And what it meant when you spent a lifetime without love or support or the deep faith for you and in you that came from your parents.

That should always come from your parents.

But she'd had that. She'd had it every day of her life. So she did the only thing she knew how.

She moved toward him, wrapping her arms around him and holding him close. "I'm sorry that it happened, but I'm more sorry you have to live with that knowledge. But it doesn't define you. And I won't let it define us."

He held himself stiff, his arms still at his sides, as she whispered the words over and over.

And finally, when she thought he'd pull away, he put his arms around her, holding on tight.

Charlotte didn't let go, and she didn't move away. Instead, she knew the only thing she could truly give him was the knowledge that he wasn't alone in this. That she wouldn't leave him alone to deal with it.

It didn't change their fight, but it did give her more perspective.

So for now, she'd take what they were tentatively building—what was truly good and real—and would let it be enough.

It had to be.

Chapter 17

∿

"Horses in New York City. It's crazy."

Chance eyed the mounted police walking down the street and couldn't believe his eyes.

Or the fact that he was here.

Bea had worked her producer magic, and once she'd gotten it in her head to help film the opening drone shot for the ball, she'd been unstoppable. As the coordinators of the ball, he and Charlotte had gotten to come along for the ride to her production meetings in New York.

All in all, not a bad way to spend a few days, he had to admit.

"The mounted police are a key element of patrol in the city. They sit up higher so they can see over a crowd, and it also gives people a way to see an officer nearby if one's needed." Bea added a smile. "But you do need to keep a watch behind them."

Charlotte walked beside him as they followed Bea toward her production offices in an area of the city she had called Chelsea. "I've only been here once before, years ago with my mother. It's so wild to think that you live here. Or sort of live here," Charlotte said as an afterthought.

"*Sort of* is probably the right phrase. It's complicated."

And yet it wasn't, Chance thought, as Bea leaned down and kissed the top of Penelope's head where she was strapped to Carter's chest. When she pulled away she looked up at her husband. "You really can come in. Everyone wants to see the baby. You and I are just the sideshow now."

Carter bent down and gave her a kiss before Bea added, "Let me amend that. My hot cowboy husband is still of interest, but Penelope takes first place."

"As she should." Carter smiled down indulgently at his sleeping daughter. "Me and baby girl are going to go get lost up on the High Line for a while. The last time we came in, no one let us leave. We'll bring up the rear after your meetings are done."

"Sounds like a plan."

They all waved Carter and the baby off and then followed Bea into the building. "This was the old Nabisco factory." Bea shook her head with a rueful smile. "I'm sorry. I'm doing that irritating New Yorker thing where I'm both tour guide and walking encyclopedia."

Charlotte gave her friend a stern look. "There's

nothing like this within a thousand miles of Montana, and I'm probably underestimating that distance. Please. Talk away."

Bea took Charlotte up on her offer and began to explain about the building they were in. That it had been the Nabisco factory early in the prior century and that the High Line that Carter had referenced was the old elevated train tracks that used to bring in the flour to the factory and over the past fifteen years had been turned into a lush, aboveground park and walking path.

"Chance, you'll be interested in this. We're also close to the Meatpacking District just a couple blocks away."

"Right here? In the city?"

"Not for a long time now, but for years this part of the city was where the cattle industry was centered."

Chance took it in, amazed that this place where they stood, as far from a pasture in Montana as anything could be, was as much a part of his industry as Beaumont Farms. "It's something else."

And proof, he admitted to himself, that people and life found a way. In the middle of the western reaches of the country in places like Montana and in densely populated areas like New York City and everywhere in between.

People built lives. Had homes and families.

They survived.

It made the juxtaposition of Bea and Carter's life that much more amazing, he admitted, when you considered how vastly different the places were that made them. Yet they'd found their way and created a new generation out of all they both were.

A true testament to their commitment to each other and their family.

Was it luck?

Because he believed in commitment in every way—and he wanted no one else but Charlotte—but he still couldn't quite see his future.

They'd talked through their fight over the oil but had, to his frustration, settled into a strange sort of limbo in the three weeks since.

She hadn't stopped pushing him or talking to him about anything and everything. They spent nearly all their free time together, and they made love every night, but he also couldn't shake the sense that she was careful about what she said.

That she was careful with him.

It was something entirely new between them. A dimension to their relationship he couldn't explain but knew he didn't like.

And he had no one to blame for any of it but himself.

CHARLOTTE TOOK IN that heavy, slightly sweet smell of roasting chestnuts the next afternoon and breathed deep. "Oh, that is such a heavenly smell."

"What is it?" Chance asked.

"Something that, sadly, tastes nothing like that scent promises it will."

"I see you speak from experience."

She thought again about the trip here with her mother and couldn't help but smile. "When my mom brought me to New York years ago, we had taken a horse-drawn carriage ride here through Central Park. And the whole ride we kept smelling those chestnuts so we decided to buy some. And they were so disgusting."

"That's a disappointment."

"You have no idea."

Chance pointed to the nearby vendor cart. "I keep eyeing those hot dogs, but now I probably need to prepare for disappointment, too."

"Oh no, they're wonderful. Should we get a couple?"

"Mustard?" he asked with a ready grin.

"Eww, no." She shook her head. "Just ketchup for me."

"Be right back."

She took a seat on a nearby bench and watched Chance exchange pleasantries with the vendor.

And considered all the ways things had changed.

The past few weeks had been good ones, with less of the fraught tension they seemed so good at and more of the getting to know each other, deeply.

She was happy.

So why were there things she now refused to say?

Eggshells is what they were. Every last one of those unsaid items. And she'd carefully walked her way over them since all Chance had confided in her outside the Branded Mark.

But what was to be done about it?

She knew the things that upset him, and she wanted to give him the space to work through them. But what was the answer? Because it also felt like a cop-out to leave someone she cared about—someone she was building a relationship with—to navigate it all alone.

It chafed, subtle yet irritating, like a hangnail she kept worrying, even as she appreciated there was so much good right now.

The development of the ball was going so well. Even this quickly planned trip and all they'd done the past few days had been amazing. A visit to New York had been a good one for both of them professionally. The meeting with the network had ostensibly been to negotiate rights to the drone footage Bea had volunteered to capture for the Cattle Baron's ball, but it had morphed into so much more.

She'd walked out of their meeting yesterday with a PR assignment for a new network do-it-yourself show taking place in Montana. After all the success of Hadley's show, the Cooking Network's sister station, Fix It, had decided there was something very appealing about Montana living.

Chance hadn't walked away empty-handed, either. When one of the show executives talked him up about his sustainability program, the man had negotiated with him about making Beaumont Farms' beef an exclusive for an upcoming conference and network event that was traveling to twelve cities in four weeks.

And to top it all off, she and Chance had landed a premium sponsorship for the ball with the network buying two tables.

Not a bad day's work, all in all.

"That's a happily smug smile if I've ever seen one."

"Oh, it's very smug and very happy." Charlotte reached up and took her hot dog from Chance. "I was sitting here thinking about our meetings yesterday and how we walked out with a hell of a lot more than some drone footage."

"I've always been in awe of Bea, but I now realize she's not just good at what she does, she's also a product of that environment. The woman gets it done, and she's supported by an environment that gets it done." Chance took a bite of his hot dog and chewed, considering. "I asked that executive if he needed to get competitive bids, and he was all, 'Nah, knowing I have a sponsor locked in and getting it done quickly is more important.' Can you imagine?"

It was impressive, and it made that meeting she'd had a few weeks ago with Tom and Merrill stick out in her mind once more. "How do we bring some of that to the ball? To the story we're trying to tell our community?"

"To get people to change their minds?"

"That, too, but to better help them understand the world's moving around them, and there's an expectation they'll move, too. I couldn't get the Harveys to look at a prospectus to help their business. But an hour with the network team and they saw the benefits of what we offered." Charlotte shook her head. "We're going to work our asses off for it, but it's an opportunity. And it's action."

"You're amazing."

Charlotte caught a look in Chance's eye. It wasn't something she'd seen before, and it stopped her. Stilled her, really, so that everything inside sort of slowed down, even as her heart sped up at his intense scrutiny.

"Thank you."

"No, I mean it. It's something I said to Zack. That night your family had me over for dinner."

"Yeah, yeah, that night my brother grilled you about us."

Chance smiled at that as he wadded up his napkin. "Yes and no. He had a base level of brotherly concern, which wasn't misplaced because, you know, brother. But he did force me to explain what I see when I look at you."

She didn't think her heart could beat faster, but at his words, Charlotte felt a distinct uptick. "What do you see?"

"That you have an amazing combination of ambition and heart. They're not separate for you. You're not driven by money or status but by an excitement for this vision you have in your head. Of how something can be. Of all it can be. It's special, Charlotte. You're special. You're beautiful and smart and the whole package and all, but that's not the whole of it. It's your heart. That's what makes the difference."

"THANK YOU." SHE gave him one of her dazzling smiles. The ones that telegraphed her happiness and her contentment. "That's one of the loveliest things anyone has ever said to me."

"It's true."

And I love you for it. I love who we are together.

That idea hit him, hard and swift, filling up his mind as a light breeze whipped around him.

Should he tell her?

Could he?

Although they'd grown closer over the past three weeks, there were those layers. The things that were unsaid.

The rush of living in the moment and not thinking too hard about the future.

But he loved her.

He'd felt it after the first time they'd made love, but in reality, he'd known it long before that. He'd tested its limits, but he'd also felt it grow in her open-armed acceptance when he'd both confessed and apologized to her at the Branded Mark. And he'd felt it in big moments and small moments throughout most of his life.

He *loved* her.

Hadn't that been why he'd loved sitting next to her in grade school? Or why he sought her out on the playground, always for some reason or other that he somehow manufactured in his mind.

But it had all coalesced since that crazy, unplanned kiss under the stars last spring.

The rest had sort of steamrolled from there.

And no, he didn't have his future planned out. But none of it changed how he felt.

How he felt about her.

They ate their hot dogs in silence, and once they finished, she leaned her head on his shoulder, that pretty breeze drifting around them.

Despite that nagging, lingering worry about a future he couldn't see, Chance couldn't help but marvel at all he felt but simply had no words for. The need he had for this woman—both for her and for all she made him want to be.

And the fact that no matter what they experienced, it was always better when they were together.

"I recognize this is between you and Charlotte. But I'd be lying if I didn't tell you that she's different when she's with you."

"Different how?"

"She's more settled when she's with you. Which makes no sense, since the two of you swipe at each other like two pissed-off wet cats most of the time."

It wasn't just Charlotte who was different, Chance acknowledged to himself as he remembered Zack's words about his sister.

He was different.

Every moment in her presence made him better. Stronger. Made him want to work harder on pushing away that voice inside that said he wasn't worthy.

And helped him see, more every day, that he was Chance Beaumont and not Trevor Beaumont's son.

He'd never understood how badly he needed

that until he'd given in to what was between him and Charlotte.

So he tightened his hold and pulled her a bit closer.

Because now that he knew how much he needed her, he had to make sure he did everything in his power not to screw it up.

CHARLOTTE CARRIED A large plate of corned beef out through the swinging kitchen door into the cozy dining room in the brownstone in Brooklyn.

And nearly turned around at the loud scream that emanated from the very tiny human in Carter Jessup's arms.

"Is she okay?" Charlotte asked, doing her level best not to grimace, all while hoping like hell the plate in her hands didn't crack in half at the noise.

"She's just hungry," Carter said in a calm, even tone despite the fact that his daughter's shrieks and screams were roughly at the decibel level of a ship's horn pulling into port.

"Her lungs are impressive."

Carter calmly tried to insert a pacifier once more in his daughter's mouth, despite the fact that Penelope was having none of it. "Bea'll be down soon, and then she'll return to sweet-angel territory. These bouts are just so her mom and I don't get too complacent."

Carter bent down and nuzzled his daughter's red face. "Isn't that right, sweetie?"

Charlotte set the platter down on the middle

of the table, amazed at the long, lanky cowboy who'd literally transformed into a father before her eyes.

She'd known Carter for a lot of years, and the man who'd always been her brother's right hand—his steady, stoic, calming force around the ranch—had somehow channeled all those same patient qualities into fatherhood.

Without giving it a second thought, she walked over and dropped a kiss on his head. "They're lucky to have you."

He grinned up at her. "The luck's all mine."

Charlotte suspected there was a lot of luck all the way around, but she couldn't quite shake off the strange melancholy that blanketed her shoulders.

What was wrong with her?

She'd had an amazing time in New York. She and Chance had grown closer: that had been evident in their time together. Even those quiet moments in the park had been simple and easy and just about *being*.

Together.

They were together.

So why couldn't she take the proper comfort in that? In what was between them?

Their time in the park had been followed by a lovely sort of quiet, practically spellbound lovemaking in their hotel room before getting ready to come to Bea's family home for dinner.

Which made this odd mooning ridiculous and pointless.

And yet . . . as she watched Carter's patience with

the baby and the simple joy he had being with his daughter, she acknowledged to herself what she refused to say to anyone.

Being with Chance and getting to know him hadn't fully erased the years between them. They still hadn't dealt, all the way down deep, with the hurt he lived with. They'd addressed it, but they hadn't eradicated that demon.

And as she struggled to understand how to help him do that, she lived in a sort of permanent present, not pushing too hard and only taking what he could give.

Could she live with that?

Could she be in a relationship with a man if that never changed or healed?

The real living, day in and day out, when life wasn't even necessarily hard, but when it was routine. When the days passed and you found a way to get through them.

When it wasn't Hollywood glamour or New York City pizzazz.

When you looked yourself straight in the mirror each morning and determined all you could do was your best.

For all her pursuit of Chance, Charlotte had to admit that she hadn't given much thought to the day-to-day. They'd done their level best to avoid that through the years, popping up into each other's life after time spent away. Even the past few weeks had been out of the ordinary.

The newness of their relationship, coupled with his oil discovery and the planning for the ball. It had all moved so quickly. So determinedly forward.

But that would fade.

The madness of planning and prepping would die down, and they'd move into whatever came after.

Plenty of time for him to revert back to being a Beaumont and her back to a Wayne.

And that's what scared her. That when the time came around for real life to settle in, they'd be right back to where they started.

Her thoughts were interrupted by Bea's brisk walk into the dining room, her arms already outstretched for the baby. "Oh, my sweet girl, Mommy's sorry." Bea rolled her eyes. "My brother-in-law has cornered Chance out in the garage, determined to get his opinion on some old riding lawn mower he bought at a yard sale."

"What does he need a riding lawn mower in Brooklyn for?" Charlotte asked, genuinely confused. "Why does anyone need a riding lawn mower in Brooklyn?"

Bea shook her head. "One never knows."

"I'll go save him from Rick's well-meaning yet misguided welcome." Carter was already up and out of his chair. "The first time I met him he regaled me for an hour on how they mowed the great lawn in Prospect Park."

"Why?"

"I think he thinks he's bonding with the out-of-towners. Clearly my work on a ranch means I'm well versed in lawn care the world over."

"I love you!" Bea hollered to her husband's re-treating back.

"I'm making you prove it later!" came winging back, leaving Bea and Charlotte laughing.

"Come on," Bea whispered over Penelope's wails. "Come with me while I feed her and es-cape the madness when my sisters walk in." Bea looked down at the baby. "If you think she's loud, you'll get a sense of what makes up half her ge-netic material in no time."

Charlotte didn't need to be asked twice and followed her friend up two flights of stairs in the house.

"This place is amazing. A real, honest-to-God brownstone." Charlotte stood by the window looking out over the street below, utterly fasci-nated with the view.

"It's been home my whole life, so it's always fun to see it through someone else's eyes."

"Thank you for having us." Charlotte took a seat on the edge of the bed while Bea rocked a quickly gulping Penelope at her breast. "This week's been more than I could have ever expected."

"I'm glad it's been productive." Bea glanced down at her daughter before looking back up. "I know we've only recently gotten to know each other better, so if I'm overstepping please tell me, but . . . I sense there's something wrong. And I wanted you to know that I'm here to listen if you need it." She rushed on. "And I'm a vault, too. I won't tell anyone, not even Carter, if you want to keep this between us." She blew out a hard, angry breath. "I swore that once I was in a relationship I wouldn't do that to my friends, so you can trust me to keep a confidence."

"Thank you. Really, thank you."

Charlotte was prepared to brush it off. Not because she didn't trust Bea or thought the details would get back to Carter or to her sister-in-law but because she didn't need to share anything.

A fine thought, Charlotte realized, until three weeks of upset and worry and anger spilled out. Even as something even deeper inside of her was surprised no tears spilled out along with the words. All through the retelling, her eyes remained dry as a bone.

She continued to keep the details about his father's attempts to cheat Chance out of the oil a secret—she was a vault, too—but the rest of it all came out. From when they were kids to all that had happened since the trip to Bozeman.

"I know I need to be understanding. It's like you said a few weeks ago at the Branded Mark. Baggage isn't something you set down or set aside. There's a weight on him, and each pound's been layered on over a lifetime. I understand that. Or I think I do."

Charlotte stopped. "It's selfish, right? I'm being selfish because I want him to be one way, and he's another. I'm doing that thing I said I'd never do, which is get someone in my life and then try to change them."

"I don't think you're trying to change him.

You're not sitting here telling me about habits Chance has or a style that you want to be different. You're upset that he's hurting. That he continues to hurt. I don't think it's the same."

"It's just that he's my friend, too. He's a person I thought I knew. Well."

"Is that maybe part of the problem?"

Bea's earnest tone cut through Charlotte's confusion. "In what way?"

"You've had feelings for each other. And a lot of that got wrapped up in the excitement and energy of the sex dance. Which, don't get me wrong, is great."

"It is great." Charlotte couldn't hold back the smile.

"So great." Bea smiled down at her daughter before looking back up. "But it's like our discussion at the bar a few weeks ago. There was something I didn't say then. When I talked about the baggage."

Charlotte nodded, suddenly curious. Bea was such a straight shooter that it seemed odd to think the woman had held something back.

"Those emotional burdens might not be something we can easily set down, but their weight is also a mean, nasty liar."

"How?"

"It wraps itself around your shoulders and tells you that you're not good enough. Worthy enough. Smart enough. That the things that have happened to you are somehow all your fault, even when they're the actions of another or the circumstances around you. The only person who can work through that is Chance. But you . . ." Bea shook her head, clearly trying to find the words. "But you can't take on those same behaviors yourself. Chance, for all his troubles and challenges, is making these decisions. You're not the owner of them. He is."

"He keeps calling them ghosts. That the ghost of his father won't let him go."

"That works, too." Bea reached out a hand and laid it on Charlotte's knee. "You can be there to help him exorcise it, but you can't take it on. It's not yours to carry, Charlotte, no matter how much you love him. No matter how much he loves you."

Penelope's light coo drew Bea's attention, her daughter happy and smiling now that she'd been fed. Bea quickly rearranged her over her shoulder, rubbing her small back and settling her tummy after eating.

Charlotte stared at the baby, so small and innocent, and couldn't hold back the question. "How do we start out like that and end up like we do?"

"It's the great mystery of being human." Bea pressed a kiss to her daughter's head. "But if we have any luck, we get people around us who love us, who want the best for us and who make the right decisions in the end."

Luck.

There was that word again. The idea of how much you made versus how much you got as a matter of chance.

She'd hit the luck lottery when it came to family

and friends. Maybe she just had to keep holding that truth tight and use it as her weapon of choice. Because no matter what happened between them, Charlotte would never, ever discount how lucky she was to have Chance Beaumont in her life.

Now she just had to find the way to make him understand, in those deeply haunted places he had way down inside, that he was lucky, too.

Chapter 18

"You ready to run back to Montana yet?" Carter grinned as he handed over one of two longnecks in his hand.

Chance took the offered beer. "Nah, I'm having a good time. I'm just grateful to be here and fully recognize my role is to smile and nod. All. Night. Long."

Carter glanced out the back of the small, one-car garage of Bea's childhood home and scoped out the now-empty driveway. "It's the only way to survive getting cornered by my brother-in-law."

"He's a good guy. But, man, does he come up for air?"

"Only when his wife's talking." Carter shook his head. "And I know that's nasty of me, but it is the God's honest truth. Bea's family has accepted me, even when they could have been pretty pissed

I got their daughter-slash-sister pregnant and effectively homebound more than two thousand miles away. So I do a lot of smiling and nodding myself. But damn, these people could talk paint off the wall."

"Bea? Producer Bea? Would anyone ever call that woman *homebound*?"

Carter grinned at that. "Not in the least, but that doesn't mean weird definitions don't take root and grow in family dynamics."

"I suppose."

Not that he was one to talk family dynamics. Aside from the raging dysfunction that was he and his father, it wasn't like there were a hell of a lot of other people around growing up to have dynamics with. He supposed he and Gray had formed a sort of brotherhood, bonding in childhood over equally shitty upbringings. And he'd been friends with several of the hands on the ranch as he got older.

But a real family?

Not by a long shot.

"It must be good, though, to see where your daughter comes from."

"Bea's family are wild about Penelope. My mother, too. She's eighty-two, and you'd think she was fifty the way she's constantly running around, buying up half the toys in Montana." Carter smiled broadly. "It's a good problem to have."

"It's amazing you and Bea somehow found each other. I always knew Montana and New York were physically far away, but it wasn't until this trip I realized how emotionally distant the two places are, too."

"Proof that when things are right, they're right." Carter took a long pull on his beer before laughing. "Who am I kidding. I had the hots for the woman for years before I got up the nerve to hit on her at the Branded Mark. And I'm not sure it can even quite be classified as *hitting on her* since I just went over to talk to her when she was there alone."

"And now here you both are."

"Now here we are."

"It's the damnedest thing, Carter. Are you and Bea the poster children for safe sex or the very embodiment of a happy family pictured in a Christmas catalog?"

A hard laugh escaped Carter, and he slapped his leg. "Bea'll love that one. And for the record, I can wholeheartedly say we're both."

His smile faded, his gaze going distant. "It's the oddest thing, but I had no idea, not a one, that I could be this happy. I'm not saying I never thought I'd find someone, but I got older and the ranch just became more and more of my life. And now I'm a husband to the most amazing woman and a father to the most incredible daughter, and I have days where I pinch myself thinking it's not real."

"What do you do about those moments?"

Even as he asked the question, Chance realized he was desperately hoping for a pearl of wisdom or two he could adopt as his own.

Because he understood that feeling. Those moments when he looked over at Charlotte and caught her looking at him or they laughed about something or he couldn't help but just watch her focused and concentrating on her computer. Those and a thousand other moments that had already become a part of his life yet still seemed so unexpected as to be surreal.

"I take 'em. I just breathe them in and take each and every one of them for the unbelievable miracle they are."

"WHO HAS A riding lawn mower for a postage-stamp lawn in Brooklyn?" Chance shook his head as he tossed his wallet and loose change on the hotel-room dresser. "I mean, to each his own and all that, but damn, that man could *talk* about a lawn mower."

"I got the sense from Bea he bought it to restore it." Charlotte couldn't hold back the giggle at the weird conversation. "I think they were trying to make us feel welcome, and lawn equipment was the chosen way in."

"I was waiting for him to bring out the big words like *fertilizer* and *crop rotation*, but thankfully Carter stepped in and saved me from his well-meaning brother-in-law," Chance said. "The sad part is if he actually saw the tractors we use to take care of the pastures, he'd realize what a ridiculous conversation it was."

"Crop rotation." Charlotte smiled and walked over to wrap her arms around his waist. "Horse name?"

"You're nuts with that."

"It's fun. And sooner or later we'll settle on one."

"I'd rather settle on you."

He bent his head, his lips finding hers, and Charlotte sighed into the kiss. It had been a long day for both of them. A good day, but a long one, ending with the stressful smiles and the strange questions from people that seemed to think they were from another planet instead of across the country.

Even if the conversation she and Bea had shared upstairs continued to haunt her.

Was she pushing too hard? And less on Chance and more on herself?

Because as she'd sat and listened to all those odd questions aimed at better understanding her, Charlotte had begun to wonder if maybe she was pushing everything too quickly.

Rushing things with Chance so that she could get to a place in her mind that was somehow perfect.

Sort of how Bea's family thought they could get over years of not knowing each other in a single, well-meant evening.

Was it simple impatience to push because things with Chance were finally moving in a forward direction? Or more of her innate drive that, while effective in some areas of her life, might not be the best fit in others?

They were together. They were getting to know each other as a couple, not as two people who were attracted to each other.

Wasn't that enough?

His hands slipped beneath her shirt, drawing

the material up and over her head. He barely
broke the contact of their mouths as the material slipped away. He'd already come to know
the exact perfect places to touch her. And when
they were with each other, pleasure their sole focus, Charlotte forgot about all her worries and
the anxiety that she might be doing something
wrong.

That she might be pushing him too quickly.

Because when it was just the two of them, like
this, it was easy to forget anything else waited
outside the door. Unwilling to think anymore
about what awaited them when they got back to
Montana or even what was to come a month from
now, Charlotte leaned into all he offered.

Tonight it would be enough.

Long, smooth strokes stole over her body, and
she matched his movements with her own explo-
rations. Their clothes fell away as they touched
and stroked one another, and as his large body
pressed against her, the strength of his arousal
firm against her belly, Charlotte understood another facet of what they shared.

For all his strength, Chance was exceedingly gentle with her. Not careful, like she'd break, but gentle
in a way that showed how much he cared. Gentle
in a way that suggested she was precious. It was in
the physical that she had hope for all that did await
them back home.

If he was able to show how much he cared here,
surely he'd find a way to truly live that in other
areas of his life?

That weight around his shoulders that Bea spoke of. He could find his way past that. Or around it or over it or through it. She knew he could.

And while she couldn't take on that journey for him, she could be by his side.

That's where she needed to focus.

As they fell deeper into each other, Charlotte vowed she'd find the way.

GAGE WARNER PRACTICALLY bounced on his feet as he stood beside Charlotte and watched the footage from the drone flying over Beaumont Farms.

It had taken a lot of planning, but when they'd finally gotten everything scheduled for the video shoot, Charlotte realized it would be a real miss if Gage didn't have an opportunity to see it.

Especially since his work had served as inspiration.

"This is really some amazing stuff. What a setup!" Gage moved in and around the equipment, looking at everything, yet respectfully not touching. "The network's resources are like a whole 'nother level."

"It really is something. They use drones on my sister-in-law's TV show, but I never really understood all the ins and outs of it. It's quite a production."

"It's really something else that you got the Cooking Network to help with this." Gage shook his head. "Chance and I have talked about it, a few times over the years. How the public has just taken to your sister-in-law and her cooking."

"I'm so proud of her and what she's built. She's a force of nature, that's for sure. But what she's created—" Charlotte looked around. "It's an endless source of amazement how her success has rippled out to so many."

Gage nodded. "That's what you and Chance have brought to the planning this year. I hope you don't mind my saying so. And I'm truly sorry for the reason Loretta had to step aside." He stopped. "That was unkind of me."

"You're not wishing her circumstances on her." Charlotte patted his hand. "And you'll be glad to know I talk to her regularly, and her doctor is pleased with her progress and the baby's health. So bed rest was the right course of action for her."

"That's good." Gage nodded. "Even if what I'm about to say isn't."

His discomfort was palpable, but he continued. "I've struggled for a long time with what our industry refuses to see as some of our key challenges. Not everyone in the world loves what we do, and they don't have to. But we could do a heck of a lot more to talk about the good things we are doing. The responsible things."

"My brother has spoken about that often. It's one of the reasons he's been as patient with my sister-in-law's show as he is. It's a big production to bring onto a working ranch, yet he's also used his position in it to bring awareness to the work."

"You have a vision for our industry, Charlotte. Just because there are ways of doing something doesn't mean those ways can't be made better." He broke off, blushing. "Sorry, but you got me all keyed up on a topic I'm passionate about."

"It's hard to ask you to stop when you've given me such a compliment. I hope I can live up to it with what we've got planned for the ball."

She and Gage talked easily, exchanging ideas. In it she found some of the same excitement and enthusiasm she'd so hoped to find in Tom Harvey.

"It's also pretty great that you found a way to stay associated with the industry, even if you decided ranching wasn't for you. Most people don't find a way to blend their interests like that."

"I'm fortunate," Charlotte said and knew it to be the truth. "My father was totally supportive of whatever I wanted to do. That included leaving the business *or* staying if I had wanted to. Not every woman in this industry can say the same."

"The legacy of the Western cowboy hangs on, without regard to women or those who don't quite look the part." Gage laughed before patting his flat stomach. "Let's just say there's a mythos and an expectation, and ninety-eight-pound weaklings aren't quite the image Hollywood goes for."

"I saw the way you and Chance handled that bull earlier that was brought out for the opening shot. Clearly, looks are deceiving."

A fact Gage more than proved later when Hadley's lunch setup was all spread out and he ended up eating three plates of enchiladas.

"That man's impressive." Hadley shook her head as she discarded several disposable serving pans that were now empty. "I thought Gar had a remarkable appetite, but Gage made him look like an amateur."

Charlotte laughed, thinking of Zack's ranch hand with a long, lanky build about as slender as Gage's. "The Warners are good people. I've enjoyed getting to know Gage and his wife, Selma, through this process."

"Zack's incredibly excited over this drone technology. He's walked around muttering for three days how he never considered it for herd management despite the fact that there have been drones from the whole *Hollywood Shitshow*"—Hadley made air quotes—"on the damn ranch for years now."

"Sounds like my brother."

Charlotte helped with the rest of the cleanup, then joined Hadley in her SUV as they bumped over the paths that crisscrossed the ranch back to the main house.

"It was really sweet of you to make everything for today."

"It's the least I could do. And I really want to support Chance's work as well as what you're doing for the ball. It's a win in every way."

"I can't believe all this work, and now it's only three weeks away. It's gone by so fast."

"You've had a lot to keep you busy. The professional *and* the personal."

Charlotte saw the hopeful look on her sister-in-law's face. "I am not telling you any more sexy stories."

"It's not like you've really *told* me any, anyway."

"You've got a one-track mind."

Hadley shrugged. "So I've been told."

Charlotte thought about the talk she'd had with Bea a few weeks ago in New York. True to the woman's word, nothing had gotten back to anyone else about the conversation, and Charlotte considered saying something to Hadley now.

Even if by doing so she had to accept the details would get back to her brother.

It was the one thing that had kept her quiet, even as she would have loved talking to her friend about this mixed bag of emotions she wasn't quite sure what to do with.

Especially because, while Bea had made every kind of sense, Charlotte had chickened out on any conversation with Chance that got too close to the real discussion they needed to have. Instead, she kept using their physical intimacy as the bridge to believing everything would work out.

Even as she had no idea if it would.

So she maintained that careful distance, just as she had since the night at the Branded Mark, where she continued to risk her heart and hold it back, all at the same time.

It was exhausting.

And a weird sort of half-life that wasn't at all what she'd expected when she finally fell in love.

Hadley made the last turn toward the main house and the stables and slowed down at the sight through the front window of her SUV. "What's that all about?"

Charlotte leaned forward, catching sight of it all about half a second after her sister-in-law. "I have no idea."

There had been a lot of commotion on the ranch all day with the shoot, but the line of cars and people milling around them didn't look like they had anything to do with the teams of production people. In fact, Charlotte realized as she took in the camera equipment and large microphones, it was press.

Press who'd just caught sight of their arrival.

"How'd they get in here?"

Hadley's own trials with the paparazzi had given her the experience to instantly assess the situation as well, and she slowed, hitting speed dial on her dashboard. Zack answered in one. "Hey, darlin'. How's the drone shoot going?"

"Honey, I think we have a problem."

"What is it?"

"There's a bunch of cameras over here at Chance's. Charlotte and I just got to the main house, and they're everywhere."

"Call the cops and stay put. I'm on my way."

Charlotte already had her phone out as well, dialing Chance, but his phone went straight to voice mail. "It's me. Call me as soon as you can."

"What do you think they're here for?" Hadley asked as she tapped the number for the local precinct.

"I think we're about to find out."

CHANCE LOOKED AROUND at the setup near the edge of his property and had to laugh. He'd heard Zack make jokes through the years about what he called the Hollywood Shitshow but had never really appreciated it until these past few weeks, both for its efficiency and its sheer size and scale.

That shitshow had given him that solid business opportunity in New York and the help here for the Cattle Baron's ball, so he could hardly complain.

But damn, it was a production.

He'd waved off Gage earlier before riding out once more with his team to make sure the herd was settled. They'd remained fairly oblivious to it all—one more point in drone technology's favor—and by his last check were grazing comfortably. He had been shortchanged out of Hadley's reportedly delicious lunch while taking care of a few things, so he was anxious to get home, get cleaned up and finally eat.

For the first time since he'd agreed to take on the ball with Charlotte, he could really see it all coming together. Her vision had been extraordinary, but watching the work today, he knew they were going to make a difference for their community. The show was an opportunity to feature the new and different and shine a spotlight on all the good work being done.

Work that he was a part of.

And for the first time in a long time, he felt a measure of ease in his chest. The money from the oil was going to go a long way toward making Beaumont Farms all he dreamed, but it was more than that.

All the work and sweat and effort finally seemed to have a purpose. Like the universe had finally caught up to his dreams.

Hell, if he were honest with himself, it might be whispering that he hadn't dreamed big enough.

And wasn't that an amazing kick in the ass?

It all comes together with Charlotte.

And suddenly, he couldn't wait to get back to her.

He mounted Squash, his directions to the horse minimal as they navigated toward the stables. And as they rode in the dying light of a fall afternoon, Chance acknowledged his new reality.

She was never far from his mind.

And how humbling it was to realize that the best relationship of his life was the one he'd determinedly run away from.

Pushed aside, more like.

And now that she was here, it was impossible to imagine life without her.

Although he'd see her in less than a half hour, he was suddenly impatient to hear her voice. He

dragged his phone out of his breast pocket, surprised to see several text messages and a few
missed calls. What had he missed?

Even as he asked himself the question, he remembered the buzzing in his pocket when he
was saying goodbye to Gage and waving the man
off. He'd thought to go back to it and then had
gotten waylaid in several odds and ends with the
production crew.

He scanned the messages and saw the increasingly panicked ones from Charlotte, the last one
being COME TO THE BIG HOUSE AS SOON AS YOU CAN.

What the hell was going on?

He already had Squash in motion, the horse
deeply in tune with Chance's physical guidance
as he picked up speed.

They moved over the ground, Chance's mind
whirling with possibilities. What had happened?
What the hell could have possibly happened in
an hour?

It was only as he and Squash crested the last
ridge before the house that Chance saw it. Even
from a distance he could see the throng of people
milling around the front of his property, a line of
cars stretching down his driveway. Police lights
were visible in the distance, bumping down the
long length of driveway from the road, and he
pushed Squash even harder to get there.

Had something happened to Charlotte?

Was someone hurt?

He'd had a shocking number of people over

his land all day. Was it something to do with one of them?

All of it whirled through his mind as he rode up to the scene. He was already off Squash and hastily tying him to the paddock rail when he saw Charlotte and Hadley in the distance, the distinct sight of a blond head and the shorter red one easy to pick out.

Both stood there, surrounded by people with cameras and microphones, and he raced over, desperate to know what had happened.

It was only as he got closer that it all finally became clear.

"Chance!"

"Mr. Beaumont!"

"Hey!"

A cacophony of shouts and attempts to get his attention filled the air, camera flashes going off in the dying afternoon light.

"How does it feel to be sitting on a gold mine that's not yours?"

"What do you say to the real businessmen of Montana who are owed a lot of money?"

"You've stolen mineral rights from legitimate investors!"

His only goal was to get to Charlotte, but she was too far away, separated by the screaming, shouting people.

What was this?

But it was only as one more crafty person slid into a small space by his side, a microphone just shy of hitting his chest, that he finally keyed in to what was being said.

What all the shouting was about.

"Mr. Beaumont, how does it feel to know you've struck oil on land that rightly belongs to someone else?"

Chapter 19

Charlotte watched Chance pace the length of the kitchen and back again, the overhead lights casting his features in harsh relief. He'd taken a quick shower when they'd come inside, but she didn't miss how he kept wiping his hands over his jeans, as if they were still dirty somehow.

It was silly of her—and it likely meant nothing more than he was nervous—but she couldn't shake that image from her mind. Couldn't quite remove the unsaid notion that he felt tainted.

They'd been holed up inside the main house for the past two hours, the police still outside dealing with the last of the consequences of the trespassing paparazzi, information dribbling in as they had it. Confusion had been the order of the evening, and she and Hadley had ended up reheating the leftovers from lunch to share with the Rustlers Creek cops who'd come out to help.

In the end, they'd discovered the real culprit behind the arrival of the paps on private property. Chance's new security team, now duly chastised, hadn't understood the press passes flashed at them weren't tied to the production going on at the ranch that day.

For his part, Chance had remained calm—eerily so—through the telling and the subsequent conversation with the head of the security firm he'd hired.

A mistake, he'd agreed, over and over. A simple mistake.

One that had revealed a far bigger issue swirling in the air.

"I don't understand this." Her father shook his head. Charlie and Carlene had come over at Zack's insistence, and Chance had given him the survey details to review. "I'm no lawyer, but I don't understand this. The survey's clear. The deed here is equally clear. This is your land, Chance. Those mineral rights are yours."

"Then what was everyone screaming about?" Charlotte tapped the top of the old deed certificate, clearly noting Chance's grandfather's name. "They kept saying the land doesn't belong to Chance."

"That's a load of bullshit," Zack bit out. "Who the hell else does it belong to?"

Although he'd been quiet up to now, Chance let out a harsh laugh. "My father was up to his eyeballs in so much bad business, who the hell knows what deals he made or what commitments he intimated to others."

"Talking a good game's not a contract." Charlie shook his head. "Your inheritance has been through probate. This land is yours."

"I'd like to believe that, but my father's been playing fast and loose with the strings on my *inheritance*"—Chance spat the word—"for years. Why should it change now?"

Charlotte caught her mother's eye before quickly looking away. "This will all be clear in the morning. Chance's lawyer can straighten this out and get rid of whoever thinks they have any right to the land."

Chance's voice was dry, devoid of any inflection when he finally spoke. "Right. Because it'll be that easy."

Charlotte didn't think it would be easy, but it would be handled. To her father's point, the courts had already acted. People could make all the claims on the property they wanted, but it didn't change the reality that Beaumont Farms was rightfully owned by Chance.

Charlotte's phone rang, and she briefly considered letting it go to voice mail when she saw Loretta's name on the glass screen. Excusing herself, she headed out to the living room to take the call. They exchanged some quick pleasantries, including the good news that Loretta's pregnancy was going well, when the conversation took a sharp turn.

"Um, Charlotte, I'm sorry to call this late, but I do need to talk to you."

Charlotte heard the hesitant tone as a wash of something dark and cold crept over her spine. "Of course."

"The committee, they—" Loretta changed course. "I want you to know, none of this is my doing, and I've said my piece that this is the wrong move, but, well, I was overruled."

Overruled?

"You see," Loretta kept on in that same steady, cheerful patter, "the committee's not sure Chance Beaumont should be part of the ball in a few weeks."

That dark cold turned to ice as Charlotte considered how to play this. It was only her years of PR training that had her keeping a clear, even tone.

"Whyever would they think that?"

"Well, sweetie, it's just that with the news today, the committee thinks now's not a good time."

And they were so considerate they made a woman on bed rest make the call, Charlotte thought with no small measure of disgust.

"News that's been a simple misunderstanding. Chance Beaumont is the rightful owner of Beaumont Farms."

Loretta's nervous laugh had Charlotte gritting her teeth. "It's not a misunderstanding to Boone Webber and his family. Boone's one of the biggest contributors to the Cattle Baron's ball, and he claims that he had a lock on Chance's land before Trevor up and died."

Up and died?

"Trevor died of cancer, Loretta. I realize it happened very quickly, but if Boone Webber was such a good friend and business partner, perhaps he'd have spent time with a dying man to resolve any outstanding questions."

"Yes, well, that's not for me to say."

"No, Loretta, it's for you to do the dirty work of a bunch of old bastards who don't have a fucking leg to stand on. Men who've suddenly become the thieving cattle barons they take such pride in pretending not to be."

"Charlotte!"

"I'm sorry." Charlotte reined in her emotions. "Again, my apologies. You're just the messenger here. And now clearly you'd like me to play messenger to Chance."

"Well, if you could, it would be so helpful."

"Sure, Loretta. I'll handle it. I suppose you'd like me to tender my resignation for the ball as well."

"Oh no, no." Loretta was quick on that one. "You're a Wayne, Charlotte. Your family's been a part of the Montana Ranchers' Association for years. You're above reproach on all this."

"I see."

"Look, Charlotte, I'm sure this will all blow over. Boone's an old man, as you say, and he's looking to pick a fight. Probably, when all's said and done, we'll find out this is some vendetta over a hand of cards he lost to Trevor Beaumont a million years ago. You know how men are, hanging on to their convictions and their grudges." That annoying titter was back in her voice. "We just need to get through this, and by next year I'm sure it'll all be back to normal."

Just get through this?

"Again, Loretta, as I said. I'll handle it."

"Of course. And don't forget, the run-throughs for the presentation start next week. The committee will be in touch with your practice time. I know they're looking forward to your final product."

Charlotte disconnected and stared at her phone. She'd been in PR for over a decade. She knew how to do the hard work. The tough work. The *uncomfortable* work.

But until today, it had never—not once—felt dirty.

"That was fast."

Chance stood at the entrance to the big, sprawling living room, laid end to end with dark hardwoods and various animal skin rugs across the expanse.

"It was Loretta."

"I assumed as much. Nice speech, too, about the thieving cattle barons."

"You heard that?"

"As I was walking down the hall."

She wanted to move—wanted to go to him—but something about the way he stood there, isolated in the doorway, his hands shoved deep in his pockets, held her still.

"She called with some news."

"I'm out of the committee and off the cochair responsibilities for the ball."

That same stillness she'd seen all evening seemed to permeate through him, his shoulders set in stone.

"Yes, that's right."

"Naturally, I'd expect no less."

"Look, Chance, I can resign, too. There's no reason for me to participate."

"Of course there is. This is a huge opportunity for you. You can't walk away. Besides, you've got a smelly bull coming to you." He flashed a grin that never reached his eyes. "Good horse name?"

She'd forgotten about the reward for chairing the ball, but at its mention realized there'd likely now just be one bull given.

"You're still getting mine."

"I'm not so sure about that. If Boone Webber has his way, there isn't going to be a ranch to put said smelly bull on." He glanced around the living room, his gaze skirting the floor, the walls and then the furniture before coming to rest on her. "I always hated this house. At least I can get that albatross off my neck."

"Chance—"

"Besides, this screams *rancher chic*. I'm sure whoever takes over will feel right at home in this decor."

"Chance, please stop saying that. This is your home. Your land."

He glanced around one more time before shaking his head. "No, it's really not. It never has been."

CHANCE KEPT WAITING for the anger to penetrate through the raw shock that had filled him since riding Squash back to the main house. If it wasn't going to be anger, he'd have settled for frustration or even a solid sort of annoyance.

But nothing came.

Nothing penetrated the empty that seemed to fill him up.

He only remembered one other time he'd felt this way. The day his mother died. He'd been coming home from school, he'd just lost a tooth, and he was so excited to tell her about it, ready to hand it over so they could prepare it for the tooth fairy.

Only, he'd gotten off the bus and walked into the house to find their housekeeper crying on the sofa. Great big heaving sobs, with tears that streamed down her face. Kate had called him over from where he stood in the front hallway. Her voice had been gentle as she'd pulled him into a tight hug.

And as she held him, she told him his mama had died. None of which had made any sense since his mother had been right as rain that morning over breakfast, but by early afternoon she had died.

He'd learned years later, when he was old enough to understand, that she'd had an ectopic pregnancy that had been caught too late. Her fallopian tube had ruptured on the way to the hospital, and by the time they'd gotten her there it had been too late to save her.

A waste, people had said as they shook their heads. Others called it a shame.

But all he'd known was that one morning he had a mother and the next he didn't.

Charlotte was still looking at him from across the room, her gaze dark with worry. It was amazing, he realized, how much she said with her eyes.

Windows to the soul and all that.

It had always been that way. He'd talk to her at school, and he'd think about all the things her eyes said, even when her mouth said other things.

Sassy things that, in no uncertain terms, told him what a jackass he was.

But her eyes always said something different. Sometimes they looked hurt. Sometimes challenging. And there were times—usually when he walked over to her on the playground, before he'd gotten around to running his mouth—they even looked hopeful.

But he'd never quite seen the look she wore today.

Nor could he fully place it, but he had a sense that she was wary, and that was a new one.

"This is all just a ridiculous misunderstanding. This is your home. Or if not this," Charlotte said and waved a hand at the surrounding room, "the ranch certainly is. The cabin is your home. The land is your home." She finally moved, coming to stand before him, laying a hand over his heart. "Here. Right in here is where you know that. I *know* you know it."

"I know a lot of things. I know what it smells like before a snowstorm and how many labored breaths a cow takes right before she delivers a calf. I know just that perfect shade of green in the grass that says we're going to have our first real spring day." He moved in closer, pressing his lips to her ear.

She pulled back, even as he saw desire stamped in her eyes. "Chance. My parents are down the hall, and so is my brother."

"And you think it's some sort of surprise we're sleeping together?"

"No, but I'd rather not broadcast the specifics."

He didn't want to broadcast them, either, yet he couldn't deny this strange, dark need to brand her.

Even as those dark whispers rose up in his mind that he didn't deserve her.

Wasn't that why Loretta had called? Why the committee had made their decision?

He didn't fit, and he never would.

And just like he never seemed to run far enough or fast enough away from who he was, he never quite got past that desperate need to push her away.

No matter how badly he needed her.

Wasn't that the real rub?

He'd spent a lifetime wanting her yet keeping her at arm's length. Because he knew they came from vastly different backgrounds, and if given enough time, his would taint her.

And he'd got a dead-center bull's-eye on that one.

Even now, with the stink of his Beaumont name as bad as it could be, the Wayne name was pristine.

Chance knew damn well Charlotte would take the specifics of that conversation to the grave, but Loretta Cox Hardwick wasn't a quiet woman on the best of days. Even without the speaker on, her nervous voice had streamed out of Charlotte's phone clear as a bell.

So clear he hadn't missed one goddamn word.

You're a Wayne, Charlotte. Your family's been a part of the Montana Ranchers' Association for years. You're above reproach on all this.

Above reproach.

Something he would never, ever be.

CHARLOTTE HADN'T KNOWN what to say or do to help Chance understand that she was there for him, but after they'd spoken, he made an excuse that he needed to see to Squash now that the excitement had died down outside.

It wasn't exactly a lie—he had rushed the horse into the stables earlier to get him out of all the commotion. Only now as she went to the window and looked out over the property, she couldn't help but think it was also a convenient excuse to leave.

"Charlotte?"

She turned to find her mother and Hadley in the doorway. "Hey there."

"Hey," Hadley said, her expression dark. "I, um . . ." She glanced around. "Is Chance here?"

"He went out to take care of the horses."

"It's probably just as well. I just talked to Bea and needed to share something."

That same sense of foreboding that had come over her at Loretta's call struck once more, and Charlotte realized as her sister-in-law started in that she likely could have scripted this.

Word for freaking word.

"Bea's pissed, but it seems that one of the production crew today found out what was happening with the paparazzi and already shot word back to corporate. She's trying to hold them off until Chance can talk to his lawyer, but the corporate folks are looking at pulling Chance's sponsorship."

"Over a little dustup with some Montana media outlets?" Charlotte asked, well aware news like this shouldn't have that sort of impact.

Especially news that was all unsubstantiated speculation.

"The fact that the cameras caught me as part of this has added to the attention." Hadley looked ready to cry. "Oh, Charlotte, I am so incredibly sorry."

"There's nothing to be sorry about. You didn't do anything."

And she hadn't. But for the first time, Charlotte saw the absolutely ugly side of Hadley's fame. The thing her brother had lived with and fought through—all on his own—had suddenly taken on a very real twist.

Carlene patted Hadley on the back before stepping in. "We can stay if you need us to, but

I don't want to be an intrusion if it's better we leave."

"I'm sure Chance is glad you came over. I know he values Dad's insights on this."

Carlene looked indecisive, which was not a trait Charlotte ever associated with her mother. Hadley must have sensed it, too, because she quickly excused herself, leaving them alone.

"Do you want to come home with us tonight? Or we could drive you home if you want."

"I should probably stay."

Her mother nodded, nearly turning to go before she seemed to think better of it. "I know this hasn't been easy. These past few months. The two of you finding each other after all this time. I know you love him."

"I do, Mom. I really do."

"I said something to you. That night after I watched Penelope when you all went out."

"I remember."

"Do you? Because I've felt bad about it ever since."

Charlotte thought about their conversation, there in her parents' driveway, and couldn't remember anything Carlene should regret.

"You told me that our hearts have a way of pushing forward when we're in love. Regardless of the signs around us. I don't think you're wrong about that. In fact, I'd say you were spot-on, since that's exactly what I've done, consequences be damned."

"I think I might have made it sound like a warning or that you shouldn't try. I—" Carlene took a deep breath. "The two of you have something special. You've always known that. And no matter what comes out of all of this, you acted in love."

Charlotte looked out the window once more before crossing over to the couch and gesturing for her mother to sit as well. She waited until Carlene was settled before asking, "Do you think this is going to have a bad end?"

"I think you and Chance are going to go through more difficulties before anyone can know that, baby."

Her mother was nothing if not honest, and it gave Charlotte the leeway to ask what had bothered her for so long.

"He's convinced himself somehow that he's not worthy. That our family and our local status make it so."

Carlene frowned at that. "I'm sorry that's what he's taken away. From all of us." She sighed. "But I can't say I'm surprised. And I'm sure Trevor didn't help that in any way."

"Before, that was Loretta Hardwick, calling me about the ball. They've asked Chance to leave the committee."

Carlene sucked in a hard breath. "Of all the things!"

"When I suggested I should resign, too, he didn't want me to. Said I needed to do this."

"That's your decision to make. Though, I would hate to see you give in instead of doing the show the way you've planned and sweetly shoving all their antiquated notions up their collective asses."

For the first time, Charlotte felt a glimmer of a smile hit her lips. "There is that."

"You took this opportunity for a lot of reasons, but one that has become clearer and clearer is that you want the ranching community to look to the future."

"I think we've done that with the work."

"Then don't give up on that piece. Be mad and work over the next few weeks to make it even better, but don't give up. Because if you walk away, no one has any hope in hell of getting a new perspective."

"I don't know if it's that easy, Mom. Chance and I have spent the past few months together. Real, honest time together. But he still seems stuck in the past that haunts him." She shook her head. "No, in a past that seems to *define* him."

"I think there's one difference you're forgetting."

"What's that?"

"The work you've been doing for the ball? It's about changing hearts and minds. Chance has proven he understands that. That he knows it's important. If some old rancher who doesn't know a sustainable strategy from his ass just needs to be persuaded enough to open his pocketbook, think what Chance can ultimately do."

"But this is different. This isn't his livelihood, it's him. How he sees the world. Who he thinks he is."

"You're working against a lifetime of pain and

scars he likely doesn't even realize he has. They're going to take a bit more time to work past."

"What if I'm wrong? What if I can't get past it? If we can't get to the other side?"

"Then you'll dust off your four-inch heels, kick his ass with the pointy toe of one of them and climb over him as you walk away."

"You make it sound easy."

"It's not easy, baby. Love never is."

Charlotte laid her head on her mother's shoulder and had the fleeting memory of watching Penelope lie against Bea's shoulder. As she did, her friend's wise words echoed through her mind.

It's the great mystery of being human. But if we have any luck, we get people around us who love us, who want the best for us and who make the right decisions in the end.

She'd gotten the best, Charlotte knew. The very best. And that was the gift no one on the outside actually saw or even understood. The fancy Wayne family with the big ranch and the industry name meant nothing without the love that had always raged strong and true inside their four walls.

Love didn't mean you never had a problem.

It meant you dusted yourself off and kept at it. It meant you kept coming back, over and over, to the people you cared for the most.

That's the love she had for Chance.

She *knew* they could be amazing.

But if he ultimately walked away anyway?

Then, Charlotte figured, she'd take the advice of a very wise woman and kick a dumb cowboy's ass to kingdom come and back with her pointy four-inch heels.

Chapter 20

❦

Chance came back into the house expecting to find it empty, maybe a note on the kitchen table. Instead he found Charlotte curled up on the couch in the living room.

It was jarring to see her there, her blond hair splayed out over the thick brown leather.

Had he really expected anything less?

He stood there for a moment, looking his fill at the woman who had so thoroughly turned his world upside down.

How did she manage it?

It felt strange to remember being ten so vividly— the feelings he had for this woman were so much more complex and intense and *adult* that it almost seemed wrong to compare—yet there was no ignoring it. Even before the Valentine incident, she'd been there.

She was in his life, and she always had been.

During the times when she was his whole focus.

Or the times when he tried to forget her.

His Charlotte.

She didn't stir when he came farther into the room, so he turned on a small lamp and switched off the overhead lights. Then he went to kneel beside the couch, shaking her gently.

"Charlotte. Hey there, wake up."

It took him a few tries, but eventually her eyelids popped open, and she stared at him, vaguely confused. "Where were you?"

"Just finishing up in the stables." At her fading confusion, he added, "Or hiding out is more like it."

Since that didn't appear to come as a particularly big surprise, he dropped back onto his ass and pulled his knees up to his chest, crossing his arms overtop.

"My parents mean well, but until you talk to the lawyer, it's a lot of people shouting about a lot of things without answers. I get why you needed a break."

"I appreciate your family's help and their attention on this. More than I can say."

"They're happy to help." She reached out and ran her fingers through his hair before cupping his cheek. The move was sweet and tender, and he couldn't help but lean into her touch.

"You don't have to handle this alone."

"Yeah, actually, I do. My ranch, my business, my asshole father."

"No, you really don't. Beaumont Farms is your

business and your livelihood, but you have a support system. Wasn't that evident earlier? My parents came, and so did Zack and Hadley. Gray and Harper would have been here, too. You have people who care about you and want to see you succeed."

"I know."

"Do you? Really way down deep, do you know that?"

She asked too much. Truly, she did. Yet as he sat there, staring into that heartbreaking face in the muted light, how could he walk away?

He'd considered it, as he brushed down Squash and took care of the horses for the night. One of his hands had already come in and handled the work, but he'd stayed, hiding out just as he'd said. With each step he'd paced in the barn, he thought about walking away from Charlotte and her family and his friends, too. Because if he destroyed what was between them, he'd effectively remove all those people from his life anyway.

So he'd stood there, talking to Squash and trying to make sense of it all. And in the end, he thought of the people sitting inside his home, right now. Not just Charlotte but her family, too. People who'd supported him and wanted what was best for him.

And then he thought about ghosts and those notes about his inheritance and Gray's words, so matter-of-fact and so true.

I get it because no matter what you do, no matter how hard you work or how many years pass, it's there, man.

It's in your head. It talks at you in ways you can't always fight. And it's especially hard, and that voice gets extra loud, when the world around you is changing.

He had let the voice get too loud.

And he'd given it way too much of himself.

"I do know that, Charlotte. You've shown me that. Your father has. Each person in my home tonight has let me know, in one way or another, that I'm important. That I have value. It means—" He broke off, trying to find the words.

The ones that no longer made him feel small or less-than.

"I had a parent who bullied me. Who believed in belittling to make a point instead of teaching or coaching or even gently reprimanding when you inevitably messed up."

"I'm sorry, I didn't know. I didn't—"

He reached for her hand and held it. "I let that voice have too much room in my head, too often. But I'm working on it."

"And moments like tonight, with Loretta's phone call?" She asked the question, her voice soft. "It makes that voice too loud?"

"It does. But I realized something, out there in the barn."

He smiled at her, pleased when he saw a gentle, sweet smile come winging back.

"What's that?"

"It's time to fight it back. Each time it rears up, it's time to push it away. Time to remind myself that I have a life and people in it who want good things for me."

A tear shimmered in her eye, and he brushed it away with his thumb.

Charlotte wanted good things for him. So did her family and his friends.

And so did he.

And maybe, Chance realized as he leaned forward to press his lips to hers, that was what really mattered.

It was time to rise up against that voice.

To fight every one of those emotions, battered into him as a child, because Charlotte meant more than all of it.

She meant everything.

CHARLOTTE BREATHED A small sigh of relief when she woke up in Chance's bed, the comfortable decor in his cabin reminding her of the night before. She'd stayed after her family had left, and although she hadn't expected to fall asleep, the events of the day had left her exhausted.

But it had been those shared moments after he came in that Charlotte finally felt they'd turned a corner. She'd questioned herself all evening as she'd waited for him, using the time after her family left to assess her future.

She and Chance were linked—they always had been. And all this careful management of their relationship had begun to take a toll. Feelings and emotions and all the pain a person carried inside mattered.

His feelings and emotions mattered.

But so did hers.

And then he'd come back inside, and whatever he'd needed that quiet time for, it had clearly paid dividends. After sharing that terrible overview of his father's approach to raising a child, his eyes had cleared, almost as if he'd finally put the ghost of the man behind him. His gaze was clear, and he spoke of the upcoming discussion of the property and the fight he was prepared to have once he went over everything with his lawyers. He had no doubt the ranch was his. People claimed a lot of things—especially when money was involved—but it was damned hard to question the clear rights of heredity and landownership.

He told her he supported her decision to stay on the committee. And he'd told her to give 'em hell.

And then they'd found each other, in the quiet and the calm.

In the acceptance.

In that link that was uniquely theirs.

It felt right, Charlotte thought as she imagined the day ahead. She'd see him off to the lawyer before settling in with her own work finalizing the details for the ball. She had a meeting in town with the production crew to look at the footage taken the day before. After their consultation, the editors would build out the four-minute video she'd specified for the opening of the ball.

Hadley had even volunteered to do the voice-over.

Charlotte sat up and stretched, the sound of

the shower turning off rumbling through the cabin walls.

She might have a to-do list to fell mere mortals today, but she was going to damn well enjoy herself until that time. She was going to draw in every last bit of joy and happiness she could before she had to go face the vipers disguised as caring committee members.

And she'd smile all the way through the meeting, sure in the knowledge Chance had still won.

Padding over to the door, she flipped the handle and opened the thick wood on a rush of steam. He stood in front of the mirror, his truly supreme ass high and tight against a simple white towel, and Charlotte felt her knees give way.

Good God, the man was gorgeous.

His back muscles rippled as he rubbed his wet head with another towel, and for the briefest moment she was able to drink him in before he realized she was standing there.

"Hey." His eyes met hers through the smoky fog of the mirror.

"Hey yourself."

"I—" Whatever he was about to say vanished as she dragged his T-shirt she was wearing up and over her head, leaving the material to fall away.

"I thought you might be lonely in here." She moved a few steps closer, trailing her fingers down the long length of his spine before she got a solid fistful of towel. She tugged it off with a hard yank.

"I didn't realize I was," he drawled, his eyes

darkening. "But consider me a man who knows how to pivot when presented with a new truth."

"What's that?"

He snaked out an arm, dragging her close before lifting her up and planting her ass on the counter. The cool marble was at odds with the thick, soupy steam in the room and the even hotter body pressing against her. "I was very, very lonely."

He moved in to her, nuzzling her neck and getting her wet with the moisture still clinging to his body. The firm, wet planes of his chest slicked across her breasts, teasing her nipples with the motion. She lifted her legs to wrap around his waist, pulling him closer so that even more of that glorious, slick wetness pressed against her body.

She reached down, running her hands over his thick erection, using the wetness from his shower to slide skin over skin, taunting them both with what was to come. He groaned her name, whispering against her ear even as his breath quickened at the steady, insistent motion against his flesh.

Everything she felt—all the emotion and need and sheer, desperate craving for him—coalesced in that moment.

Body pressed to body, she spread her legs wider to allow him entrance. And then, with her thighs wrapped tight around his hips, her calves pressed to his lower back, she took. Great, greedy gulps of all the magic they made between them. She allowed him to set the tempo, mindlessly meeting him thrust for thrust as she took him in.

As she gave him everything.

It was only as he shouted her name, pulling her hard against him as he reached for his release, that Charlotte felt her own in return. She reached for that same release, wave after wave cresting then crashing through her as she held him tight against her.

She was greedy—mindlessly so—for all of it.

Every last bit she could take away with her.

Because like those memories that had danced in her grandmother's eyes over lunch, Charlotte understood these days didn't come around often. When they did, you needed to hold on with both hands.

CHARLOTTE CLICKED THE lock on her car and headed for the welcoming lights of Rafael's. She was meeting Chance for dinner and was anxious to hear how his latest meeting had gone with the lawyer. She also had some of the drone footage on her iPad and already had it cued up to show him.

True to his word, he'd continued to support her work with the committee, doubling down on his encouragement and his desire to see her kick ass with the event.

One more thing to make her smile, after a day happily full of them.

She'd had lunch with Harper, who was increasingly exhibiting signs of Mamma Wayne behavior. God help them all when Harper was ninety. Charlotte felt a small shudder race through her as she pulled open the door to the restaurant.

Even if she couldn't hold back the smile at their remembered lunch.

"On the bathroom counter after a shower. It's like a sexy game of Clue." Harper took a sip of wine, considering. *"Maybe that's the next big idea. I can have sexy date night at the coffee shop. 'In the solarium while role-playing mistress and butler.' Ooh, even better! 'In the library playing sexy nursemaid with the aging mansion owner.'"*

"Way to make it gross, Harper." Charlotte rolled her eyes. *"And a bit too much on the role-playing, thank you very much. I thought you ran a quality establishment."*

"Oh, come on, I'm entitled to a little fun. And I finally got a sexy story out of you."

To be fair, Charlotte considered, she hadn't meant to confess about the after-shower sexcapade, but since she hadn't stopped thinking about it for the past two days, she also hadn't stopped blushing about it and her ever-observant friend had finally called her on it.

"I knew it was a problem to let you day-drink."

"Hey, you're looking at a girl who just beat her fourth-quarter projections more than a month early. And that's before the holiday bump that was factored into those projections."

"What? When? Wow!" Charlotte lifted her glass and clinked Harper's.

"Coffee 2.0 is shaping up to be the second-best decision of my life."

"And we know what was the very best," Charlotte teased. *"Your aging butler."*

"That was the aging mansion owner or the young, sexy butler. But yes, you got the basic gist." Harper took a bite out of one of the burgers she'd picked up on her way over to Charlotte's. *"I can't believe how much has changed. And so quickly."*

"You guys were meant to be. You just had to make a few stops along the way."

"Like you and Chance?"

Was it like her and Chance? Charlotte wondered as she looked around for him, not immediately seeing him. After asking at the host desk, she was taken to their table and told that Mr. Beaumont would be seated as soon as he arrived.

Charlotte ordered a glass of wine and settled in to wait. And still, her best friend's enthusiastic comments kept her company as she—damn Harper!—imagined a sexy maid costume she still had in the back of her closet from a Halloween party ages ago. Perhaps she needed to toss it in her overnight bag next time she headed over to Chance's place . . .

"Charlotte?" The sound of her name pulled her from her thoughts, and she looked up to see Tom Harvey standing next to her table.

"Tom, how are you?"

He bent down and pressed a kiss to her cheek, lingering a fraction too long. She ignored it, unwilling to make a scene, and pasted on a big smile.

"I'm good. Real good. Heard this restaurant was a new hot spot. Thought I would check it out."

"It's great. I was here with some friends about

six weeks ago. We enjoyed ourselves quite a bit. Make sure you save room for dessert."

"I'll be sure to do that." His gaze was appreciative as he looked at her. It was a lone moment of speculation that put her antennae up before he firmly dropped into the chair opposite her. "I don't care for how we left things a few months ago, and I'd like an opportunity to give you my apology."

Between the lingering kiss and the extra heat behind his gaze, she'd rather that he just moved on, but she notched her smile down to polite. "Whatever for?"

"I made some unpleasant insinuations the last time we were together. About your work. It was wrong of me."

"Thank you." She nodded. "Really, Tom, thank you. It means a lot."

He glanced around before settling his gaze back on her. "I would like to make it up to you. Can I buy you a drink?"

"You apologized. That really is enough. We'll put it behind us." She did a quick glance but didn't see Chance yet or her waiter to flag him down for an imaginary problem. "It was nice to see you, but I'm waiting for somebody. I hope you have a nice evening."

"If you're waiting for someone, where is he? A man knows he's got a beautiful woman waiting for him, he gets his ass in gear and gets to the restaurant on time."

Just like that night in Bozeman, Charlotte felt

genuine surprise crater in her chest. She'd always thought Tom was a decent sort. Maybe a little old-fashioned, but decent. This made two times she'd misjudged him entirely.

She wouldn't make that mistake again.

"I was a bit early."

"Well, then, you've got more than enough time for a drink."

"I believe she very kindly told you no."

Charlotte registered Chance's arrival and barely veiled threat a hair's breadth before Tom. But whether it was the challenge or her second rejection or the drink Tom had clearly already imbibed at the bar, the man stood up loaded for bear.

"What the hell does it matter to you?"

"I'm the late sonofabitch who kept a beautiful woman waiting."

Tom shot her a dark look before turning back to Chance. "This is who you're waiting for? A damn land thief who got kicked off the Cattle Baron's committee?"

"Tom, I'll kindly ask you to lower your—"

Her hissed request meant nothing as Tom moved up into Chance's space, crowding him with his chest. She'd estimated he was one drink in when he walked over, but the rapidly degenerating situation and the wild swing that went wide had her reconsidering.

But it was Chance's quick move, grabbing Tom's swinging hand and pulling it behind his back, that saved the moment. For all the potential for spectacle, Chance deescalated it quickly, holding the man tight despite his attempts to struggle.

A few of the waiters had seen what was happening and quickly came over, taking over the struggling patron and insisting they'd refresh his drink at the bar.

All of which left her and Chance alone, whispers and furtive glances shooting their way.

He dropped into the chair opposite her and reached for her glass, taking a large sip. Although he projected a calm outward demeanor and a veneer that suggested nothing fazed him, she didn't miss the way his leg bobbed beneath the table or the way his fingers tapped his thigh.

But it was the rakish grin and lazy voice that let her know just how upset he really was.

"I think we finally found our horse's name."

"Name? What?"

"Land Thief has a nice ring to it, don't you think?"

CHANCE WANTED TO leave. Every instinct he possessed was screaming to pay the check and walk out of the damn restaurant with his head held high.

And yet, somehow, that felt like running away.

Like the outcome Tom Harvey would have planned if he could have scripted the evening.

So he gestured to Charlotte to order a fresh drink, and he got one of his own and sat there. And ignored the whispers and kept his head high just like he wanted to.

And stared across the table at the woman he loved.

Love?

Was it that simple?

Was that the real secret to exorcising the ghost?

As they sat there, sharing their day, Chance knew it for the truth.

He'd always loved her, in a way that spoke of fondness and friendship and care. But these past few months? Ever since that night in Bozeman when everything changed?

On an inward laugh, Chance had the odd thought that perhaps he should reverse course and buy Tom Harvey a drink.

"What's that smile for?"

"I'm not sure this is the time or place to say it."

Charlotte leaned forward, her smile conspiratorial. "You can tell me."

Which was how he found himself leaning forward, too, reaching for her hand across the small space.

"I love you, Charlotte Wayne."

"Oh." She sat up straight, her eyes going wide.

There was a part of him—the very large part that had dominated much of his adult life—that wanted to ask her how she felt. But then he realized there was another part of himself, smaller but growing bolder by the day, that could wait for the answer.

He loved her, and it was enough.

It had always been enough.

Especially when she leaned across the table once more, her gaze locked on his. "I love you, too."

Chapter 21

Charlotte floated through the Cattle Baron's rehearsal, her heart light and happy.

She was in love.

Which she'd known and yet somehow hadn't. Or hadn't let herself really feel it was maybe the better description.

She loved him; of that she'd been sure. She'd been sure at ten, and the feeling had only grown ever since.

But she was *in* love with him. And it was that *in* part, Charlotte acknowledged to herself, that made all the difference.

"Can we run it from the top, Charlotte?"

The voice-of-God floating out of the speakers pulled her back from the trippy sensations that kept tap-dancing through her chest, and she focused on her show notes after hollering her agreement in the show producer's general direction at the back of the room.

It still pissed her off that Chance wasn't here to share this with her, but she was determined to make the best of it. The drone footage had come out amazingly well, and while they were only working with a rough cut at the moment while Bea had the full piece edited in New York, the committee had been thrilled by their preview of the work.

"We're going to run the last ten seconds of the footage with the lights down and then follow my cue as the lights come up."

Charlotte nodded and waited for the lights, hitting her mark on that run as well as the three additional takes as they played with lighting cues. Until, *finally*, she was done, the producer calling a wrap from his place in the back of the ballroom.

Charlotte gathered up her things, suddenly anxious to get out to the parking lot to meet Chance for their planned lunch date, only to find Boone Webber standing at the edge of the stage, his large form dominating the space.

"You're going to give your sister-in-law a run for her money, that's for damn sure."

Anger fired, quick as heat lightning, in her blood.

She'd been raised to be polite. To respect her elders.

But as she took in the sight of the broad-shouldered cowboy who had made Chance's life a living hell, she couldn't find an ounce of charity in her body.

With careful steps in her heels, she moved down the metal stairs at the edge of the stage, ignoring his outstretched hand to help her, before she brushed past him in her rush to get away.

"Is that how you're going to play it? A cold shoulder and a sassy attitude, not even an ounce of gratitude in you for the opportunity you've been given?"

The accusation was heavy, the implication she should be grateful to work her ass off for the committee loud and clear.

"My gratitude isn't the problem."

"No, your slumming with Beaumont's son is."

Charlotte would have been less surprised if he'd actually reached out and hit her, the force of those words so unexpected—so raw—it put her on her back foot.

She stilled, her body going taut. "Excuse me?"

"You heard me."

Charlotte turned, slowly, so that she had the time to take one long, deep breath. She might have been raised to be polite, but she'd also been taught to fight.

Never corner anything meaner than you.

It was one of Mamma Wayne's favorite phrases, and Charlotte had no idea why it had settled in her thoughts like a war chant. But in that moment she was deeply aware that *she* was the meaner one in this fight.

"You want to put your balls on and say that to my face?"

Her own verbal slap hit its mark, and he took a step back, his tone dark. "You heard me."

"No," Charlotte said. Despite the hard pounding of her heart, her tone was calm. Deadly so. "I heard a coward insult someone I care about deeply. Which is why I'm giving you one chance to apologize."

"I don't apologize for speaking the truth. And I ain't a coward."

"So says the man who's trying to steal someone else's land."

"Chance stole it from me!"

"That's not true at all, and everyone knows it. If you had any claim to that property, you'd have crawled out on your yellow belly a hell of a lot sooner than the week after Chance discovered oil."

Webber doubled down, and Charlotte wondered what streak of misplaced male pride allowed something so blatantly false to pick up steam. "Trevor lost that land to me in a card game!"

"Trevor is dead. If there ever was a card game, and I doubt very much that there was, Chance would have known about it a lot sooner than now."

"It was his property. A man has a right to do what he wants with what's his."

"Exactly, Mr. Webber. Chance Beaumont is the rightful owner of Beaumont Farms. And he has every fucking right to make it a wild success. Because it's his, and it always has been."

She turned back around and headed for the exit.

And came face-to-face with Chance as she hit the doorway.

"WHERE ARE WE going?" Charlotte asked.

Chance was surprised she even needed to ask, but he kept his voice level. Calm. Even as he wanted to rage against the scene he'd just witnessed.

The only thing that had stopped him from marching over to Boone himself was the clear sign Charlotte had the situation well in hand.

Hell, if he wasn't so upset he'd have been laughing at the sheer brilliance of her insults.

You want to put your balls on and say that to my face?

Was there another woman like her?

He hadn't needed to see his whole life on display, one more fucking slap in the face, to know the answer to that question was—as always—an unequivocal *no*.

"Back to Rustlers Creek."

"The restaurant we agreed on for lunch is in the other direction."

"And your home is in Rustlers Creek. Which is where I'm taking you."

"Why?"

"You stood there firing verbal bombs at Webber, and you have the nerve to ask me that?"

"He's an asshole, pure and simple."

"He *is* the ranching association, Charlotte."

"So?"

So?

How could she say that and dismiss it all so easily? Worse, how could he have forgotten, so clearly, what he'd been battling against for forever?

It didn't matter what he did. It didn't matter what he achieved or earned or worked for. He was Trevor Beaumont's son.

And Charlotte Wayne was slumming with him.

He made the turn into Beaumont Farms and wished like hell he hadn't driven her that morning. It would have been easier to drop her home.

"Chance, can we talk about this?"

He pulled up next to her car, turning his truck off, and gazed at the land that spread out before him, still in dire need of upkeep and maintenance and attention. Then he shifted his focus to his run-down foreman's cabin. The one the *land thief* had chosen to make his home.

And finally, he turned to look at the woman he loved, with her heartbreaking face and warm brown eyes and her way of looking at him that made him forget all those truths of his life.

So he pulled his gaze away and shook his head.

"No, Charlotte. I want you to go home."

CHARLOTTE FELT THE first shots of real, bone-deep panic as she saw Chance jump from the truck and slam the door.

What was this?

They'd talked. He'd told her how hard he was working on the hurts of his childhood and she'd believed that was all well and truly behind them.

Only it wasn't. It wasn't at all.

Because, once again, things had gotten hard.

Never corner anything meaner than you.

Her grandmother had always meant the lesson as a warning, but Chance had learned it at the hand of the meanest snake this side of Montana.

She climbed out of the car, desperately trying to think how to play this. She would not corner him. Not because he was meaner than her but because that had been the persistent lesson of his life and he deserved so much better.

He always had.

"Chance. Please."

"No! You don't get to turn those freaking heartbreaking doe eyes on me and tell me I don't get to feel this way. You don't know what it feels like."

"What *what* feels like?"

"That no matter what I do, people look down their damn noses at me like I'm pond scum they sucked off Town Lake after the spring snow melt."

"Boone Webber is an asshole. Worse, he's a greedy bastard who took a dishonest shot at trying to steal some land. Why would you give a single word out of his mouth any space in your head?"

"He said those words to you."

"And I know the truth."

"You don't understand."

He turned but she followed him, her breath streaming out in puffs in the cold air. "Then make me understand."

Harsh, craggy lines carved their way into his face, his pursed lips tight with his anger and frustration.

"It's not just the words. It's more of my father."

He took a hard, pained breath. "More of that endless humiliation."

"I'm sorry for that, Chance. In every way, I am so sorry you had to live with that. Through that."

"Yeah." He laughed, more of that hard brittleness that seemed to encase him in its thrall. "Me, too."

"None of it matters. Not between us."

"It all matters. Every bit of it. It's why I can't do this. I thought I could. That I could hold my head high and brazen my fucking way through it. But I can't."

And in that moment, she saw the little boy who'd rejected her Valentine's card, the teenager who'd given her a wide berth around town, the young buck who'd teased her each time they met up at the Branded Mark.

None of them were the man she knew, yet each was a part of him.

Just like the girl who'd given him that card, the teenager who'd stared longingly at him during Friday-night football games, the young woman whose heart had fluttered when he swaggered up to her with a longneck in hand were a part of her, too.

"Do you know why I want you?"

"Charlotte—" He stared down at her, his eyes a deep gray that matched the heavy sky around them.

"You're not the only one with pain. Or sadness. Or experiences that make you feel less-than."

"You can't understand this, Charlotte."

"Of course I can. I'm human, Chance. I've had

hurts and disappointments and setbacks. And while I'm not comparing them to your father, I've had pain, too."

"What hurt you?"

"I was almost eight when my triplet sisters were born. And they were small and perfect, and holy shit, there were three of them. They spent some time in the NICU before they came home, which meant my parents weren't around a lot. And when they came home, everything changed."

"Well, yeah, new babies."

"All the excitement I had while my mom was pregnant changed. Because I realized those innocent, precious babies had taken her away from me. I was ashamed of it then, and I still am."

"You were a kid, Charlotte."

"But they were my family, and I felt that way." When he only stared at her, she pressed on, determined to see this through, to share the memory that still shamed her to this day.

"I used to go to school, and there was this boy in my class who made me laugh and said silly things to me and looked at me like I was still special. Every time."

"You were special." He scrubbed a hand over his cheeks. "You *are* special."

"But I didn't feel like it. In fact, I felt pretty bad inside, because while I loved my baby sisters, I was angry they were there. But most of all I was angry that they took my mom away."

"But you moved past it. You clearly don't still think that. You had the normal feelings of a child."

She took a deep breath, desperate to make him understand what he'd always meant to her. "*You* were the one who moved me past it."

"Me?"

"My mom made Rice Krispies Treats for me to take in for my birthday, and you were so excited. And you told me how lucky I was that I had a mom to make them for me." Charlotte felt the hot tears splash over her cheeks, quickly cooled by the air.

"At first I felt ashamed. And then I realized that I had a mom who loved me. Who was alive. And who made me treats to take to school. And this sweet, amazing boy who always looked at me like I was special didn't know how awful I'd been in my head or the mean things I'd thought."

"Charlotte . . . *God*, Charlotte."

He moved a step closer, but for reasons she couldn't describe, she stepped back. "So when you talk about how it felt when you were young, about how that lives with you, I get it. And I know. I've always known that you had hurts. That you were sad in ways a child shouldn't be. But I love you anyway."

She took another step back, even though he didn't move. "It's why I have to go now. Because I can't be in this place where you don't understand how special you are. Where you don't see the amazing, wonderful person I fell in love with before I even knew what that meant." She exhaled a hard, quavering breath. "Where you don't see that you gave me my mom and my family back."

And as she took one last look at him, standing there under an overcast sky, his face set in that odd mix of wonder and sadness she had always equated with him, she saw the little boy she remembered.

The one she carried in her heart.

CHANCE WENT THROUGH the motions, day by day, through Thanksgiving and the end of November and on into the first week of December. It snowed like a bitch the first Tuesday in December, and he'd spent hours shoveling out, desperately hoping the cold would give him some reprieve from the fire that burned in his head and in his chest and in every freaking memory that rolled through his mind.

Charlotte had destroyed him.

Word by word, she'd torn him down and built him up in equal measure.

And then she'd walked away.

Not that he blamed her. He'd gone to that place he was comfortable in. The one where he hid when the voice of his old man got too loud. Worse, he hadn't trusted her enough, and that was his real sin.

He kicked at a clump of snowpack as he came out of the stables. They'd had a sunny stretch that had melted most of the snow, but it had turned witch-tit cold, and he was freezing his damn balls off. Kate had made soup this week, and he'd already figured on eating about a gallon of it while he watched one of the Saturday-night NFL games.

Charlotte's brother was playing, which was oddly cool and horribly torturous all at once.

But it was something to do.

His head was down, but the sound of his name pulled him up short.

"Chance."

Chance stopped, face-to-face with Charlie Wayne. "Mr. Wayne."

Charlotte's father stood there, arms crossed as he settled against the front of his truck. "*Charlie* still works for me, if it does you."

"Yes, sir."

"Heard you messed things up pretty badly with my girl."

Since he had nothing else, he just nodded and agreed. "Yes, sir."

"You stupid?"

"I'd say *yes*, sir, but I suspect the question was rhetorical."

A small, sly grin lit the corners of Charlie's lips. "No one knows I'm here, by the way."

"Why are you here?"

"Because I think it's a damn shame you messed things up with my girl, and I'm here to help you fix it. And that means you're going to a ball."

However he'd imagined his evening, Charlie Wayne arriving like his fairy godmother wasn't it.

"I don't think so."

Charlie ignored Chance turning him down and kept right on talking. "Since you're a guest at my table, you'd better get your ass inside and cleaned up in twenty minutes."

"Look, sir—Charlie. I was uninvited from the event and kicked off the committee. And it's Charlotte's big night. She doesn't need me there messing it up."

"You're not messing it up if you make all this up to her."

"This is her big night. After all that happened, with my ranch and some of the senior members of the committee, it's just not the right time or place."

Charlie puffed up his chest. "I'm one of the senior members of the committee, and there's nothing I'd like more than to stick it to Boone Webber. I'm also looking forward to gloating and telling him to put his balls on." Charlotte's father laughed at that one. "Bet you don't want to miss that."

Chance felt the first real smile he'd had in days tug at the corner of his lips. "Since I had the pleasure of watching your daughter say the same, I'd definitely be up for a repeat show."

"So get in there and get ready." Charlie wagged a finger. "And start thinking up how you're going to make this up to Charlotte."

"How am I going to do that?"

Charlie's eyes narrowed, and in the set of the man's jaw Chance saw the same determination he'd seen in Charlotte's face pretty much his whole damn life.

"You've been moping around this ranch for

more than two weeks. Surely you've thought up a grand gesture or two."

"I have, but I mean—"

"Do you want to fix things?"

He'd gone through every scenario in his mind. All the reasons why he should stay away. All the reasons she was better off without him.

And he still came back to the truth, every damn time.

No one would ever love her like he did.

No one.

"I do."

Charlie pointed toward the house. "Get in there, get cleaned up and be at my house in under an hour."

He considered arguing, but what was the point?

Besides, he *had* thought up a grand gesture or two.

And really, if you'd obliterated a woman's heart to smithereens and her father still came over to drag your ass to go make it up to her, didn't you sort of have to go?

"I'll be there in forty-five minutes."

CHARLOTTE TOYED WITH the gold bracelet at her wrist and fought the urge to twist her note cards. She'd planned and prepped, and her three run-throughs with the committee had gone flawlessly.

She could do this.

She'd made a commitment, and she could get through this. Her family was here. Her friends were here. It was just time to get it over and done with and go back to her life.

Oh, and somehow figure out how to get the bull—who truly did have a powerful odor, evident even at a distance from where he was currently penned in the hotel parking lot outside—to Beaumont Farms.

She'd get Zack to do it. She'd bribe him if she had to. Besides, he had all the equipment.

Satisfied she'd at least checked off that chore and dumped it on her unsuspecting brother, she turned to find Hadley, Harper and Bea all waiting for her from the wings.

"You look gorgeous." Harper pulled her close for a tight hug.

Although she'd confessed to all three women what had happened, Harper had also been drafted for two different crying sessions as well as an ice-cream binge over the past two weeks. She'd held up admirably, but even Charlotte had grown sick of her own maudlin attitude toward everything.

So it was time to get through this, get over Chance Beaumont and move on with her life.

Oh, right. And kick her own self-righteous ass for thinking it would be easy to just go back to being friends with the man after the past three months.

Since she had plenty of time stretching out in

front of her to worry about that one, she resolved to think about it later and focused on her friends. They wore variations on a holiday theme, one in silver, one in red and one in green. It had made Charlotte's own choice of a shimmery champagne seem pale by comparison. Yet when they'd taken some photos earlier, she was happy at how they complemented each other.

They gave her hope and support and friendship.

And where she'd struggled with their romantic relationships even a few months ago out at dinner, she'd come to see all of them in a new light. It *was* possible to find forever. To find the person who'd check the proverbial *yes* on your heart. You didn't need a Valentine card for that. You just needed the right person.

She wasn't ready now, and she probably wouldn't be ready for a while, but someday, in some way, she wanted that, too.

But right now, she had a ball to kick off.

"I have to get out onstage. Go ahead back out to the tables, and make sure you don't drink all the champagne."

"You do realize who you're talking to?" Harper asked her. "I make no promises."

"Me, either," Hadley said.

"Me three," Bea chimed in.

Their presence and their solidarity and even their threats to drink all the booze were strangely comforting, and Charlotte blew them all kisses as she shooed them off backstage.

And then it was time.

The music she'd heard in rehearsal began just as they practiced, the steady, rising crescendo on the orchestra's cymbal rousing the crowd and setting the stage for her to go out. She took her mark, and as soon as she heard the cymbal crash she moved toward the curtain as it slowly opened.

And came face-to-face with her community.

The good and the bad, the old and the young, the earnest and the cocky. These were the people she'd grown up with. The people she admired, and the ones she'd gladly see never mark another head of cattle again.

But they were here, and they welcomed her on-stage with a round of applause that seemed to roll through the ballroom, toward her and back out again.

Oddly buoyed, she smiled and took it all in. Whatever else had happened the past several months, she'd worked for this. And it was time—

The noise shifted, taking on a new sort of energy as whispers began along with the clapping. Charlotte looked down at her notes as well as the teleprompter set up at the base of the stage, but all she could see was the continued instruction to wait for the applause to stop.

What was going on?

It was only when she caught sight of her grandmother, standing and clapping as hard as the rest of the room, that she registered Mamma Wayne's tilted head. Charlotte was confused until the woman stopped applauding and pointed to Charlotte's left.

And that's when she saw Chance, standing at the edge of the stage.

Her heart was already racing from a mixture of nerves and adrenaline, but the moment she saw him, something started to beat hard through her veins before divebombing her stomach.

What was he doing here?

She was supposed to say a few words and then turn everyone's attention to the screen for the video they'd created, but he seemed to be changing the script. Or she thought that might be what was happening because he was talking, but she couldn't hear over the wild applause. It was only as he stopped before her, a microphone in hand, that she finally registered what he was saying.

A feat made easier by the sudden collection of indrawn breaths in the room of six hundred.

"Good evening, Ms. Wayne."

She nodded, not sure what this was but willing to play along. "Mr. Beaumont."

"I realize this is your moment, and I'm not here to stop it, but I was hoping I could get a minute of your time."

A minute?

Her mind whirled, but she fought to keep her smile in place. She was in PR, after all. Weren't these the moments she was supposed to live for?

When they happen to other people, her conscious screamed, but still, she kept that smile firmly in place.

"Of course."

"I came to a startling realization about something. Rather recently, in fact."

She took him in as he moved a few steps closer. His black tux fit perfectly, and his jaw gleamed from a recent shave. His gray eyes held a note of mystery as he stared at her across the stage, but they also held longing.

Glorious, beautiful longing she knew was reflected in her own eyes.

"A realization?" She pasted on a smile and turned to the audience. "I wonder what about?"

Those bated breaths released, a rumble of laughter rolling through the crowd, and she took heart that he might be getting a warmer welcome than she'd have expected for the man unceremoniously kicked off the planning committee.

He winked at the audience before turning to her. "You asked me a question once upon a time."

Whatever she thought he was going to say about his apparent realization, something steady began to pulse in her chest at his mention of a question. Because she'd only ever asked him one question.

Just one.

And she hadn't liked his answer.

Only, now he was here, onstage, and he was bringing it up to her in front of all these people.

"Do you remember?"

"I—" Charlotte swallowed around the sudden dryness in her throat. It was only when someone in the crowd shouted "Come on, Charlotte! Surely you remember!" that she forced air in and out of her lungs and gave him an answer. "I do remember."

"Then you probably also remember I was too stupid to give you an answer."

He mugged for the camera on that one, eliciting a few half-hearted boos and a lot of groans from the audience.

"Fortunately, I'm not so dumb anymore."

Before she could even register what he was doing, he opened his suit jacket and pulled out an oversize pink card. The edges were frayed, but the droopy-eared puppy was still visible on the front.

As she watched him open it, she remembered the moment she'd seen the card. How she'd believed it was perfect, just the right amount of cute, and good for a boy since it had a dog on it.

She'd figured he'd like the dog.

He held up the card and turned toward the audience once more. "Now, this is a bit private between me and Ms. Wayne. I'm not sure if I should embarrass this lovely woman like this."

The audience was having none of it, a variety of whoops and hollers echoing in the ballroom.

"Read it!"

"Tell us!"

"What's the question?"

The shouts came from the audience fast and furious at his subtle teasing, and Charlotte knew he had his audience exactly where he wanted them.

Just like he had her.

He opened the card and put on a serious face. "The card reads, *Chance, Will you be my Valentine?*"

A few *awww*s echoed from the crowd, and he continued. "That's not the only question. I was given a multiple choice."

Chance moved a few steps closer. Still too far away to touch but close enough she could see the hope shining in his eyes.

"Today? Tomorrow? Forever?"

He turned the card so it faced out. The cameras set up to broadcast the event and give people in the back a better view caught the inside of the card, and it was clear to see the boxes were still empty.

"It's a good thing I have a pen." He reached into his pocket and pulled out a thick marker.

And in front of everyone in the audience, he put a big *X* over the box next to *Forever?*

The distance between them narrowed to nothing as he moved to her, and she moved to him.

But this time when he spoke, it was words for her ears only.

"Forever and ever, Charlotte. I wanted to check that box twenty-two years ago. I want to check it today. I want to check it forever. Because you're the only one I want."

To the crowd's great delight, she pulled him close for a kiss.

But it was the words she said in return that were only for him. "Chance Beaumont, you're my forever."

As she kissed him to shouts and applause, the key lights on them died down, and a large screen came up above their heads. Hadley's voice rang out through the ballroom as the video she'd voiced over began the tale of the Montana ranching community and what it provided to the world.

Charlotte heard very little of it as she pulled Chance toward the edge of the stage and out of view of the audience.

"I'm sorry, Charlotte. For all of it. For not believing in us. For making you spend even one single second feeling like you didn't matter to me. Nothing is further from the truth."

"Chance, I—"

"You mean everything to me." The fervor in his eyes knocked the breath right out of her. "I will spend every day showing you that." He leaned in and kissed her before laying his forehead against hers. "Every. Damn. Day."

And if the evening weren't already perfect enough, he went and sealed the deal.

"Not only do I love you, I think we found our horse name."

"Oh?"

"What do you think about Forever Valentine?"

"It's perfect."

As he pulled her close, wrapping her tight in his arms, Charlotte knew the real miracle of the night. They had, indeed, found their horse name. And so much more.

They'd found forever.

Have you read the previous books
in the Rustlers Creek series?

THE COWBOY SAYS YES

and

FORGET ME NOT COWBOY

Available now wherever books are sold!